Warren Cooper, owner of Twin Oaks, has passed away, and now the secret is finally out! Warren, and not Lawrence Webb, was the true grandfather of the three Webb siblings. Private detective Mark Solomon is about to deliver the news that will change the lives of three people forever. But little does he suspect that his life will be thrown into turmoil, too.

Sally Webb and David Miller haven't seen each other since she was thirteen and her grandfather sent her brother's best friend packing. Now, years later, David finds an older Sally suddenly seeking comfort—in his arms!

Richard Webb is the consummate playboy, going from one woman to the next without any thought for the future or long-term plans. Until Janelle Jamison stuns him with her news—he is the father of her twin boys!

Diana Webb has sworn off men—forever. They have caused her nothing but grief and heartache. Then one day she discovers on her doorstep the man she spent one passionate night with four years ago. Diana can't figure out how he found her, especially since they never exchanged names.

Old Warren Cooper may have left more of a legacy than he originally planned!

Muriel Jensen is the award-winning author of over sixty books that tug at readers' hearts. She has won a Reviewer's Choice Award and a Career Achievement Award for Love and Laughter from *Romantic Times Magazine,* as well as a sales award from Waldenbooks. Muriel is best loved for her books about family, a subject she knows well, as she has three children and eight grandchildren. A native of Massachusetts, Muriel now lives with her husband in Oregon.

Bobby Hutchinson is the author of over twenty romance novels and is a resident of British Columbia, Canada. To her, writing a story about a baby is a really good time. When she was a little girl, she used to tell anyone who asked that she wanted to get married and have twelve babies. Well, she grew up and had three fine sons, and of course reality set in. Luckily her daughters-in-law have been generous, giving her four grandbabies, but she's still an incurable baby junkie!

Kristine Rolofson read and analyzed over two hundred Harlequin romances before beginning to write and sell her own first novel. Now the author of over two dozen books, she is the winner of the Holt Medallion and the National Reader's Choice award. Kristine lived in the mountains of northern Idaho for twelve years before returning to her native Rhode Island. Having married her high school history teacher at the age of eighteen, she has now been married for twenty-nine years and is the mother of six. The Rolofsons were named Rhode Island's Adoptive Family of the Year!

Kristine Rolofson
Muriel Jensen
Bobby Hutchinson

A Wedding at
Cooper's Corner

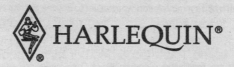

HARLEQUIN®

TORONTO • NEW YORK • LONDON
AMSTERDAM • PARIS • SYDNEY • HAMBURG
STOCKHOLM • ATHENS • TOKYO • MILAN • MADRID
PRAGUE • WARSAW • BUDAPEST • AUCKLAND

Special thanks and acknowledgment are given to Muriel Jensen, Bobby Hutchinson and Kristine Rolofson for their contribution to *A Wedding at Cooper's Corner*.

ISBN 0-373-83505-1

A WEDDING AT COOPER'S CORNER

CONTENTS

Dear Reader,

I love this anthology and the upcoming COOPER'S CORNER series because it puts me back in Massachusetts, where I was born and spent the first ten years of my life.

It was also great fun to delve into the fantasy of an old, unresolved attraction, a traumatic discovery and a heroine six days away from her wedding who wakes up in a Las Vegas hotel room married—but not to her fiancé!

Caught between a wealthy, demanding father, an understanding fiancé and a new husband determined to hold their marriage together at all cost, she must find her way.

We should all have such problems!

Happy reading!

Muriel Jensen
P.O. Box 1168
Astoria, Oregon 97103

STOP THE WEDDING!

Muriel Jensen

CHAPTER ONE

SALLY WEBB STUDIED the slight swell of her breasts above the bustier top of her wedding dress and frowned at her friend's reflection in the antique French Provincial cheval glass.

"You're sure it isn't too...sweet?" Sally asked. The beaded ivory top bared her shoulders, except for two two-inch wide straps, and the snug waist and bouffant skirt lent her an ingenue look that was at odds with the organized and efficient woman she really was.

"You are sweet." MacKenzie Danforth Drake, who owned the Fantasy Bridal Shop in Harwich on Cape Cod, had brought the dress for Sally's final fitting. She folded her arms and nodded with satisfaction. "The dress is perfect. When the eastern Massachusetts gentry see you in my dress, my business will triple. It is too bad you cut your hair, though."

What had been a yard of glossy brown hair rippled with mahogany was now a short, thick cap that skimmed Sally's eyebrows and the tops of her ears, and was tapered to a mannish cut in the back.

"I had hoped it would make me look more mature," Sally said with a wry twist of her lips. The cut had had just the opposite effect. It exposed the curve of her neck and shoulders, and with her fresh good looks, made her appear vulnerable. "My grandfather counts on me to keep his schedule and this estate, yet I swear he still thinks of me as the two-year-old he took in when his daughter died, instead of the twenty-eight-year-old woman who keeps his life in order."

MacKenzie rifled through a box of tissue on the bed and held up a beaded bolero. "You're not going to prove anything with a haircut, Sally. You're going to have to get tough. Here. Try this on if you need modesty in church."

Sally dutifully held her arms back as MacKenzie slipped on the little jacket. "Mac, Granddad learned 'tough' from some Saxon ancestor who took no prisoners. You don't build an international conglomerate like Webb Worldwide by being soft." Her grandfather had named his company to make clear its global holdings. He considered its similarity to the ever-expanding electronic network a happy accident.

"Is that why you're marrying Brandon Pryer III, the king of the stock market and the Dover Country Club?" Mac tugged the bolero into place, intrepidly meeting Sally's eyes when Sally spun away from the mirror.

"I'm marrying Brandon," Sally said firmly, "because I love him, and don't start with me about this a week before my wedding!"

"Fine." Mac turned Sally back toward the mirror. "I think he's a self-centered snob, and that you love *him* because you know your grandfather approves of him. You like the jacket?"

"I like the jacket. And I love him because he's very loveable." And he made her feel safe in an environment where young men often sought out her company because they hoped to share the social spotlight or the wealth that made up Lawrence Webb's world. Brandon's father was a state senator whose family had made a considerable fortune in Massachusetts's textile mills, and Brandon had come into an enormous trust fund when he turned thirty. Thanks to the Yankee work ethic, Massachusetts society welcomed the working rich whether or not their ancestors came over on the *Mayflower*. Brandon wasn't marrying her for wealth or position. He had his own.

Sally caught Mac rolling her eyes and frowned

at her. "I could get another maid of honor at the last minute, you know," she threatened.

Mac stepped back to get a full view of the dress. "Yeah, yeah. We've been friends since college, Sally. I have enough on you to make you keep me as your friend until we're sharing the same front porch swing at Silly Acres Retirement Farm."

"Most of the trouble I got into," Sally reminded her, unable to hold back a grin, "was following you." They'd roomed together at Sarah Lawrence; Sally and Mac had nearly been suspended for selling black market cigars to other senior girls, though Sally hadn't even known Mac had them. Fortunately, their English Literature professor had pleaded their case and they'd been allowed to remain. He'd also claimed the cigars.

"That won't matter to your grandfather. Have you gotten Brandon to pin down a honeymoon destination yet?"

Sally hesitated, knowing an answer to that question was going to earn her more grief. She'd pretended for weeks that their destination was undecided, hoping Brandon would change his mind. But he hadn't and Mac was waiting for her reply.

"We're going to Boston," Sally replied with a broad smile intended to convince Mac that she loved the idea. She didn't, but she was resigned to it. She loved Boston; she just preferred not to do business there on her honeymoon.

Mac slapped both hands over her eyes. "Boston! Our Boston? The forty-miles-away Boston?"

Sally carefully pulled off the bolero, concentrating so that she could avoid her friend's eyes. "He's on the program at a lawyer's conference that weekend."

"Then why on earth did you schedule your wedding for the same time?!"

Because he'd considered it efficient. "We'll honeymoon for a few days while we're in Boston," he'd said. "Save us another trip. And we're not much for sand and salt water and the gaudy tropics, are we?"

Actually, she had a drawer full of brochures about the gaudy tropics, but then common sense asserted itself and she realized that with the time she saved spending a few days in Boston as opposed to three weeks on an island somewhere, she could search for another location for the animal sanctuary she'd worked tirelessly for for more than a year. She'd picked out a spot on the

Cape, but recently learned that it was owned by the Coastline Corporation, who refused to even discuss its sale.

Meanwhile, geese, pheasants, rabbits, deer, woodchucks, turtles and toads struggled in an ever narrowing habitat which was increasingly encroached upon by residents and tourists.

Mac walked around behind her to unzip the dress. "Sally, I'm not trying to be critical of Brandon, I promise. But, sweetie—" she turned Sally around again and smiled gently "—have you really *thought* about this? I mean, where's your sense of wonder at the most important step of your life? Where are the dewey-eyed dreams of romance and excitement?"

Sally sighed at her friend's attitude. "We have dreams of security and contentment instead," she said. "Brandon will make important contacts at this meeting. He doesn't have time to think about me right now."

Mac looked horrified. "If he doesn't have time to think about you days before your wedding, when will you get his attention?"

Sally stepped carefully out of the dress as Mac held it. "I have his attention. He loves me. We just don't think he has to prove it every moment in fussy, sugary gestures."

"Really." Mac went to the bed where the plastic sleeve lay and put the dress back inside. "I can't help it, Sally. I think that's sad."

"If it was sad, I wouldn't be so happy," Sally insisted, pulling on her yellow cotton shirt and shorts.

Mac walked into Sally's wardrobe closet and hung up the dress on a rod at the back reserved for evening gowns. "I don't think you know what happy is." Mac came out again and closed the door. "You've lived your entire life according to your grandfather's wishes." When Sally would have protested, she raised a hand to cut her off. "I know, I know. It's because your brother's not remotely interested in the business or behaving as though he cares about the Webb family's status, and your sister's a rebel who prefers to stay as far away from your grandfather as possible. So you're the one who's always trying to make up for them. You're the one who tries to hold the family together. Well, when is there time for you?"

Sally rolled her eyes and embraced her friend. "Mac, it's sweet of you to worry about me, but I have never felt deprived. My grandparents have been wonderful to us, and if Granddad is demanding, it's because he wants us to be happy and he knows…'' She laughed lightly. ''Well, he thinks he knows what'll bring that about.''

''But he never thinks to ask you what'll make you happy.''

''Because I've always been happy.''

Mac shook her head pityingly. ''You don't even know that you aren't.'' She picked up her purse off a brocade slipper chair and Sally walked her out into the hall, thcn down the wide, carpeted staircase to Oak Meadow's foyer and the front door.

Sally stopped her before she opened the oak door with its leaded-glass window. ''Mac,'' she said reasonably, ''your life is filled with drama. You have a romantic and mercurial temperament, an exciting career dealing with life's most beautiful moment. You need that edge-of-your-seat emotion. I don't. I'm happy keeping Granddad's busy agenda straight, dealing with the practical matters that keep this place running smoothly and looking out for animals.''

Mac pointed a finger at her. ''You just said it yourself, Sally. I deal with life's most beautiful moment. Think about that. What is supposed to be your most beautiful moment will be followed up by your groom appearing at a conference of lawyers, and probably thinking about it while he's repeating his vows. And while he's making love to you *if* he can find the time!''

She cut off Sally's counterargument by wrapping her arms around her and hugging her fiercely. "But I love you, and if that's what's going to make you happy, that's what I want for you. I don't understand it, but if you do, that's all that matters. I'll be back Friday to steam the skirt for you."

Sally blew her a kiss as she ran across the deep front porch and down the steps to her bright-yellow sportscar.

Sally was about to close the door when she noticed a strange car coming up the drive as Mac drove out. Mentally, she ran through the afternoon's schedule. There were no guests expected, no one from Webb Worldwide, coming to pick up or retrieve documents. She watched the car pull neatly into a spot in front of the house.

"I'll take it from here, Sally." She was pulled aside by Hartfield, Oak Meadow's butler, who'd been with her grandfather for thirty-seven years. "When you don't know who's approaching, you don't stand in the open doorway waiting to be kidnapped for an obscene amount of money." He shooed her toward the kitchen. Hartfield was a former mercenary trained in the martial arts. Her grandfather had hired him after a friend's son was kidnapped and held for ransom.

These days, Hartfield counted on his gray hair and wire-rimmed glasses to delude potentially dangerous strangers into dismissing him as a threat or a deterrent.

She smiled affectionately at the butler. "You're just afraid my ransom might come out of your retirement."

"Precisely," he said. "Now, will you please get out of sight?"

"Too late," Sally said quietly. "He's already seen me."

In the time they'd been arguing, a very tall, thick-shouldered man had climbed out of the car and was taking the few steps to the veranda lined with colorful pots of flowers.

The man offered his hand to the butler. "Alistair Hartfield?" he asked.

After a moment of suspicious surprise that anyone outside of the house knew his first name, Hartfield shook his hand. Sally suspected Hartfield thought he could throw the man in an instant if he was trouble. Sally had faith in Hartfield, but this man must be at least six feet four inches tall.

"I am," Hartfield replied.

The man nodded. "Mark Solomon," he said,

smiling politely. "I'm a private detective." He handed Hartfield his identification. Hartfield examined it, then handed it back.

"I'm looking for Sally Elizabeth Webb," Solomon said.

Before Sally could admit to that identity, Hartfield asked coolly, "For what purpose?"

Solomon held up a manila envelope in his left hand. "I've been asked by my client to deliver this."

Hartfield held out his hand. "She's out this afternoon. I'll accept it for her."

Solomon withheld the envelope with another smile. "I'm sorry. I've been asked to put it into her hands." He turned the smile on Sally. "I understand your caution with strangers, but I assure you I'm here on business, Sally." When Hartfield stiffened, Solomon explained easily, "My client gave me photographs."

He put the envelope into Sally's hand, gave her a polite bow, shook Hartfield's hand again and loped back to his car. He was off with a brief wave through the windshield.

After a puzzled look at the departing car, then at the envelope in her hands, Sally turned back to the house.

Hartfield held a hand out for the envelope.

"I'd like to open it for you. Just open it. The contents will remain private."

"Hartfield..." she began, a little impatient with his overprotection.

He took advantage of her distraction to nab the envelope from her grasp. "There are all kinds of crazies out there, some with a grudge against your grandfather, some with a grudge against anyone with money. Envelope bombs are not uncommon." He made a pushing gesture with his open hand. "Step back, please."

Reminding herself that if there really was a threat in that envelope, he was bravely taking the risk for her, Sally took several steps back.

Hartfield reached for his pocket knife and slit open the flap end of the envelope. Despite herself, Sally felt a moment's trepidation.

But nothing happened. She reclaimed the envelope. "Thank you, Hartfield. Now, if you'll excuse me, I'll take this into the library. Undoubtedly it contains compromising photos of me and the lover I've kept from Brandon all these months, and I'm sure they would horrify you."

Hartfield frowned. "As hard as your grandfather was on you children, it amazes me that you've all still managed to grow up with so many ill-mannered traits. *Yours* being a smart mouth."

Sally laughed and hugged him, and as she did, the enveloped held loosely in her hand spewed its contents onto the wide planks of the porch. She stooped to pick them up, then knelt in the middle of the pile in puzzlement. She began to realize that they were all photos of herself at milestones in her life, artwork she'd done at school, newspaper clippings. She gathered them up, wondering who Solomon's client was that he'd had these mementos of her youth. The upper left-hand corner of the envelope read: "Warren Cooper, Twin Oaks, Cooper's Corner, Massachusetts."

She found a piece of watermarked stationery folded in three and opened it.

It began: "My dearest granddaughter, Sally."

CHAPTER TWO

GRANDDAUGHTER.

Sally reread the salutation in confusion. What was her grandfather doing at the home of Warren Cooper, whoever he was? He was supposed to be in Connecticut for the weekend with friends. Since when did he refer to her as *dearest?* And why was he sending her photos of herself?

She read on.

I will be gone when you read this letter. My life's only regret is that I've never been able to look upon your face, or those of Richard and Diana, but circumstances made that impossible.

Never looked upon her face? What…?

Finally grasping that this was not a letter from Lawrence Webb, Sally put a hand to a tremor beginning in her stomach and read on.

I loved Helen Aster most of my life. She knew Aster had been her grandmother Helen's maiden name. *But I had a limp from a childhood injury and a shy nature, and never collected the cour-*

age to tell her—not until she'd married Lawrence Webb and he'd been reported missing in action and presumed dead during World War II.

She'd been in need of comfort and I'd always been in need of her. When we later learned Lawrence was alive, she knew her place was with him, though I know she left some of her heart with me. Your mother, Donna, and her sister, Diana, who died in infancy, were the part of me Helen took with her.

Lawrence had no idea when the twins arrived early that they were mine and not his.

I hold Lawrence in high esteem because I know that your grandmother was happy with him. When she passed away several months ago, I felt the loss as though she'd spent her life with me rather than with Lawrence and you children. Knowing she lived, even apart from me, gave my life its purpose.

Now that that's gone and my own life slips away, I wanted you to know that I am your blood, that I gave life to your mother, and that I've loved you all these years.

I know your life with Lawrence has been privileged, but maturity brings struggles for all of us. If you ever feel sad or defeated or brokenhearted, lean on my love for you. I planted an oak tree in

*the back garden at Twin Oaks when each of you
was born. They stand at the edge of the garden,
and when I stand under them at night after my
work is done, I can feel all of you with me.*

*When you're beleaguered, think about your
oak and know that I'm with you.*

Love, your grandfather, Warren Cooper.

Sally made a sound that was part gasp and part
sob and looked at the photos and memorabilia
spread around her. Everything seemed to spin.
She had a sudden, completely unrelated memory
of having heard something in a college science
class about polar reversal, a theory claiming that
at some time in our prehistoric past the poles
shifted or even completely reversed themselves.

She felt as though that had just happened to
her. She knew she personally hadn't changed, but
everything around her was suddenly alien and
somehow hostile to her identity because so much
of her was Webb—or, so much of who she'd
thought she was.

"Sally?" Hartfield stood over her worriedly.
"What is it?"

She looked up at him, wanting to tell him,
wanting to share this shocking news with *some*-
one, but she remembered that the letter said her
grandfather hadn't known when the twins ar-

rived, that they were not his. And Hartfield was as loyal to her grandfather as any member of the family. If he knew something had upset her, he might tell him and what if he still didn't know?

"It's from...an old flame," she said, grasping for a good excuse. She gathered everything up and tucked it back into the envelope.

"With whom you've shared all your childhood treasures?" he asked skeptically, picking up a brightly colored, poorly executed Primitive of their home, with her, her siblings and her grandparents lined up in front. She'd done it in second grade.

She snatched it from him. "Yes. Excuse me, Hartfield. I'm going to make a phone call."

Sally ran across the foyer and into the library that she used for an office. She sat at the huge slate-top desk near the window, pushed aside the contributions printout she'd been working on before Mac arrived, and speed-dialed her sister's number. Diana lived in a cottage on Nantucket.

"You've reached Diana Webb," the voice on the answering machine said. "Leave a message and I'll get back to you when I return in June."

June! Sally broke the connection, then dialed Richard.

A busy signal beeped repeatedly in her ear.

She slapped the phone down on its station, ran out of the library and up the stairs to her room. She changed her shorts for jeans, pulled a red fleece sweater off a shelf, snatched her purse out of its nest in a cubbyhole in her wardrobe. Then she caught sight of her wedding dress at the back of the closet and stopped in surprise. Her reality had so shifted in the last few minutes that it took her a moment to register why it was there.

She ran down the stairs to the front door.

"Sally!" Hartfield called after her worriedly.

"Don't count on me for dinner!" she shouted back and ran for her car.

Richard lived in a bungalow on the Charles River, a short distance away. Sally drove with a mounting sense of shock and disbelief. Lawrence Webb was not her *real* grandfather.

"Well, of course he's your *real* grandfather!" she told herself, forcing herself to be levelheaded. "He'll always be the real one." Just…not her biological one?

Did Richard know this? Did Diana? Had they gotten letters just as she had? Where was Diana, anyway? She had a penchant for taking off on a whim without telling a soul. Sally scolded her for that but had always secretly admired that quality. She always felt so tied to everything and everyone, so responsible. Sometimes she wondered what it was like to be secure enough to be that free.

She pulled into Richard's driveway, screeched to a stop, ran out of the car and to the back door family and friends always used.

Sobs rose in her aching throat and tears filled her eyes, making Richard's door look as though she saw it underwater. She shifted her weight on the porch, impatient for him to open the door.

She reached a fist up to pound again just as the door opened. The sense of desperation she'd felt upon reading the letter, and the emotion building up during the drive combined to make her tears spill over as she flew into his arms.

"Richard!" she wept. "You won't believe what's happened!"

Strong arms closed around her and she held tightly to the neck that leaned over to accommodate her. "Granddad isn't our grandfather! I mean, not by blood! It's somebody named Warren Cooper and he wrote me this letter. Did you get a letter? I can't believe it! Why didn't anybody tell us. Why did—?"

She stopped abruptly when she realized with a sudden jolt that she was not holding on to Richard. This man was just as tall, had the same big shoulders, and, curiously, the same comforting way of saying nothing, but simply holding her while she poured out her troubles.

But Richard had an allergy to silk and never wore it. Yet, she felt its cool smoothness under her hands. And on the sofa behind him was a Seattle Mariners baseball cap. Richard had been a Red Sox fan since they were children.

Sally dropped her arms in sudden alarm and pushed herself away.

"Hi, Sally," a handsome, dark-haired man said with an apologetic smile. "Don't be frightened. It's just me."

She took another step back, now embarrassed as well as horrified. "Me" was David Miller, Richard's good friend who now owned a multibillion-dollar computer and software company in Seattle that often bought the computer games Richard designed. She knew he came at least once a year to visit Richard, and sometimes Richard flew to Seattle to sail the Sound with him. In high school, she'd had a painful crush on him that she'd kept to herself.

Her grandfather had disliked David not because of anything he had done, but because of where he came from—his father was a penniless drunk. She remembered that Richard had invited him to a costume party at Oak Meadow one Halloween against her grandfather's wishes. When her grandfather had discovered David, he'd allowed him to stay, but told Richard afterwards that he would not be welcome at Oak Meadows again.

Though Richard had vehemently protested, her grandfather had insisted that while David had done nothing to them, he had undesirable parents and was therefore not desirable company for them.

But, as she studied him now—long, slender legs in black slacks, his formidable chest and biceps covered in a black silk T-shirt, and those sympathetic hazel eyes studying her in an angular face with a cleft in its strong chin, she thought her grandfather was completely wrong.

She found David *very* desirable.

Very.

CHAPTER THREE

SALLY WEBB HAD grown into a remarkably beautiful woman, David Miller thought as he caught her hand and drew her into the kitchen so that he could close the door. She was average in height, her soft dark eyes on a level with his chin, which she seemed interested in at the moment. Her nose was small and straight above beautifully defined plum-colored lips now trembling with residual emotion.

He'd dreamed of this day—Sally coming to him and telling him she didn't care that her grandfather disliked him, that she'd secretly loved him since the day he'd worn the Dracula costume and kissed her under the apple tree. He'd pretended he was about to bite her neck, but he'd stolen a kiss instead.

And then—moments later, Lawrence Webb had discovered his presence and made it clear he wasn't pleased to see him. Richard had later explained that David could not revisit Oak Meadow.

She didn't know that at that moment he'd made a silent vow to one day come back for her, armed with social position and a stock portfolio, and no one would be able to turn him away.

He had returned about seven months ago— right after the deal he made to supply United Oil with his specially designed software made the nightly news—only to discover that she was engaged to Brandon Pryer III. He debated fighting for her anyway when he ran into her at a local restaurant. Then he saw her look into Pryer's eyes with love and decided that that would only hurt her. So he'd gone home to Seattle, bought another small company, developed new products, made more money, held more press conferences and tried not to think about her.

But here she was, on his doorstep. Well, Richard's doorstep, but that didn't matter. Of course, this wasn't quite an "I realize I've always loved you" scenario because she'd come in search of Richard, not him. But he'd take what he could get. The kid of a drunk father and a dissolute mother who'd abandoned him when David was ten, he'd learned to take his advantages where he saw them.

He hadn't seen Sally since then and was overcome by the power of her femininity. Even the short bob and the leap into his arms didn't diminish the grace with which she moved. And she had such a disarming sweetness under the strength she seemed to be trying to pull together.

"Where's Richard?" she asked, looking around.

"He's gone fishing for a week," David replied, pulling a chair out at the oak-and-white farm table in the middle of the kitchen. "Sit down. I'll pour you some coffee." Then at her distressed expression, her eyes still pooled with tears, he asked, "Or do you need something stronger?"

She nodded without hesitation and sank into the chair. "Please. Where did he go?"

"I don't know." He took orange juice out of the refrigerator, vodka from a cupboard where Richard kept liquor, and took down a barrel glass and pushed it under the ice maker. He began to assemble a Screwdriver. "He's just finished this game he asked me to look at because he knew I was coming to town. But he was feeling stressed and tired, so he took off for a while without his cell phone and no real destination."

"He invited you here, then left you alone?"

"That was fine with me. I like to keep my hand in Research and Development, and I'll do a better job of checking over the game if he's not looking over my shoulder, or planning changes while I'm still working on it." He turned to smile at her. "Your brother's obsessive-compulsive, you know."

The drink made, he carried it to her and placed it in her hand. "There. Now, what's happened? Richard's out of reach, but maybe I can help."

She took a long pull on the glass, then put it down and shook her head. "I don't think so. It's family stuff."

He took the chair at a right angle to her and tried to coax without pressuring. "What kind of stuff?"

She took another long drink and put the glass down to study it moodily. "I need a sympathetic ear," she said, lifting the glass again to down the rest of the Screwdriver. "And you won't care because you don't like him."

"Who?"

"My grandfather."

"You have that reversed," he corrected gently. "He doesn't like me. What did he do?"

She opened her mouth to speak, then shook her head and handed him back the glass. "Could I

have another one? And if you're going to insist
that I tell you about it, would you join me?''

"Okay." He drank very little as a rule, having
learned early on that alcohol and clear thinking
were not compatible. But she obviously needed
to talk and he wanted to make it easy for her.
Remembering the swiftness with which she
downed the last one, he'd make them in tall
glasses, using a little more ice and a lot more
juice. He gave her another drink and took his
place, sipping at his as he prepared to listen.

"My grandfather isn't my grandfather," she
said, taking a long gulp of the drink. She
frowned, studied it, then pushed away from the
table and went to get the vodka. She poured a
generous portion into her glass, then the same
into his and sat down again, putting the bottle in
the middle of the table. "Someone delivered this
letter today...." She pulled a manila envelope
out of her purse and reached into it for a docu-
ment folded in three. She handed it to him. "It's
beautiful, really, but it pulls the ground out from
under my life! I'm not me, anymore!"

She drank as he read the letter. By the time
he'd finished, she was already topping up their
glasses again, long on vodka and short on juice.

"Of course, you're you." He handed back the

letter. "It doesn't really matter who made you what you are, does it? You *are*."

"But I'm not! That's the point," she said, making a gesture with her right hand that was a little sloppy. "I'm not Sally Webb! I'm really Sally Cooper!"

"Your name didn't make you, either," he said forcefully. "It identifies you, but it doesn't define you. You're Sally, and whether it's Webb or Cooper, you're *still* Sally."

Large tears slid down her face. "I can't remember my mother's face," she said, her voice tight and starting to sound a little strange. "Though I have photographs to tell me what she looked like. But sometimes, I think I remember her voice." She stopped, cocking her head slightly as though she were listening. Then she focused on him. She seemed to have difficulty doing it. "She and my father had a band, you know."

He nodded. "Richard told me."

"And sometimes at night—" her voice fell to a whisper "—I think I can hear her when everything's quiet. She's singing a lullaby."

"That's probably a memory from when you were a baby. One you didn't even know you'd stored."

"But her father wasn't really her father. I—I used to feel connected to her...through him, but now—" she shook her head "—I find out her father was someone I've never even seen. And now he's gone. Just like her. Just like my father."

"Look." Her right hand fidgeted on the table-top and he covered it with his own. "In some cases, good stories about your parents told to you by grandparents—blood or not—are better than memories of the real thing when your parents don't really care that they have a child. Trust me on that. I'm sorry you didn't know yours, but I knew mine and I'd rather be in your position."

He was a little surprised to hear those words come out of his mouth. He'd put his childhood behind him—way behind him—and he seldom dragged it out for purposes of philosophy or anything else, but it seemed to make a point here. He thought it weird that it still had the power to hurt him. Then he remembered that he'd decided not to let it. He pushed all thoughts of his past away.

"What was it about your parents?" Sally asked. "I sort of remember that it was them..." She seemed to lose her train of thought for a moment, then waved a finger in the air and nodded. She was getting sloshed. "Yes. It was them, and not you that he didn't like. My grandfather. Who isn't really." She rubbed a hand in the air as though erasing the last few sentences. Then she studied him with surprising lucidity. "Tell me. If I'm sharing, you have to, too."

Oh, God. He hated this. That is, he liked her this close to him and wanting to talk, but he hated that she wanted to talk about his parents. But he'd brought them up. He drew a breath, closed off all connection to the hurt, and said calmly, "My mother was promiscuous and took up with anybody and everybody, and left when I was ten with a guy who played the sax at The Whale and Whistle. My father drank to forget, and it worked. He managed to forget me completely."

She stared into his eyes with a clarity that was astonishing considering the amount of vodka he knew she'd consumed. "You love him, anyway, though, don't you?" she asked quietly.

And that was what unglued him. How in the hell did she see that? He didn't even admit it to himself. He built computers, the most fact-demanding, mathematically based occupation in the world, so how could he do something so intrinsically nonsensical as love someone who'd never loved him?

He reached for the bottle. They were down to ice now and no juice, he noticed. She held out her glass.

He hesitated. "Sally, you're getting drunk," he warned.

She shook her head, twice quickly and once very slowly. "I'm not. I was too busy to eat today, and I took an antihistamine because the wildflowers were driving me crazy." She sighed as though the explanation were an effort. "And I don't usually drink, so it's hitting me. But, I'll be fine."

Apparently impatient for his compliance, she took the bottle, poured more vodka into her glass, then topped up his.

"Go on," she commanded.

Fighting her seemed futile, so he did as she asked.

"He worked two jobs to keep it together for us," he said, remembering how often his father was gone, and how his father had arranged for the woman who lived next door to feed him dinner when she fed her children. "When he was around, the place always reeked of beer, and if he did speak to me, it was to bark at me to do my homework, or finish my chores. I remember wanting to tell him that I was on his side, that I understood how hurt he must be, but when he wasn't barking at me, he was asleep or drunk.''

Sally shook her head sadly. ''Out of reach,'' she empathized, ''just like my mother and my grandfather. The one that is. Cooper. But it's okay that you love him anyway. You appreciate that he tried...even...even if it wasn't enough.''

He didn't understand how she could seem so lucid one moment, then slur her words. And her face had a tendency to blur. Of course, that could be his problem. She was drinking a lot, but he'd been keeping up with her.

''It's stupid.''

''It's what people do. I wanted to be a vet.''

He tried to relate that to her previous state-ment—or to any part of the conversation— and couldn't. That didn't matter, he guessed.

''The first time I saw you,'' he remembered, his recollections clear though things were fuzzy at the moment, ''you were trying to lure a fawn out of the woods with rose petals.''

She giggled. ''The deer love our roses. Hart-field says he's forgotten what color the roses are in the back of the house because we never get to see them. They eat them while they're still buds. Are you hungry? I'm starved!''

Food. Food was a good idea. It would dilute

the effect of the vodka. For a man who didn't like to lose control of things, intoxication was unsettling.

"I know a great place for dinner," he said, pushing his glass away.

She giggled again. "Good. But I don't think I can drive."

David stood, tested his balance and decided he could get to the phone if he didn't have to do it in a straight line.

"I'll call a cab," he said.

She leaned back in her chair and spread her arms wide. "I *love* cabs."

Then call *me* a cab, he said silently to himself, thinking he couldn't be that under the influence if he could still make a joke. Such as it was.

CHAPTER FOUR

SHE WAS DEAD. Sally couldn't think of anything else that could be responsible for this total blackness.

The pain in her head must have been the cause of her death. That had to be it. She throbbed from ear to ear both across her forehead and over the crown of her head. It felt as though the pain had cleaved... Wait a minute!

If she felt pain, she couldn't be dead. This headache might have resulted in death, but then she wouldn't feel anything.

So, she was still alive, but she was blind!

No. Not entirely. There seemed to be light from beyond a kind of veil. An involuntary fluttering told her that that veil was her eyelids.

She wasn't dead or blind, she was simply caught in some kind of REM sleep paralysis.

She forced herself to remain calm, to relax. "Open your eyes," she mentally told herself. "You can do it. You can do anything. You taught yourself that long ago. You can do it. Open your…there!''

Her eyes were open just a slit, but they were open. Through the slit, she saw… What was that? A coffered ceiling? It was beautiful. Oak Meadow had a coffered ceiling, but it was in the dining room. Had she fallen asleep in the dining room?

Of course not. There were no beds in the dining room.

She opened her eyes completely, startled by the anomalies of her half-asleep investigation. She saw ice-blue watered silk fabric on the walls, the top of a large, oak-framed mirror, the pointed top of a cathedral-backed chair and French doors that opened out onto… Where was she?!

She sat up abruptly and saw what appeared to be the Taj Mahal beyond her window, the Eiffel Tower, and a Gothic spire.

She caught sight of the scrollwork sign on the nearest rooftop and blinked to clear her sleepy eyes. The L-a-s space V-e…Las Vegas!

"Oh, my God!" Sally whispered, bringing her hands up to her mouth. As she did, her right hand collided with something warm and suedelike beside her in bed. She looked down and choked back a gasp. Her eyes focused on the floral bedcovers that were pulled up to a navel between angular hip bones. There was a line at a flat waist where the white skin below it changed to a café-au-lait color above it, the jut of a strong, tanned rib cage and a pattern of dark hair that started in a point and opened into a broad V shape over strong pectoral muscles.

She felt the scream starting in the pit of her stomach.

Almost against her will, she made her eyes follow the line of a strong throat up a chin…a chin with a cleft in it!

David! She'd slept with David!

She put one hand over the other to stop the scream. And as she did, she scratched her right hand with something on her left. She brought her hands up in front of her eyes, wondering what had done that, and saw a large, probably two-karat diamond ring on her left hand—and a band that matched it inset with small diamonds.

One fact stood out clearly in a brain muddled with horror and confusion. That was not the diamond Brandon had given her.

She dropped her hands to her lap, felt bare skin and looked down to see that she was completely naked.

"No, no, no!" she told herself, swinging her

legs out of bed. A sheet of parchment propped up against the base of the lamp caught her attention. A moan began in her throat as she leaned closer to see it more clearly.

"Marriage Certificate," it read, "Sally Elizabeth Webb to David Elliott Miller on this day of our Lord..."

SOME FIEND had implanted a fire alarm in his ear. David turned over, only to discover the same vile crime had been perpetrated in his other ear. As the sound forced him out of sleep to wakefulness, he began to realize that the awful sound wasn't an alarm at all, but a woman's screams.

He sat up abruptly, wondering what on earth was going on. He never brought a woman home. He often worked at home and one provided too much of a distraction from the other.

The first thing he saw was his naked upper body reflected in a large oak mirror atop a completely unfamiliar dresser, in a room he didn't recognize at all. The only part of the picture he'd ever seen before was the woman reflected beside him, the blankets pulled up to her breasts, her mouth wide open in a scream. She was Sally Webb.

What in the hell...?

The first thing he had to do was stop the sound; his head ached abominably. He turned to clamp a hand over her mouth and demand in a harsh whisper, "What is the matter with you?"

Her eyes wide and clearly horrified above his hand, she held up her left hand and pointed to her third finger. There was a large diamond on it...and a wedding band. Oh, God. He couldn't remember how he'd gotten here, but it was pretty clear they'd spent the night together. He dropped his hand.

"You're married?" he asked in disbelief.

She made a sound of disgust, shoved him back to the pillows, turned to grab something off her bedside table and kneel over him, holding it to his face. "To you, David! I'm married to you! How could you *do* this?!" She scrambled off the bed, either unaware or unconcerned about the fact that she was completely naked. Certain that was bound to occur to her at any moment, he leaned up on an elbow and let himself enjoy the view of her tight little backside walking away from him, then her flustered turn that brought small, high breasts into view, a neat waist above the slight flare of hips, slender thighs and... Well. Best not to go there.

Although...the only thing he could remember

about last night was that he already had. He felt a weakening along his spine that was usually foreign to him. That memory blossomed in his mind, her legs wrapped around him, her small hands on him, her voice in the darkness whispering his name.

Just as he'd suspected, she suddenly looked down at herself, made a disgusted sound, and snatched a long dark-blue terry robe off the foot of the bed and cocooned herself in it.

"How could you *do* this to me?" she demanded again. "You're supposed to be my brother's friend! And I'm supposed to marry someone else in a week!"

"Okay, wait a minute." He spoke firmly. He had every intention of using this turn of events to his advantage, but if she suspected that, she'd do everything she could to fight him. So he had to pretend the same horror over the situation that she obviously felt until he could figure out how to make her see that this was a good thing after all. "You're not the only one whose plans this has upset. I was in Massachusetts on business and I'm supposed to be at the governor's mansion for lunch tomorrow. If you just stay calm, we'll figure out what happened and how we can get out of it."

She glowered at him and sat down on the edge of the bed. "You made the drinks, as I recall," she accused.

"You're the one who kept adding vodka," he retorted, "and no juice. We must have gotten here on my plane." He looked around the room, spotted his cell phone on the bedside table and reached for it.

"Who are you calling?" she asked.

"My pilot." He stabbed out Charlie Walker's cell phone number and Charlie picked up instantly.

"Ready to go?" Charlie asked.

"Where are you?"

"Spent the night at the Airport Hawthorne Hotel." David heard a chuckle. "Not remembering much this morning? You and the lady did consume a bottle of champagne on the flight from Dover. And you were already under the influence when we took off. You took a cab into town from the airport."

"That was wise."

"It took you to the Desert Sands Bridalorium. I asked the cab driver to let me know where he took you. You didn't get...married?"

"Oh, yeah." David reached for the front of Sally's robe and as she tried to slap his hand away, he read the embroidery on the pocket. "We're at the Firenze. We're going to get something to eat, then we'll be at the airport in about an hour and a half."

"I'll have us ready to go."

"Thanks, Charlie." To Sally, he said, "Get dressed, we'll have breakfast, then we'll head home and figure out what to do."

She put a hand to her head and held on to the bed post. "I can't even think about food," she grumped. "I think I'm going to be sick."

"That's because you have nothing in your stomach." He climbed out of bed and went to the chair for his clothes. She watched him, her eyes wandering over him with sudden interest. When she realized he was aware of her study, she said irritably, "Would you please put something on!"

He grabbed his briefs and jeans and grinned at her. "If you're sure you've had your fill."

She snatched her things off the foot of the bed and shook them at him. "We're going home and have this marriage annulled!" A sheer, purple-blue-and-pink-flowered bra fell to the floor. With a growl, she picked it up.

He pulled on his briefs and pretended to look regretful. "I'm not sure how the law reads, but I don't think we can get an annulment after last night.''

She looked puzzled for a moment, then realized the significance of that detail. She hesitated, as though analyzing her body and how it felt. Then her eyes met his and her cheeks flushed. She tossed her head and continued to hold his gaze, though he knew she wanted desperately to look away.

"Then we'll get a divorce,'' she said, her voice strained, and stormed into the bathroom.

The moment that made annulment impossible came back to him as she slammed the door behind her. He sat on the end of the bed, feeling weak as he remembered it.

It was probably the importance of her touch on him that had brought him out of his vodka-champagne stupor. He'd come to awareness suddenly and found himself in the middle of the bed with Sally kneeling astride him.

It was clear that she wasn't entirely aware of what she was doing. Her eyes had a dreamy, faraway look, and her whispered endearments were slurred. But her touch was sure, her gestures sweet with yearning.

Still—she was Richard's little sister. She was

a vulnerable woman in a dangerous situation. He could easily deter her from her purpose.

And he was about to when she lay her upper body atop his, the beaded tips of her cool breasts pressing into his pecs, her short, silky hair rubbing against his cheek, her lips moving over his jaw as she said his name over and over.

Then it seemed suddenly noble and right to let her do as she pleased. There was no danger here because he'd loved her forever, and all he'd ever wanted was to care for her and love her as she deserved.

That purpose settled inside him like a creed to live by as he pulled on his clothes and socks and shoes. He gathered up his watch, wallet and cell phone from the bedside table.

She was now Mrs. David Miller, and she was going to stay that way.

All he had to do was make her realize that she wanted that, too. He'd turned major corporations to his way of thinking, certainly he could change the mind of one small woman.

It would occur to him later that it was probably that kind of optimism that had defeated Samson when he was dealing with Delilah.

CHAPTER FIVE

SALLY BRUSHED her hair with shaking hands, feeling completely out of control. She'd slept with David Miller! She could feel the difference in her body, the…the…slight physical pressure, the weird feeling of…of emotional exhilaration.

Ha! She dropped her brush in her purse and stared angrily at her reflection. "You idiot!" she told herself. "That isn't exhilaration, it's simple satisfaction because you made love with a man you've secretly lusted after for years! But you missed it!" And that was unfortunate, because Brandon never approached it with quite the enthusiasm she felt it deserved. Brandon. Oh, God!

She yanked the bathroom door open and marched to the outer door, stopping to accuse David as he tucked his shirt into his jeans, "I can't believe you let this happen!"

He smiled pleasantly. "You underestimate your own powers of persuasion, Sally."

She opened her mouth to offer a retort, then

stopped, momentarily off balance. Brandon's casual approach to their lovemaking always led her to believe she didn't have any.

But she pushed the thought away. She did not need more confusion.

She yanked the outer door open and caught a glimpse of a crowd of men and women gathered in a semicircle in front of the door. Then lights went off in her face, blinding her, as a female voice said, "Miss Webb. Congratulations on your marriage! How long have you and David Miller been involved?"

As she blinked to restore her sight and swallow a gasp of desperation, other voices asked other question.

"Will you keep your name?"

"Will you continue to manage Oak Meadow? Will you live there?"

The press was always eager to report David Miller's latest accomplishment, she thought grimly.

So much for trying to fix everything before anyone noticed.

"You're all on your toes," David said with lazy amusement. He came up behind her and placed his hands on her upper arms, rubbing gently. For their benefit, she wondered, or to relax her? "How did you find us, Baldwin?"

A seasoned veteran of the paparazzi that Sally had seen hovering on the fringes of parties and charity functions replied from the middle of the crowd. "I was covering the arrival into town of Ruby Ryan and her current boy-toy, and had the good fortune of seeing your pilot walk into the Airport Hawthorne hotel. I figured you had to be around somewhere and just scoured my sources until I discovered you and Miss Webb got married last night at the Desert Sands Bridalorium." He looked around at his companions, giving them a look that was slightly superior, yet somehow fraternal. "And this pack is always watching me to find out what's going on, so when I learned you'd registered at the Firenze, they followed me here."

"Well done," David praised, his manner light and cordial. "So, there's no point in telling you we're just good friends, and we're working on a charity project together?"

A young woman in the front of the crowd held up a photocopy of their marriage certificate. "Don't think that'll work, Mr. Miller."

Someone else asked, "What about your engagement to Brandon Pryer, Miss Webb? Does

he know that you've married someone else a
week before your scheduled wedding to him?
You've invited over three hundred guests, I understand."

Sally prayed for attack from another planet and
vaporization of her body. She had no such luck.

She smiled, considering her options, and decided that appearing fickle to the national press
would probably do less damage to her family's
image and her own reputation than admitting that
she'd made a terrible error in judgment while
drunk. Lying to these people never worked. She
would worry later about how to fix it.

"No, he doesn't," she said candidly, "but I'm
sure he'll react with the grace for which the Pry-
ers are known and respected."

There were greedy looks of anticipation in the
crowd, mad scribbling, the clicks of tape record-
ers, and more flashes in her face.

As she backed away from a particularly bright
flash, David tucked her protectively into his
shoulder. "All right," he said to the group.
"You've got your story. Now, if you don't mind,
we're off to breakfast." He tried to move through
the crowd, but they pressed closer.

Baldwin asked, "Does this mean you won't be
keeping your date with Governor Brooke tomor-

row to talk about getting computers into the hands of underprivileged children?''

"That's become a priority for me, too, as well as for the governor." David replied patiently. "I'll be there."

"Will Mrs. Miller be accompanying you?"

Sally opened her mouth to reply, but all the ramifications of a yes or no answer ran through her mind. If she said no, she'd look like a less than enthusiastic newlywed, but if she said yes, she'd have to go to Boston with David instead of regrouping and trying to figure out how to repair what she'd done!

Somewhere in the back of her mind, a thought not hampered by her challenging circumstances reminded her that Anne Marie Brooke was an avid advocate for animals.

Apparently deciding she was taking too long, David squeezed her closer. "Can't let her out of my sight. Now please, before she collapses from hunger…'' David put a hand out in front of them and literally pushed his way through the crowd to the elevators.

The elevator doors opened as they approached. A bellman, surprised by the crowd, got off with a full luggage cart, forcing the crowd apart. David bustled Sally onto the car, pushed the button

to close the door, then glowered at a lanky reporter who tried to follow them but apparently
thinking better of the impulse, stayed back.

The doors closed and the car began to move
downward.

Sally felt the nausea rising in her throat. "I'm
going to be sick," she said, putting a hand to her
mouth.

"Take a deep breath," David suggested, putting an arm around her shoulders. "We'll be outside in a minute."

"What have I done?" she demanded in a raspy
whisper, willing to admit to herself for the first
time that it wasn't all his fault, that this was the
result of that letter from Warren Cooper and her
own immature reaction to it.

She waited for the quiet condemnation her
grandfather would have offered, or the carefully
worded criticism that was Brandon's way of reg-
istering disapproval.

But David said simply, "You did the best you
could in a sticky situation. That's all anybody
could ask."

"I got drunk and married you!" she reminded
him.

He laughed lightly. "And I got drunk and married *you*. We got in it together. We'll find a way out together.''

Having someone take half the blame for her behavior when she'd spent most of her time trying to blame it all on him, was new in her experience.

"I'm not going to be able to eat," she said, picking a topic she understood.

"We'll get a couple of bagels to go, and take a cab to the airport. You have to have something in your stomach for the flight."

She hid from reporters in the ladies' room while David went to the coffee shop for bagels. Then he sent one of the desk clerks in to tell her he was waiting for her outside with a cab.

The air outdoors was like the inside of an oven, but once the cab got moving, she hung out the side window, breathing in the fresh air, hoping it would settle her stomach. She felt David's hand rub gently up and down her spine. She rested her head on her folded arms on the lowered window, feeling more wretched than she'd ever felt before.

She was just beginning to see all the holes in her plan for dealing honestly with the press. Now Brandon would probably hear on the news that she'd married another man in Las Vegas. Be-

cause David Miller was involved it was undoubtedly on CNN already. Brandon would have to
explain to his father, who was about to announce
his candidacy for the United States Senate.
Maybe her decision favoring her own change of
heart over the excuse of intoxication had been
stupid after all.

But, then, Brandon's mother headed up a committee called Pledge To Be Sober, encouraging
young people to pledge sobriety throughout high
school. She'd gained national acclaim for her efforts. Maybe the decision had been right after all.

Hardly right, but maybe the best of the poor
choices left to her? And she would get to speak
to the governor's wife.

She pushed Brandon and his family out of her
thoughts and concentrated on her grandfather's
reaction to her marriage. She could imagine him
sitting at the breakfast table with his friends and
reading the morning paper. "Webb Heiress Weds
Computer Mogul Miller" would leap right out at
him. He would probably even presume it was Diana, the rebel, until he read on and found Sally's
name. If he didn't suffer a stroke on the spot, she
would certainly be in for the sharp edge of his
disapproval and probable disownment when she
got home.

Only she wasn't going home. Was she?

They pulled into the airport and up to a very efficient and sophisticated-looking personal jet. The word *Lear* was painted in script on the tail. A man about David's age wearing khaki shorts, a T-shirt and a baseball cap with the word *Millerware* on them walked around the plane to meet them. David shook hands with him, then drew Sally forward.

"Sally, I'd like you to meet Charlie Walker. Charlie, my bride, Sally Webb Miller."

Charlie had a strong handshake and a bright smile that seemed to annoy her hangover. "We met yesterday afternoon," he said, shaking her hand. "But you probably don't remember."

"I don't," she said, returning his smile. "I apologize. Was I obnoxious?"

He looked surprised. "Not at all. Just a little giggly."

Giggly. Sally Webb, Lawrence Webb's estate manager and doyenne of the ecologically minded social set had been *giggly.* She sighed and allowed David to lead her to the fold-down steps.

"Go on up," he said, "and make yourself comfortable. I'll be right behind you."

"If we're going to Boston," she said, remembering that important little detail, "I'm going to have to stop at home first, talk to Brandon and my grandfather and pick up some clothes.''

He nodded. ''We're stopping in Dover, then driving to Boston. Your grandfather's meeting us at the airport with your clothes. A driver I sometimes hire while I'm here is picking him up.''

She blinked at him, then regretted it. The action hurt.

David continued, ''I called him while you were waiting in the ladies' room in the hotel. I didn't want him to hear it on the news before we had a chance to explain.''

She was torn between irritation with him for usurping a chore that should have been hers, and appreciating the fact that he'd taken the responsibility especially when she hadn't had an opportunity but had been concerned about it. It had been both heroic and thoughtful of David.

''What did Granddad say?'' she asked, not certain she wanted to hear.

He grinned. ''Not for a lady's ears. Go on up.'' He handed her the bag of bagels. ''I bought you tea instead of coffee. Thought that might settle your stomach.''

She went, happy to put thoughts of her grandfather out of her mind for the moment.

She'd noticed last night in a soft-edged haze

that the interior of the plane was surprisingly roomy. It was fitted with armchairs and a sort of settee with seat belts making it look like some-one's living room. There was wallpaper patterned with ivy vines, cozy wall lamps and carpeting that matched the ivy.

She took a single chair, pulled her tea out of the bag and placed the paper cup in a little well carved out of the table near her chair. Sitting back, she grabbed the airplane phone and called Brandon's private number, she got his answering machine, then called his office and got his voice mail. She hung up without leaving a message.

She took a sesame seed bagel, ignored a paper container of strawberry cream cheese, and tried to force her brain to adjust to what had happened. Had it been only about twenty-four hours, since yesterday, when MacKenzie was helping her try on her wedding dress and harassing her about Brandon?

She'd been so sure she had the answers then, but Mark Solomon's arrival with the letter from Warren Cooper changed everything.

No. That wasn't accurate. Her grandfather Cooper's letter unsettled everything, but it had been her choice to run to Richard in alarm. Find-ing David there instead had changed everything.

So, here she was, one brief day later, sitting on a Lear jet eating a bagel—and married to David Miller.

She suspected Diana had just lost the title of rebel.

CHAPTER SIX

LAWRENCE WEBB was furious. Sally withstood his withering glare and his wooden, unbending stance as she stood on tiptoe and reached up to hug him. All six feet of him remained regally stoic. His iron-gray hair contributed to the impression he made of steely implacability.

The long, black limousine David had arranged to pick up Lawrence Webb and drive him to the airport stood by.

David turned to Charlie, who waited behind them. "We're taking off to eat," he said. "It's been a long day and we're famished. We'll see you when we get back from Boston in a couple of days."

"Sure," Charlie replied. "I've got a few things to do. I'll wait for your call."

David ushered Sally into the back of the limo. Lawrence followed her in and sat facing her while David settled beside her.

"Nice to see you again, Mr. Miller," the driver said, then asked, "Where to?"

"Butler's Grille, please, Henry."

"Sure thing, Mr. Miller."

As the limo glided away, Sally met her grandfather's angry stare intrepidly. She knew the man, any sign of weakness and she'd be dead.

"If I'm to have any respect for you in the future," he said, "you will have this marriage annulled. I don't know how we'll handle the scandal, but we'll worry about that later. Right now, I need some reassurance that you haven't completely lost your mind!"

Of course she understood his anger and confusion. It just couldn't be handled as easily as he thought.

"I've already called Dan Paige," he said. Dan Paige was his lawyer. "He can arrange for—"

"An annulment isn't an option," she said quickly and with a firm gaze.

He raised an eyebrow that she'd questioned his solution, then she saw the horrified disbelief in his eyes when he realized what she meant. Her cheeks flushed vividly, but she made herself hold his condemning stare.

"And I'll deal with it. It's my life, my...my marriage."

"Very well," he said, looking out the window as though he couldn't bear to look at her. "It'll be interesting to see how you get your life on track again. If you can."

"She's been pretty busy keeping your life organized," David interjected calmly. "She's had little time to even find a track for her own life."

"Well, it isn't just her life involved here, is it? I can't imagine how poor Brandon's feeling right about now. I've tried calling him and can't reach him."

"We've tried, too," Sally said. "He isn't answering his cell phone or his pager."

"It's comforting to know you've at least thought of him," Webb retorted. "Even if it's a little after the fact."

"Mr. Webb..." David began.

"And *you!*" Her grandfather turned his attention to David. Sally knew it was cowardly, but she was relieved. "I never liked you, Miller. But I gained respect for you as a businessman, and invited you to Dover to talk about a deal. And this is how you repay me? By stealing my granddaughter?"

Sally was about to defend David by explaining to her grandfather that he hadn't exactly stolen her, when she realized what he'd said.

He'd invited David to Dover?

They were doing a deal?

Insight fell on her like ice water from a bucket in a booby trap.

So this wild escapade that had shaken her to the core, though oddly exciting, was not the result of alcohol consumption at all, but more likely a business strategy. Her grandfather had always disapproved of David, but doing business with the old man would probably not only be extremely lucrative, but do a lot for Millerware's status as well.

The chill seeped through her bones and deep inside, sealing off her wildly beating heart.

"You married me," she heard herself ask in a flat undertone, "to insure a business deal?"

DAVID CLOSED his eyes, suddenly impatient with both of them.

"Yes, of course," he replied flippantly. "Your grandfather has always hated me, so when I'm invited to demonstrate my product to his company, I abscond with and marry his granddaughter to secure a multimillion dollar deal. Right. Sure. It's a good thing you're in fund-raising, Sally, and not business. You'd be living under a bridge by now.''

Sally pushed away from him to the end of the back seat and he lowered his arm, missing her closeness despite the glimpse of irrational thinking on her part.

''No, I did not steal your granddaughter.'' He turned his attention on Webb. ''She was upset and came looking for Richard, but he'd gone fishing and I was there, checking out his latest game.''

''Upset about what?'' Lawrence asked.

Sally turned to David, her eyes wide and pleading. It took him a moment to realize she was asking him not to mention the letter. Of course. Lawrence might not know about Warren Cooper.

He usually favored honesty, but where an old man's feelings were involved, he could see her point. Even if it was an old man who'd always considered him inferior.

''Wedding jitters,'' he said, hoping the words didn't sound as lame as it felt saying them. ''You know. I made her a drink, we got to talking and catching up and we drank a little too much.''

"Wedding jitters!" Lawrence repeated in disbelief. "Why on earth would you have wedding jitters when you're marrying a lawyer with a thriving practice, who happens to be the son of a socially prominent and very wealthy state senator?"

She looked relieved that her grandfather was buying the story. "Because there should be more to marriage," she said, her color coming back as she was hit with the epiphany, "than social position and money."

"He loves you! His diamond was bigger than that one!" Lawrence pointed to the rings now on her finger. David remembered that the ring Brandon gave Sally had probably been a karat larger with smaller diamonds on each side.

Sally ran the thumb of her right hand over her rings. "I thought these were beautiful," she said with a sincerity that surprised David. He had only the vaguest memory of shopping for them, of her picking out the simple set. She glanced at him in reluctant apology.

Webb shook his head pityingly. "You traded down, Sally," he said. "A bad move in business or in life."

They'd reached the restaurant and the driver

pulled into the valeted lot. The door was opened, and the valet's hand reached in to help Sally out.

Before Webb could follow, David leaned forward to obstruct his passage.

"Look, Mr. Webb," he said politely, but with a gravity he hoped the old man didn't underestimate. "I'm asking you to stop bullying her. I know you're her grandfather and you've raised her, but at the moment, I'm her husband, and whether or not that relationship remains when all of this is resolved, it holds for now. And while I didn't marry her to deliberately hurt you, I don't think I have to worry about 'paying you back' as you put it for inviting me to show you our product. You were smart to recognize that we offer the best computers and software on the market, so I don't think I owe you anything for wanting to deal with me."

Clearly unused to being spoken to with candor rather than deference, Webb barely held his temper in check as he climbed out of the limo.

David followed, wondering if he'd just kissed a four-million-dollar deal goodbye.

Then he thought with a private smile as the three of them walked into the restaurant like a parade, if it meant he was kissing Sally hello, it was worth it.

"You're just taking off for Seattle," Webb asked, downing the last of a glass of Madeira, "without a thought to what happens to Oak Meadow?"

"David has an appointment with the governor tomorrow," she said. "The press is going to be watching us, and David told them I'm coming along. So, I'd better go to avoid further embarrassment for all of us. Besides, the governor's wife was an animal rights activist before her husband got into the governor's mansion." She would recoup some of her losses if she could make an ally out of Anne Marie Brooke. Thinking about that helped her ignore the absurdity of her situation. Things had been bad enough when she'd thought she'd married David because they'd both been overcome by Screwdrivers. But to realize that he'd actually had a plan and that she'd fallen right into his hands was almost more than her pride could bear. "I might be able to get her help with a new site for the wildlife shelter."

"And Oak Meadow can just flounder, I suppose.'' He sounded petulant rather than angry, Sally noticed, and it served to lessen her sense of guilt. For a man who didn't believe in spoiling children or staff, he certainly enjoyed being indulged himself.

"I'll send you someone," David said.

"I don't just need *some*one." Her grandfather repeated the word disdainfully. "I need an organizer, a guardian angel, a field marshall, a—"

"Trust me on this," David insisted. "My staff are clever, intelligent people and I'll have my best help here first thing in the morning."

"I need Sally," Lawrence said, a demanding edge to his tone. "The estate cannot function without her."

"It'll have to," David said, "because she's coming with me."

Despite her sense of having been betrayed by David's failure to mention his business deal with her grandfather, Sally was impressed by his ability to stand up to him. She had yet to see anyone who worked for Lawrence Webb or did business with him challenge him and survive.

Of course, David probably wouldn't. She was sure whatever business they were doing was now dead in the water.

She excused herself from the table and went to the telephone in the lounge to call Brandon. She got the answering machine again.

She tried his cell phone and got his voice mail.

He'd either been in the courtroom all day and hadn't heard, or he had heard and was hiding out. Knowing him, the former seemed more likely. She'd never seen him get upset or even raise his voice, but this was a unique situation. It could be that he'd holed up somewhere in order to deal with his fiancée's defection with another man.

She hung up the phone, then her attention was caught by the sound of her name in the bar. She peered in to see her face on television and the recreation of the scene in the hallway on the twenty-ninth floor of the Firenze.

She looked desperate and terrified; David looked relaxed and amused.

"Brandon Pryer, III," the reporter said, a pretty little blond with knowing blue eyes, "who was Miss Webb's fiancé until this sudden turn of events, has not been reached for comment. His parents, Senator and Mrs. Pryer, are hiking in the Adirondacks with members of a Newburyport halfway house for alcoholics. The house is a pet project of Mrs. Pryer's. They are also unavailable for comment.

"Lawrence Webb, Mrs. Miller's grandfather, refused to speak to our reporter.

"This wedding seems to have sent a lot of people into hiding," she said in closing. "Or into denial. This is Annabeth Barrett from Dover, Massachusetts."

Sally let her forehead bang against the plastered wall. Hiding and denial sounded like good options to her.

CHAPTER SEVEN

DAVID LOVED BOSTON. It was big and noisy, but its drivers were the most suicidal in the world, except possibly for Paris. Fortunately, though, he had a driver, and was able to enjoy the lights, the sights and the unmistakable flavor of a city that had reckoned with heroes and both won and lost against invaders several times in its history.

He'd looked forward to this trip for the opportunity to meet the governor and for Millerware to help children at risk to learn and grow. Then he'd intended to spend several days just playing tourist.

A lot had changed since then, but he did hope he'd still have a chance to get around the city. He'd love to show Sally all his favorite places, and have her show him hers. If she ever spoke to him again. She'd been silent since they'd left Dover, about forty miles ago.

Sally still thought he'd married her to secure his deal, he was sure. Though, why that made sense to her as a negotiating tool given the way her grandfather felt about him, he'd never know, but he had faith that she'd eventually see the large hole in that reasoning. Until then, he'd do everything he could to remind her that she was married to him, and to show her that he knew how to treat his wife.

He'd arranged for a suite at the Boston Winthrop, and the manager personally led them up, pointing out the amenities and explaining that the contents of what was usually the honor bar was in this case a gift from the hotel.

"Also," he said with what seemed to be caution, "there's a Mr. Pryer and a Miss Drake waiting in my office. I would have turned them away, but—" He smiled apologetically "—I saw the item on the evening news about…about…"

David turned to Sally. "Pryer and a young woman?"

"MacKenzie Drake. My friend. You can send them up," she said quietly to Benson.

"Very well. Enjoy your stay with us." He crossed the long living area toward the door. "If there's anything at all you need, extension 002 is my office."

"Thank you, Mr. Benson." David went to see him out, then held the door open for the bellman arriving with their bags. To the young man's credit, he didn't bat an eye when Sally led him to the main bedroom with his bags, then to a smaller room next to it with hers.

David tried not to look as deprived as he felt by that action. He'd dreamed of making love to her since he was fifteen and first laid eyes on her in Webb's garden, her hand held out to lure the deer. When he'd awakened last night to find her kneeling astride him, he'd been sure he *was* dreaming. But her touch had been too real and had brought his body awake in a way he'd never experienced before. Heaven had come down to earth for him and he knew he'd never be able to return to his old single life.

But his field was computer science where nothing could be rushed. One step had to follow another for careful but eventual success.

He could do this. He just had to think of it as one of Richard's sophisticated games. Wait out all the hiding menaces, slay the dragons, win the princess.

As the bellman opened the door to wheel his cart into the hall, a man and a woman stepped aside to let him through. Pryer and Sally's friend, David presumed. He held the door for them, then ushered them inside.

He was vaguely aware of the pretty young woman and Sally embracing in the middle of the room as he and Pryer assessed each other. David considered himself good at character evaluation. One had to do it quickly and correctly in boardrooms and private business meetings. But he found this one tough to call.

"I'm Brandon Pryer," the man said with stiff politeness. They looked each other in the eye. He had the kind of looks that seemed to appeal to women—smooth, even, affable. They were comparable in size, though David doubted that Pryer's muscle came from years of hauling in fishnets to make money for school.

"Yes, I know," David replied. "David Miller."

On the one hand, David admired Brandon's coolheadedness in light of his having stolen his bride. But on the other, he knew how *he* felt about Sally and wondered where Pryer's passion and fury were. Not that that would have helped resolve things at this point—he just wondered about their absence.

Sally approached Pryer, taking his hand and leading him off toward the room she'd chosen, leaving David with the pretty little brunette.

Expecting her friend's displeasure, he was surprised when she socked him on the arm, whispered, "Well done!" and dragged him with her into the kitchen toward the cappuccino maker. "Do you know how to drive this thing?" she asked. "I could sure use one! Preferably with caramel syrup, but I suppose that's too much to ask?"

SALLY DIDN'T KNOW where to start. She'd been prepared for fury, for accusations, for recriminations, but Brandon simply sat in the chair by the bed and waited for her to begin.

"I'm sorry you found out on the news," was the first thing that seemed appropriate to say. "I tried to call you several times, but couldn't reach you."

He nodded. His face was expressionless. "I was in court all day, then Mac came to tell me when she heard the news on television. Your grandfather told us where to find you. He's pretty upset."

"Yes, I know."

"So, what happened? Do you love this guy?"

"Of course not." Sally, sitting on the edge of the bed, rubbed her throbbing forehead and tried to organize her thoughts. So much had happened, it was difficult to remember the sequence of events.

She started with the letter. She told him about Warren Cooper, about his love for her grandmother and the relationship that finally developed between them when her grandfather was missing and presumed dead.

"But you must never mention it to Granddad," she said. "He doesn't know any of this, and I have no intention of telling him. I can't imagine how he'd feel or what he'd do."

Brandon frowned and nodded. "I understand. But...what does that have to do with—"

"Well, I was upset!" she said a little too loudly, surprised he didn't see that. Then she lowered her voice and went on. "I called Diana and she was gone, then I called Richard and his line was busy so I just got in the car and drove over there. Only Richard was away on a fishing trip, and he'd invited David to stay with him while he was meeting with...a client." She put that in hurriedly so she didn't have to think about it.

Brandon raised an eyebrow. "The governor of Massachusetts is a client?"

Sally shook her head. "No, that's something

else. They're putting together a plan that'll help poor children get computers.''

"Then, who's the client?"

There was no escaping. She had to think about it after all. "Webb Worldwide," she replied.

She expected him to find that detail as shocking as she did, but he didn't seem to. "So, you went to Richard's and David was there. What happened next?"

Ignoring her disappointment, she continued. "I poured out my problems to him—"

"To a complete stranger?"

"He's not a complete stranger," she corrected. "He's been a friend of David's for years, and I've known him since I was thirteen."

He didn't seem to be upset by that either, just pensive. "Okay. You told him about the letter."

"I was crying," she explained, "and he made me a drink. A Screwdriver. It helped a little, you know. Made me feel less stressed, so I added more vodka and pretty soon we were talking about our lives and our families—and I was drinking vodka without the juice."

Brandon leaned back in the chair. "I see," he said. "And then he proposed?"

"No. All he proposed was a great place to

have dinner. I just didn't know the restaurant he had in mind was in Las Vegas.''

After all she'd told him, he remained calm. She went on intrepidly, certain his patience was about to snap at any moment.

''I don't remember much after getting on his plane,'' she admitted. ''His pilot says he put us in a cab in Vegas, and I guess the driver, presuming we, like many others there, had matrimony in mind, dropped us at the Desert Sands Bridalorium. We don't remember whose idea it was to get married, but we did.''

She waited for an outburst. It never came.

Brandon got to his feet, paced the length of the room, turned at the foot of the bed to go toward the window, then came back again. He sat down and said in the same tone he'd used since he'd arrived, ''I guess there's nothing to do but go along with things as they are.''

She stared a moment, then realized he must mean she could just stay married to David because Brandon no longer wanted her for his wife.

But he continued, surprising her further. ''When my father gets back to town, he's going to announce his candidacy for the U.S. Senate, and mom's getting an award for her work at the halfway house. If we announce that you did this in a drunken stupor, it's bound to be harmful to both of them.''

She waited for recrimination, certain it would come now. But, all he said was, ''We'll just wait a while, then you can quietly split and come back to me.''

It sounded so logical, so...clean, but deep inside she couldn't help feeling it was somehow the wrong solution.

''But, Brandon—'' she began.

''Don't worry about the wedding,'' he said, leaning forward to take her hands in his. ''I'll cancel everything and see that all our guests are notified.''

She thought about the evening news and figured they'd all probably already been notified.

''Let me do that,'' she said, overwhelmed with guilt and a weird sense of unreality. ''It'll be embarrassing for you.''

He smiled good-naturedly. ''Nah. When you come back to me, I'll look like a hero and the best man after all.''

She could not believe or even understand his behavior. Yet, it made her feel small and mean to question it. She was the one completely in the wrong, and he seemed to be doing his best to make things right.

She touched his face. "Brandon," she said gently. "I don't deserve this understanding, this...compassion."

He dismissed that with a wave of his hand. "You got traumatic news and reacted without thinking. And...you'll come back to me when the press forgets."

Yes. When the press forgets.

"But your father's announcement will be affected adversely anyway, won't it?" she asked anxiously.

He shook his head. "Not if I behave with stoic heroism, tell the press I understand and forgive you, then get you back in the end. The voters will think it took a remarkable man to father me." He smiled, quite pleased with himself. "All modesty aside, of course."

"Of course," she said, amazed that he'd found a way to benefit from what had happened. She wasn't sure if she was proud of him or offended by him.

In any case, he wasn't yelling at her, and she was extremely grateful for that.

They left the bedroom and found David and Mac sitting on opposite ends of a flowered sofa, chatting comfortably and drinking coffee.

"I've got court in the morning," Brandon

said, giving Sally a brief hug. "We have to take off. Mac, you ready?"

Mac put her cup down, David helped her into her suit jacket, and they all walked to the door.

Brandon turned to smile pleasantly at David. "I'll expect you to take good care of her until I get her back."

"I'll take good care of her," David said.

Brandon apparently missed the subtle omission, smiled and waved his goodbye. Mac hugged Sally, holding an extra moment, then left with Brandon.

When David had closed and locked the door behind them, he turned to Sally with an expectant expression.

She spread both arms out at her sides. "He understands," she said, the shock she still felt over that noticeable in her voice. "He says the best thing to do is to keep on as we are until the press forgets us and then I can quietly leave you and go back to him."

David stared at her. "Really," he said finally.

"Really," she confirmed. She told him about Brandon's offer to cancel the wedding plans, call the guests, then handle himself like a hero in front of the press.

"Carefully thought out," David said, picking up his cup and going to the coffeepot.

"Sensible," she said.

"Cold-blooded," he corrected, coming back into the living room with a steaming cup. "And he didn't kiss you good-night."

She pointed to the spot where he'd hugged her. "He took me in his arms right there," she disputed.

"He held you," he agreed, "but he didn't kiss you."

"Same difference," she argued.

He made a scornful sound. "Hardly."

"It's body contact," she insisted. "It's the same thing."

He put his cup down on the coffee table and opened his arms. "It's not, and I'll prove it to you. Come here."

She studied him warily.

He beckoned with his fingertips. "Come on. For the sake of argument."

She walked into David's arms, unwilling to give him cause to consider her a coward, yet certain she was stepping right into danger.

His arms closed around her and held her loosely as Brandon had done. "This is affection," he said, leaning his cheek against her hair.

"It's nice, comfortable. But not even serious body contact."

"A man doesn't have to wrestle a woman," she said, already aware of little frissons of feeling stirring everywhere their bodies were in contact, "to make his point."

"Of course not," he agreed, "but he does have to make sure she understands what he's telling her. This embrace," he said, "tells her she's a sweetheart and he loves spending time with her."

"Precisely." Feeling victorious, Sally relaxed her arms, expecting to be released.

Instead, David tightened his grip on her so that her breasts were squashed against him, and his thigh was pressed between her legs. She felt her pulse race. Her nostrils were filled with his herbal scent and she could see through the dark velvet of his eyes all the way into his soul.

"This embrace," he said softly, "says 'you are absolutely everything in the world to me, my very life, and I will stand between you and anything that would hurt you, and love you with everything I possess until my last breath.'" He began to lower his mouth to hers. "The kiss seals that promise," he whispered.

And he kissed her.

Point taken, she thought, some little corner of her brain at work in a body that had completely abdicated all power in the face of David's sensory onslaught. *A hug is not the same thing as a kiss at all. Not even close.*

There was no clever movement of his mouth, no passionate cupping and pinching of private parts, only the long, slow, intense connection of two pairs of lips discovering each other. His hands cradled her so completely that she felt herself a part of him, and his body enveloped hers so that his words played over in that one wide-awake corner of her brain. *I will stand between you and anything that would hurt you. And love you with everything I possess until my last breath.*

This was adoration, veneration, and she fell for it like a tree in a hurricane.

CHAPTER EIGHT

DAVID FELT the subtle change in her. She stopped holding back, leaned into him instead of away. She responded like a woman who'd never been cherished before.

He wanted more than anything in the world to take this to its natural conclusion. But he liked to think he was smart enough to know they'd both enjoy it more if that came as a result of a point *she* was making.

He dropped his hands from around her, holding her arms only long enough to help her regain her equilibrium. Her eyes were wide with astonishment, their focus somewhere beyond him.

"Sally?" he asked.

"Yeah?" She responded vaguely.

"See what I mean?"

"Uh...yeah." She seemed to focus on him finally, her smile a little shaky, her eyes still enormous. "I'm—I'm pooped," she said. "I'm going to bed."

"Okay. We're due at the mansion for lunch, so you can sleep in a while."

"Good." Her smile dissolved and she studied him as though he were a painting on the wall she'd just noticed. Then she shook her head, blew air between her lips in a way very different from her usually ladylike behavior, then walked off to her bedroom.

He fell onto the sofa, thinking that finding the key to Sally Webb was going to be harder than creating the complex, but user friendly, software for which he was famous.

At least he seemed to be moving in the right direction. Then he heard her bedroom door close between them and thought that was little comfort to a body yearning to make love to her.

THE GOVERNOR'S mansion was beautiful. As Lawrence Webb's granddaughter, Sally had lived in and visited homes that were more splendid and magnificent, but none that were as alive with the artwork and memorabilia of the commonwealth's past. Reporters were there to film them getting out of the limo, being welcomed by the governor and his wife, then led into their home.

John and Anne Marie Brooke were in their middle forties, children of political families, having grown up attending conventions and working campaigns. They were a handsome couple, down-to-earth and completely devoted to making a contribution during John's term of office.

"Imagine," the governor said at the head of a table that had once occupied space in John Adams's residence in France while he served as Minister to the Court of Saint James, "the difference it would make to underprivileged children, if we could put a computer in every one of their homes. Those who couldn't go on to college would still have a university right there at their fingertips."

Anne Marie put her fork down and patted his hand. "I agree with him, but I think you'd have to somehow close the computer to games, because that's what any child would turn to first."

"Couldn't we create a computer specially programmed for educational purposes alone?" Brooke asked. "To only allow access to approved Web sites, and only so much game time before it closes off, or something?" He pushed his plate aside and leaned toward David. "Could we do that?"

David thought and frowned. "We could program it to include whatever you wanted, and shut off game-playing after a certain time, but whether or not it's legal is something we'd have to look in to. I mean, if a child who's gotten a five-thousand-dollar laptop for his birthday can play games whenever he wants and visit any site his parents haven't excluded, a kid who gets the computer you're talking about could cry discrimination.''

The governor shook his head. ''I don't think so. If we're giving them away as a learning tool—say to support a curriculum—then it could do whatever we approve it to do.''

Sally marveled at the ease with which David conducted himself. She had met the governor and his wife before in several social situations once because of a committee her grandmother had belonged to that had helped restore the mansion's carriage house where many of the area's historical artifacts were kept. But she'd never sat with them at a table and held their undivided attention. She was surprised to find that she was the one who was a little uneasy while David seemed completely comfortable.

A woman in starched gray and white appeared with a chocolate cake on a pedestal dish.

Anne Marie smiled across the table at Sally. ''Do you have room for dessert?''

Sally shook her head regretfully. "It looks wonderful, but I'm afraid I don't."

"Good. Then come with me." She pushed away from the table. The men stood. She gestured them down. "If you'll excuse us, while you gentlemen have dessert, Sally and I will walk through the garden. I want to hear how her wild animal shelter's coming."

The governor glanced at his watch. "Don't forget we have our Sister City committee in an hour."

"I won't." Anne Marie pointed to the cake. "And don't eat it all in case we walk off lunch and want some after all."

The garden was a formally plotted affair that took up several acres behind the mansion. There were roses in many colors, a variety of mums and daisies, stately irises in yellow and purple, and pansies and alyssum everywhere. The women wound their way through all of them, Sally surprised to know that Anne Marie knew many of the details of her efforts for animals.

"That's a shame about that property on the Cape," she said as she plucked a small purple pansy and tucked its stem into the pocket of Sally's yellow suit. "It would have been perfect. Why won't the company let you buy it?"

Sally shrugged. "They just refused to even speak to me about it. I got as far as the second in command of Coastline Corporation and he said they had plans for it and were not interested in selling." Sally rolled her eyes. "I even got obnoxious and explained why it was so perfect for us and offered to look for another property for them, but he made it pretty clear his answer was final."

Anne Marie frowned. "Well, I'll keep my eyes and ears open. My mother is still in real estate."

Sally was surprised by her willingness to help. "I'm sure with all you have to do..."

Anne Marie plucked a very elegant purple iris for herself. "We're finally getting shelters for the homeless, for women in jeopardy, for teens. Our mission—John's and mine—is children and animals."

"Big jobs."

Sally followed Anne Marie around a bright-pink rhododendron, and thought in some wonder that her husband's plans seemed to be big also. John Brooke had asked David over lunch to consider the donation of computers to the project, and David had replied that he couldn't see how else it could be done. Education budgets were strained to the limit everywhere.

John had looked at him in ingenuous shock. "You mean...you'll do it?"

David had shrugged, then said simply, "Yes, we'll do it."

"You do understand that we're talking three or four million dollars?"

"Yes, I do."

"And Millerware can afford to do that?"

"Yes."

The governor had leaned back in his chair. "You'll forgive me if I say, 'Wow.'"

David had laughed.

Just before it was time for Anne Marie to return to the house for the governor's next appointment, she ran into a small shed at the edge of the garden, emerged with shears, and cut Sally a colorful bouquet of chrysanthemums.

"THEN THE PLAN IS," John Brooke said as the four of them stood by the limousine, photographers snapping away, reporters taking notes, "that we'll meet back here in two days when I'll have Bill Marshall from Friends for Families who will implement this project. He's in New York until Friday. You'll like him. Nothing discourages him." He shook Sally's hand. "You don't mind that I'm anchoring your husband in

Boston for a couple of days? I want him to meet Bill. I think we can get this project moving much more quickly than I'd anticipated.'' He clapped David on the shoulder. "There's nothing like having four million dollars handed to you to speed up a project. Shall we name something after you?'' he asked smiling.

"Oh, no.'' David helped Sally into the car as Henry opened their door. "The only thing I want named after me is a son. Thank you for lunch, Governor Brooke. We've enjoyed your hospitality.''

"And we've enjoyed your generosity. See you in a couple of days. I'll call your hotel when Bill gets in.''

Sally carried the flowers on her lap on the drive back to the hotel, both shaken and intrigued by David's remark.

"What do you say we let Henry see that those are put in water,'' David proposed, "then wander around Boston and see what's going on?''

She shouldn't be doing this, Sally thought. She should be figuring out how to get her life back, how to repair the damage she'd done to her family and to Brandon's. Then she remembered that Brandon would be making the most of this opportunity to come out heroic. And thanks to the governor's plea that they wait in Boston until he could arrange the meeting with Bill Marshall, Sally had several days to simply think about herself. She was surprised by how much appeal that held for her—and how much she liked the idea of wandering around Boston with David.

"Do you mind doing that, Henry?" David asked the chauffeur.

"Not at all," Henry replied. "Why don't I leave you at the foot of Beacon Hill? You can get lost in the crowd, and enjoy your afternoon and evening.

David waited for Sally's reply.

"Okay," she said finally. "Let's do that."

CHAPTER NINE

DAVID AND SALLY walked companionably hand in hand down Charles Street, where a concentration of antique shops were set among coffeehouses, bakeries, flower shops and gift and clothing boutiques. It was noisy and aromatic, and Sally seemed to be enjoying herself.

David had almost regretted asking her where she wanted to start, when she immediately replied, "Charles Street." But he could see that the walking and shopping relaxed her, and she seemed to have forgotten her anger over their marriage and her belief that he'd lured her into it in the interest of business.

She even reached for him unconsciously to point out things that interested her in shop windows, or when they crossed the busy streets. He was living his dreams, he realized, and was determined to make the most of every moment.

Over her objections, he bought her a jade pendant in an oriental shop.

"The gold character in the middle of the disc," the elegant woman behind the counter said, "means *love*." She tied it around Sally's neck and the dark-green stone fell between Sally's breasts. "It's part of Ming Oh's estate," she added. "Have you heard of her?"

Sally, intrigued despite herself, shook her head as she held up the pendant to study it.

"She was one of our leading citizens who fell upon hard times, and with no family to leave her treasures to, she gave some to a museum, and sold the rest. This is one of the less valuable pieces that belonged to her great-great-grandmother, a poor girl taken as a slave and bought at auction by Brian Maloney, a ship's captain out of New Bedford."

Bewitched by the story, Sally looked up at the clerk. "What happened?"

"They had nine children," the clerk said with a satisfied smile, "and Brian was a business genius. They had a big house up The Hill, and she lived to be ninety-one and see all her grandchildren and great-grandchildren. You can't ask for more than that."

Sally clutched the pendant. "No, you can't," she said, her voice strained. "Can we stop for a mocha?" she asked David, as they left the stores.

They found a coffeehouse on the corner and sat opposite each other at a small, round table in a fenced-off area of the sidewalk. Though he felt sure she loved the pendant, she suddenly looked grim.

"The story had a happy ending," he reminded her.

She didn't smile. "I know. I was just thinking about my grandfather Cooper, who never got to know his daughter, or meet his grandchildren. He could only contact us when he knew Grandmother had died, and was sure he was dying himself. I've been happy, so it isn't sad for me. But it must have been a tragedy for him."

"Maybe he was happy knowing he was doing what was ensuring your grandmother's happiness."

"It just seems a shame that one person should be called upon to sacrifice his happiness for someone else's."

She played with the straw in her mocha and sighed. "Brandon should get something out of it, I guess. I've made him miserable."

David didn't think he'd seemed miserable, but he didn't mention that.

"Why don't we make Brandon and everyone and everything else at home forbidden subjects as long as we're here? We have an impromptu vacation, and we should do our best to enjoy it.''

"I know. I'm sorry.'' She leaned toward him, a sudden interest in her eyes he liked seeing there. "So, how is it that you can consider personally funding this program of the governor's without even batting an eye? My grandfather's a little bit of a philanthropist, but he talks over every donation with his accountants and his attorney.''

David shrugged. "Just a difference in approach. Your grandfather's a businessman at heart, and I'll always be just the kid from a dysfunctional family that made good because he found an escape in computers. I keep thinking about all the other poor kids who might find a similar way out and I don't feel as though I need to talk to anyone about it. I know what I want to do.''

She leaned her chin on the heel of her hand and smiled. "I always thought you were pretty neat,'' she said. "I just never realized that you're…downright amazing.''

"Amazing.'' He repeated that word to himself, wondering if he liked it.

Then he decided it didn't matter because she stood, took his hand, and led him back out onto the street. She entwined her fingers with his and they shopped for another few hours, stopped for dinner at a candlelit Italian restaurant, then cabbed back to the hotel.

"So, how do you feel about being married?" he asked as she kicked off her shoes and he made a pot of coffee.

When she seemed surprised by the question, he reminded her of their agreement. "Remember that nothing and no one in Dover exists for us."

She grinned, apparently willing to make that leap. "I like it so far."

"What part do you like best?"

She sat in a corner of the sofa, her legs tucked under her. "I like shopping with a man who doesn't complain every time I walk into a store. I like getting presents." She laughed softly, fingering the jade pendant. "And I love the way you always put the coffee on when we get home. What about you?"

"In Seattle," he said, pulling cups down and finding a spoon, "I have a lot of friends, but I'm lonely when I go home to my condo. I think what I like most is that every time I look up, there you are—warm and beautiful and...mine."

"But I'm not yours," she reminded him.

"Right now," he corrected, "you are. And I belong to you. I find that pretty remarkable."

Her expression sobered. "This...can't be!" she said firmly.

He smiled at her over the counter. "And yet it is."

"We're pretending it is."

He met her eyes. "Maybe you're pretending."

She got suddenly to her feet, snatched up her shoes, muttered a quick apology and an even quicker good-night, and disappeared into her room.

He shouldn't have pushed, he knew, but he couldn't help it. Sooner or later, she was going to have to face what was happening between them.

At least, he hoped she did.

HE WOKE HER the following morning with a tray full of steaming fresh food from Room Service.

She sat up groggily as he removed the domed cover.

"Eggs Benedict and cottage fries!" she exclaimed, looking as though she were prepared to protest further.

He lifted the other lid to show her the vegetarian omelette it protected. "Or, a veggie omelette with light cheese if you prefer, and a side of fruit.''

She considered, then said with an embarrassed smirk, ''You can have one of the Benedicts,'' she bargained, ''and half the cottage fries if you'll share the fruit.''

''Done.'' He sat beside her in bed, helped make the appropriate changes, and though his last choice for breakfast would be a veggie omelette, he enjoyed it enormously because she seemed happy with her Hollandaise-swathed Benedict.

They planned their day to include the uptown chic of Back Bay, the exciting architecture of Copley Square, the Boston Public Library and the wonderful art it contained.

They walked miles, found a bistro for lunch, a coffeehouse with eclairs for midafternoon, then went back to the hotel exhausted to shower and dress for dinner in the hotel's dining room.

David lay on his bed while Sally showered in the bathroom off his room. She emerged, pink-cheeked, her hair damp and curly, her body wrapped in the hotel's fluffy white robe.

''I can't believe I'm hungry,'' she said, padding barefoot toward the hallway. ''I hope the dinner dress I brought still fits.''

''A lady blossoming out of her dress is never

considered a bad thing," he assured her, heading for the bathroom when he'd much rather have followed her.

She stopped in the doorway to laugh. "Now, that sounds like a playboy's attitude, rather than a husband's."

"Well, it's your good fortune," he said, facing her from across the room, "to have a husband who still feels like a bon vivant when he looks at you."

The electricity was almost visible. It was happening, he told himself bracingly. She was beginning to look at him differently. To *see* him. The last thing he wanted to do was reverse that in any way.

He winked at her and closed himself in the bathroom.

WHEN THEY LEFT the dining room, the manager met them in the lobby and handed David a message. "I hope you're enjoying your stay with us," he said, a raised eyebrow waiting for David's response.

"We're having a wonderful time," David said. "Thank you."

The manager returned to his office looking

pleased. David read the message as he and Sally waited for an elevator.

"Bill Marshall's back a day early," David said, reaching out to hold the door of an elevator car as it opened. "He wants to meet me for lunch tomorrow. Mrs. Brooke's away, apparently, but he says you're welcome to come anyway."

She shook her head, disappointed that the day of museum hopping they'd planned for the following day had to be canceled.

"I'll go clothes shopping," she said with a wry twist to her lips. "I know it's superficial and so not academic, but I love to shop at Quincy Market at Faneuil Hall." It was famous for its designer labels.

An older couple stepped in with them, and the doors closed. The elevator began its ascent.

"You mean you won't be home pouting," David asked, sounding disappointed, "waiting for me to return?"

The older woman smiled at Sally over his remark.

"I could," Sally teased, "but I'd really rather go clothes shopping. Could I pout in the Donna Karan outlet?"

"Sad commentary on the current state of the loving little woman," the older man said, elbowing David. "Although, I must say the current physical state of the loving little woman is quite wonderful."

The older woman swung her clutch purse at his stomach as the elevator doors parted, then grinned at Sally as she preceded her husband out. "You go, girl!" she said.

"Now, where did you learn to talk like that?" they heard her husband ask as the doors closed and the elevator resumed its upward path.

Sally leaned into David, laughing. He wrapped an arm around her and they were still embracing, still laughing, when they walked into their suite.

David unlocked the door, let her in before him, then closed and locked it.

They stood together just inside the room, the moment charged with awareness. Sally wanted more than anything to make love to him while sober so that she'd remember it. Because she couldn't have this dear, lighthearted, fun-loving relationship. She simply couldn't. Her life was about finances and order and grave issues that occupied her grandfather and therefore her. It was about Brandon's life and his parents' lives and all they wanted to accomplish.

But she wasn't supposed to think about Brandon.

Couldn't tonight be just about her?

About her and David?

No, it couldn't, she told herself with sudden resolve, looking away from the longing look in his eyes. She had to fix what she'd done, and if she made love with David again, the situation would be beyond repair.

Because she had a suspicion if she lay in his arms, she wouldn't care about anything else, ever.

"I'm going to bed early," she said, pretending exhaustion. Unless emotional exhaustion was a consideration.

He smiled gently. "That's the coward's way out," he chided.

"Yeah," she said. "I know that. Thanks for a wonderful day."

"It was my pleasure." He said that as though he meant it sincerely.

She hurried off to her room, afraid to test her mettle another moment.

CHAPTER TEN

SALLY COULDN'T EVEN find a scarf to buy. The shops were filled with every beautifully designed and up-to-the-minute garment a woman could hope to purchase, yet none of them appealed to her. She tried on dozens of tops, pants, dresses, even a few bathing suits, and not one of them did anything for her.

The tall, leggy clerk who'd been helping her all morning and part of the afternoon, put a hand to her hip and gestured around the fitting room, littered with the garments Sally had discarded.

"You might consider, honey," she said in a pleasant, even compassionate tone, "that nothing's going to look good to you until whatever's put that sad frown on your face goes away."

Sally climbed into a cab, certain the clerk was right. She'd left her a large tip for her trouble. Maybe *she* could find something to buy with it.

Of course, she knew what the trouble was, she

thought as the Waterfront District sped by beyond the cab's window. She was in love with David Miller, but her grandfather disliked him, and there was every possibility that he'd married her to try to get in good with her grandfather.

Oh, hell. She didn't really believe that anymore. She was sure their marriage had squashed the deal with David's company anyway. And he'd been the kindest, funniest, most caring companion she could have asked for. They'd had only a couple of days together, but these memories seemed to stay at the forefront of her mind, pushing everything else, including her relationship with Brandon, into the background.

She'd had an affectionate friendship with Brandon that she'd thought she could parlay into a marriage, but what she felt for David was white-hot in comparison.

At the hotel, she sat in the middle of David's bed as though that could somehow bring him closer. She'd missed him horribly today, and it had been only nine or ten hours since she'd seen him.

That was silly. That was needy. She hated being either, but being both was horrifying.

She was wearing one of his T-shirts and eating

broiled shrimp from a Room Service tray when he came home. It was after seven.

He'd been heading for her room, then stopped in his open doorway when he caught sight of her propped up against his pillows.

"Got hungry?" he asked, coming into the room, tossing his jacket aside and sitting near enough to snag a shrimp. "I'm sorry I'm so late. We practically got the program rolling on our own. Everything fell together. It'll start next fall, I think."

"That's wonderful," she replied, every body process inside her humming at his nearness. "I've missed you something awful today," she said without preamble.

He was surprised for a moment, then put a hand to her bare ankle and asked quietly, "What do you suppose that means?"

"That I'm irretrievably in love with you," she said, deciding this was no time to be coy. "And I need you with a desperation I've never felt for anyone."

His eyes ignited. He picked up the Room Service tray, placed it on the dresser, and came back to her. She was kneeling on the edge of the bed, waiting for him.

He wrapped his arms around her and she reached her mouth up for his kiss. He obliged her.

"My promise," he said between kisses as she pulled his shirt out of his pants and unbuttoned it, "is that you'll never want for anything—me, particularly."

She pushed his shirt off, he helped with his T-shirt. "That's the answer I've been hoping for." She put her lips to his pectorals and he felt a weakness in his knees.

He reached under the T-shirt she wore to pull it off her, but was momentarily distracted by the curve of her hip against the palm of his hand. He stopped to explore and she leaned against him with a little sigh, her hands working on his belt buckle, the zipper of his slacks.

He drew away from her to pull off her shirt, then shed his shoes and socks, slacks and briefs, wrapped an arm around her waist and fell with her to the middle of the bed.

"I've felt cheated," she said, looping her arms around his neck, "that I don't remember the last time."

He lay beside her and drew her into his arms. "You made it memorable for me."

In a body already drunk on the sensation of lying naked in David's arms, she had to focus to realize what he'd said. "You remember it?" she asked.

He kissed her gently. "It woke me out of the haze. I recall everything you did, every way you touched me. It's made me determined that you're staying with me."

She was flattered, delighted that she'd made him want her. She'd had little faith in herself as a temptress. Brandon seemed to find making love to her pleasant enough, but there was never a languid aftermath to prolong the experience. Just a brisk return to whatever had been on his agenda, as though he were unaffected.

"I can't believe I don't remember," she said sadly.

He kissed her, then grinned wickedly. "Well, pay attention. I'll make sure you notice this time."

Then he launched a deliberate assault on her senses to assure that there was no time to think, only to feel.

He cradled her head on his shoulder, his other hand molding her hip and using it to hold her tightly to him, a thumb tracing its curve while his own body came alive to impress upon her just what she did to him.

His hand hitched up her thigh, explored it to her knee and back, then his fingertip dipped inside her. She leaned into him, making herself relax. This always took time. She tended to think about it too much, to get nerv—

His touch went deeper and she experienced a little jolt of surprise.

He raised his head from a string of nibbles along her jawline.

"All right?" he asked in concern.

"Yes," she whispered. "It's just that..."

There was no time to explain. What usually came only after much effort and concentration barreled down on her as though riding a rocket.

"What?"

"Nothing!" she breathed. "Nothing...just...just..."

SHE HELD HIM as though if she let go she would fall off into space. That was fine. He wanted her needing him.

He'd been afraid for a moment that she might have only thought she wanted him. She'd opened her arms welcomingly, traced his bare leg with her foot, then leaned into him when he touched her.

But he'd felt her stiffen, felt a sudden tension, and wondered—God forbid—if she was comparing him to Brandon and finding he had less to offer.

But she now clung to him like a little leech, her breath coming rapidly. Then he felt her shudder against him and held her as the tremors continued. A little cry seemed to catch in her throat and ended on a sigh as she collapsed against him.

"David!" she moaned softly.

"Yes?"

"I don't know," she replied. "Just...wanted to hear your name. To be sure...you exist."

He laughed lightly. "That wasn't proof enough?"

She kissed the hollow of his throat and rose over him as she'd done on their wedding night. "I think I need to explore you myself. Leave nothing to chance."

"My promise," he reminded her, trying to tip her onto her back, "was that I'll give you everything you need."

"That's generous," she said, pushing against him, tightening her knees on his waist so that he couldn't overturn her. That experience in itself was so delicious, that he stopped trying. She skimmed his lips with hers. "But it's said that a large part of giving is being able to take."

She put his arms out to the side, out of her way.

"I've heard that." His voice came out hoarsely because she was planting kisses right down the middle of his body.

He had no idea how he held himself together over the next few minutes while she did indeed conduct a thorough investigation of everything about him. Light, nimble fingers checked out his musculature, traced planes and hollows, kissed parts of him that particularly interested her.

And that was what finally undid him. He took her firmly by the waist, positioned her just where her fascination seemed to focus, and entered her just in time to take both of them out of the moment and into a place where nothing existed but them.

They soared, plummeted, caught a riffle of emotion and glided until reality finally rose up to meet them and they came back to awareness in the middle of the bed, wrapped in each other's arms.

But that was all right, he thought with a new sense of belonging to something besides his work. The reality to which they returned was that he loved Sally Webb and—miracle of miracles—Sally Webb loved him.

SALLY AWOKE to sunlight streaming through the window—and into her life. In the glow of her realization that she and David were in love, the worry about how to explain what she'd done to everyone seemed suddenly less horrid. She was in love. Who wouldn't be able to understand that as a reason for erratic behavior?

She would tell Brandon that she'd been wrong, and she did love David, and she'd explain to his parents. Then she'd find a way to make her grandfather understand.

But, she thought with a light heart, she didn't have to do that for a few more days. She and David had decided to stay the extra time even though his business with the governor was concluded. She was so happy, she wanted to shout.

Sally turned to David, and found his side of the bed empty. She could hear the sound of the shower and guessed he was preparing for yesterday's aborted tour of museums, now scheduled for today.

She got up and pulled on his T-shirt while she went to the closet in her room to select something to wear. Lucia had included sunny yellow slacks and pullover set in cotton terry and it matched her mood perfectly.

She carried them into David's room just as the telephone rang. She dropped the outfit on the bed and picked up the receiver.

"Hello?" she asked, expecting it to be the hotel manager.

"Miss Webb?" a vaguely familiar voice asked.

"Yes," she replied, though she thought a little giddily that that was no longer true. She was Mrs. Miller now.

"Miss Webb, it's Lane Carmichael."

Lane Carmichael. In her blissful state of playtime and self-realization, the workaday world seemed far away. Then facts clicked into place. Lane Carmichael was Webb Worldwide's purchasing manager.

Calling to formally cancel the deal with David, no doubt.

She was about to tell him that David would call him back, when the bathroom door opened, emitting a cloud of steam, and David, dressed in cotton stone-colored slacks and pulling on a matching cotton sweater.

She held up the phone. "For you," she said with a sympathetic smile.

"Something wrong?" he whispered, taking it from her.

"Not if you consider that we're so right," she whispered back. She hung her clothes on the back of the bathroom door, putting off her shower so that she'd be available to console David after the call.

She heard a little small talk on his side, then his mildly surprised, "Really." That was followed by, "I can put a man right on it, or if you don't mind waiting a few days, I can handle it myself." He winked at Sally. "I'm on my honeymoon at the moment."

She heard laughter on the other end of the line, then rapid conversation.

"Of course," David said. "I'll handle it myself, and we'll overnight the entire shipment. I'll be on hand for installation and setup."

Sally stared in disbelief as David exchanged business pleasantries with Carmichael, then ended the call. Her grandfather made the deal after all?

David hung up the phone, looking surprised himself. "Your grandfather's outfitting all the companies within Webb Worldwide with my computers and software. How about that."

"I can't believe it." A weird, unsettling suspicion began to cast a pall over Sally's happiness. "He must be doing it because we got married."

David, standing in front of the mirror over the dresser and combing his hair, looked for her reflection. "Hey," he said with playful displeasure. "That's no way to talk. He's buying my product because it's the best one on the market. It has nothing to do with us."

Dismay swelled inside her. "It has everything to do with us! He gave you the deal because of me."

He turned away from the mirror, a quiet calm overtaking his good humor. "No, he didn't. He invited me to Dover to show him what Millerware could do for him. That was before you got the letter and came looking for Richard."

"But he was angry with you then!" she reminded him. "He accused you of marrying me to make the deal."

A subtle change took place in his gaze. The

quiet calm became a quiet anger. "You still believe that," he accused.

"I believe," she said, unwilling to dispute that
but unwilling to deny it, either, "that he did it
because of me."

David shifted his weight and folded his arms,
looking like an impenetrable wall. "Why would
he do that? He doesn't know we made love last
night. He doesn't know you've fallen in love
with me, even though you consider me a fortune
hunter. He thinks you're going to come home and
somehow fix all this by divorcing me and marrying Brandon."

"I know how his mind works," she said
grimly. "He may have decided to do the deal to
see where my loyalties lie."

"Contrary to your suspicions," he said,
"Money doesn't figure into my love for you, and
you don't figure into my business deal. I don't
care what angle he's putting on it, and my dysfunctional family makes me value yours too
much to ever give you a him-or-me ultimatum.
Sally think!"

She squared her shoulders and took several
steps toward him. "Take the deal out of the equa-
tion," she challenged, knowing this was the only

way she'd ever feel secure about their relationship. "Turn down the deal. Then I'll know why
we're together."

"I wouldn't use you to make money," he said,
a hairbreadth from losing his temper altogether.
As it was he could scarcely breathe. "And I
won't give up a perfectly good business deal because you feel insecure." He was about to go too
far, but she'd gut-punched him, and he had to
fight back. "You claim to be the levelheaded
member of the family, the one who sticks by your
grandfather to keep the peace. But I think you
stick by him because you can't make decisions
on your own. You know I'm not going to blow
this deal—you're doing this to kill our relationship, to go back to what's comfortable and approved by Lawrence Webb. I love you, but if you
can't believe that, then go back to Brandon, who
doesn't give a rip about you!"

She glowered at him. "He kept after me for a
year when I wouldn't date him. He was understanding when I married you instead of him a
week before our wedding!"

"Of course he chased you!" He moved toward
her, but stopped a safe distance away, afraid to
get too close, afraid of the pull she had for him.

"You and your grandfather are what Brandon needs to get ahead. What his parents need to secure their own pursuits."

"They're wealthy in their own right!"

"But it's not all about wealth, is it? It's about who you know, about style and experience, and about having the right person by your side."

She became tearful and with that, defensive. "Then what chance would you and I have together? We got married because we were drunk!"

He shook his head, remaining calm. "That may have been the excuse, but it wasn't the reason. We've loved each other since we were teenagers. Even in a vodka-induced fog, you saw a chance to have what you really want instead of what your grandfather wanted for you, and you took it." Then he walked right up to her, consigning caution to hell. "And I can tell you that if you'd done that to me—married someone else a week before our wedding, I'd have murdered both of you."

She angled her chin defiantly. "That just means Brandon's more civilized that you are!"

He shook his head. "It means Brandon's feelings aren't involved and mine are. Did you tell

Brandon that we made love on our wedding night?''

She looked away, then looked back, rubbing her arms. ''I just...presumed he knew.''

''Then doesn't it bother you,'' he asked, leaning down to her, ''that it doesn't bother *him?*''

She thought about that, then said feebly, ''Maybe he just hasn't thought it through that far.''

''Then you should help him with that, and get his reaction before you marry him.'' That challenge hung in the air between them for a full minute before she grabbed her bag out of the closet and began to throw things into it.

''Please take me home,'' she said, her voice tight and high. ''I'm out of the honeymooning mood.''

CHAPTER ELEVEN

AFTER A SILENT drive back to Dover, David had Henry drop her at Oak Meadow. She noticed that Brandon's Mercedes was there.

"Where are you going?" she asked David grimly before climbing out of the limo.

"Back to Seattle," he replied tersely. "My lawyer will call your lawyer."

She wanted to protest, but that would have been ridiculous. How could she be upset about a breakup when she couldn't figure out how to support the relationship?

She stepped out of the limo and it turned back to the driveway and sped away. She felt as though someone had ripped out her heart with a grapefruit knife.

Brandon and her grandfather came to the door as she climbed the steps.

"Sally!" Brandon met her at the top and took her into his arms. "What happened? Where's Miller going?"

She couldn't reply. She simply caught his arm and led him into the foyer. Her grandfather followed and Hartfield approached from the kitchen, looking worried.

"Are you all right?" her grandfather asked. That surprised her. No criticism or recriminations, no "Thank God you're back," or "Thank God he's gone." But then he wasn't gone, was he? He'd be back to do the computer deal.

"I'm fine," she said, giving her grandfather a hug, then embracing Hartfield. "Would you excuse Brandon and me for a few minutes?"

Her grandfather looked doubtful, then nodded. "All right. I'll be working in my office when you're finished."

"Thank you."

"Shall I bring coffee?" Hartfield asked.

"No, thank you," she replied, and led Brandon to her study. It was comfortably familiar, yet somehow not—as though even the things she knew well had undergone a change in the few days she'd been married to David. Or was it she who'd changed?

She went to the pink-and-gray tapestry love seat next to the French doors and patted the cushion beside her for Brandon to join her.

"I wanted to explain to you about my wedding night," she said.

Brandon waited, his tennis whites gleaming in the midafternoon sun from the patio. He looked like an ad for men's cologne.

"David and I made love," she said abruptly, unable to think of a way to be subtle about it. She looked into his serene blue eyes, waiting for his reaction.

He look confused. She couldn't imagine what could be confusing about it.

He finally nodded. "I figured you had," he said.

She waited for more. It didn't come.

"And that doesn't matter to you?" she asked.

"Well, of course it does," he replied. "I'd prefer it hadn't happened, but since it did, we can just live around it."

Live around it. David, given the same situation, had threatened murder.

She leaned her elbow on the back of the settee and asked bluntly, "Do you love me, Brandon?"

He put a hand to her knee. "Of course, I do. We've been buddies for..."

"No." She stopped him with a shake of her head. "I don't mean buddy-love. I mean red-hot, pain-in-the-gut, die-for-me kind of love." The love she'd felt for David before he'd refused to prove his love for her by abandoning the deal with her grandfather.

Brandon was silent for a moment, then laughed a little uncomfortably, as though embarrassed for her.

"Sally, nobody really loves that way," he said, measuring his words. "I mean, we pair up for purposes of convenience and comfort and...let's face it...ready sex, and if business gains an advantage in the process, then—"

She took the engagement ring he'd given her from the pocket of her shirt and placed it in the palm of his hand. "I'm not coming back to you Brandon," she said, absolutely sure of that if nothing else. "I'm sorry. I think we've both made a mistake."

He stared openmouthed as she left the office in search of her grandfather. She found a tall, slender woman with graying red hair and bright-green eyes behind black-rimmed spectacles.

She sat behind a desk that hadn't been there when Sally left.

The woman stood and leaned across the desk to shake Sally's hand. "I'm Regina Robinson," she said with a wide smile. "David brought me from Seattle to sit in for you for a while. Your grandfather's actually in the garden."

Sally found her grandfather on a stone bench under an apple tree covered in spring green leaves, the lawn around it still sprinkled with blossoms. He held a cup of coffee.

"I'm divorcing David," she announced, sitting beside him, "but I'm not marrying Brandon."

He turned to study her steadily. "You're very decisive all of a sudden."

"I guess indulging in radical behavior," she said, "taught me that I'm not the Goody Two-shoes I thought I was. Or that I don't have to be. It was sort of fun to be bad, though I did horrify myself."

"Well, if you had such a good time," he asked a little sharply, "what are you doing back home?"

She told him briefly about the call from Carmichael and the argument with David about the computer deal.

"I thought you knew me well enough," he said, looking surprised, "to know that I never mix business with family. I'm buying his computers because they're the best. It has nothing to do with his being married to you. And I can't believe you'd ask that of him. He was smart not to cave in to you."

Now she was truly confused. "I thought you didn't like him."

He stared at rolling hills in the distance and sighed pensively. "So did I. But I've learned a few things about him in the past few days. Brandon's a smart lawyer, but he had everything on his side to become one—doting parents who gave him everything and an atmosphere that made it easy to learn. David, on the other hand, brought himself up against odds that would have squashed a lesser man, and he not only endured, but he built a great business on extensive research, hard work and good old street smarts."

"But he considers his business more important to him than I am!"

Her grandfather patted her hand and gave her a smile she remembered from her childhood. It had usually accompanied a well-deserved lesson. "No, he doesn't. I've seen him look at you. You're a fire in his eyes, but that doesn't mean he's going to let you dictate terms. Your demand was childish and insecure. You're a better woman than that, Sally. I've seen you look at him. Your grandmother once looked at me that way and it fueled my life. It brought me back from a terrible ordeal.'' He squeezed her hand. ''It's okay to be wrong, Sally, as long as you take the blame and put things right again. Here. Look at this.''

He handed her a sheet of paper—a fax, she noticed as she read the transmission codes. It was addressed to her, and it was from David Miller at Coastline Corporation.

The fax said in effect that the property she wanted on the Cape was being deeded to her.

''I don't understand,'' she said, thoroughly confused. ''I didn't know David owned Coastline.''

''Apparently Anne Marie Brooke put her mother on the case of finding you new property after the two of you talked, but her mother thought you should have what you really wanted and decided to approach Coastline Corporation one more time. And because of the publicity you and David have received in the past few days, the party you'd been talking to realized who you were and finally put your request to David. He doesn't really have much to do with the organization otherwise. You may have gotten farther more quickly.''

She checked the time on the fax. He must have sent it from the limo after dropping her off.

"I got it while you were talking to Brandon," her grandfather said. "You'd left David at that point. He has nothing to gain from this except the knowledge that he's giving you what you want." He smiled and kissed her cheek. "Go get him, or you're not the child I raised."

Sally remembered the letter and wrapped him in a fierce hug, thinking that though she didn't understand everything yet, she knew she had the unselfish love of two special grandfathers.

CHAPTER TWELVE

NOTHING WOULD EVER be as important as this moment, Sally thought as she pulled into Richard's driveway and stopped the car with a rocking jerk. Her life, her future, her happiness hung in the balance.

She was surprised to see Richard there, unloading his van. Fishing and camping gear lay all around him on the ground, and though he gave her a bright smile, he looked as though he hadn't combed his hair or shaved in over a week.

"Hey, Sis!" he called cheerfully. "Tell me you've brought food! I haven't had anything but beans or trout in a week!"

She gave him a quick hug and ran for the back door. "Where's David?"

"Gone," he said, picking up a foldaway tent and carrying it to the open garage.

Her heart sank. Gone! Of course! What did she think would happen? He'd said he was going back to Seattle.

"When?" she demanded.

He shrugged. "I don't know. The note was there when I got back. That was about twenty minutes ago."

She kissed him again and ran back to her car.

"Hey!" he called. "Stick around. You can take me to Carvelli's for dinner!"

She blew him a kiss and ground the car into reverse.

The airport was only a mile away from Richard's. It was very small with just a one-room terminal and a six-seat coffee bar.

She parked, scanned the sky for planes and saw nothing. Maybe he hadn't left yet. She didn't want to think that he was already gone.

She was running from the parking lot down the narrow walk to the terminal when she heard the sound of a familiar motor.

No, she thought, picking up her pace. *No!*

Then there it went, David's plane racing past her on the small runway, achieving lift and then climbing, a pretty metal bird against the twilight sky. David on his way home. Out of her life. Gone.

She put a hand to her heart and emitted a strangled little sound, unable for an instant to bear the pain. Tears clogged her throat, streamed down her cheeks, blinded her.

Then she pulled herself together and tortured herself with the fact that it was all her fault. She was unable to believe that she could have had what she wanted but because that would have required living up to such a gift, she threw it back in the face of the generous God who'd given it to her.

Standing all alone under a great big sky as night fell was just what she deserved.

DAVID STOOD in the entrance to the terminal, a paper cup full of coffee in his hand, and blinked, certain he was seeing things. A small, slender figure in yellow stood on the edge of the runway, watching his plane climb into the sky, heading west.

A small hand went to her heart, and her face crumpled.

A fist caught his heart and wrenched it.

He dropped the cup into a trash can, pushed the door open and walked out into the waning light. His heart was thumping. He wasn't sure why she was here, but he didn't want to blow it if she was here for him.

She was crying so hard, she didn't hear him

approach. He'd almost reached her when she turned, apparently to leave, and saw him coming toward her.

She stopped, her eyes wide with misery.

He stopped, his heart heavy with the pressure of the moment.

Then she screamed and ran to him, her arms open.

He braced himself to catch her and felt the world begin to turn again as he held her in his arms.

"I'm sorry, I'm sorry!" she wept. "It was myself I didn't trust, not you. Please don't go! Or, if you have to go, take me with you."

"Sally, I'm not going anywhere," he said, holding her tightly, loving the fact that she felt as though she needed him as much as he needed her. "At least, not for a while."

She pushed against him, to point to the path the plane had taken. "When I saw the plane…"

"I needed a couple of days here," he explained, "so I sent Charlie to see his parents in Texas."

"You need to be here when the computers arrive."

"I do, but that won't be for a week. I'm staying now, because I was trying to figure out what to do about you.''

"I thought you were on the plane.'' Her face crumpled again and she fell against him. "David, I want to stay married. You wouldn't really want to unload me and find a mature and sensible woman, would you?''

He enveloped her in his arms. "Course not,'' he teased. "I love you.''

She looked up at him with a red, puffy face to acknowledge the joke. He laughed and held her more tightly.

"Sally, I adore you, charming and contrary as you are. And I'm not letting you go. Your grandfather will just have to adjust to that.''

"He already has,'' she said, pushing away to smile up at him. "When I told him about our argument, he took your side, even over Brandon, and said I was being juvenile.''

He raised both eyebrows. "You're kidding.''

"No. He's suddenly your biggest fan. *That's* why he's doing the deal with you. It had nothing to do with me.''

He shook his head. "I thought I said that.''

She nodded in self-deprecation. "I'm generally pretty smart, but when it comes to matters of the heart, I'm not always very bright.'' She swiped the last remnant of tears from her eyes and gave him a bright smile. "Except that I married you. So, I get some credit for that, right?"

He laughed as he leaned down to kiss her. "Absolutely. Want to take a brief honeymoon somewhere for the next few days? After your grandfather's computers are delivered and set up, we can go to Europe, or on safari, or wherever you want to go."

SALLY HUGGED HIM tightly, unable to believe that what had seemed like such a disaster just a few days ago was now a great gift. She knew precisely where she wanted to go.

"How would you feel about going to Cooper's Corner?" she asked. "There's an oak tree with my name on it in the back garden where my grandfather Cooper lived. I'd like to see it."

"Then, that's where we'll go." He turned her toward the parking lot. "We can tell your grandfather Webb that we're going back to Vegas."

"Hm," she said dreamily. "Let's do that before we come home. Maybe we can get the same hotel room."

Dear Reader,

What could be more delightful for a romance writer than to weave a tale around secrets, babies and weddings? I always enjoy what I do, but I particularly enjoyed telling this story, partly because I have two rambunctious little grandsons who supplied much of the research for the twins.

Babies have so much to teach us. They live entirely in the moment, they broadcast their honest emotions loud and clear, and they love without reservation. They don't hold grudges, they have no concept of impossible or can't. Most of the time they bring out the best in us—and those rare times when felt pens and new wallpaper collide, we have a golden opportunity to recognize what's really important in life.

I hope this story brings you as much joy reading it as it did for me writing it. And, always and ever, thank you, dear reader, for giving me yet another chance to entertain you.

My love to each of you.

Bobby

OH, BABY!

Bobby Hutchinson

CHAPTER ONE

"COME TO Mommy, Max."

Janelle Jamison, still dripping water from the dive she'd just completed, reached her arms out to her wailing fifteen-month-old son.

Betsy handed him over, and Janelle propped him on one narrow, neoprened hip and kissed the bump rising on his forehead. "What'd you do to yourself this time, reckless?"

"He was running to meet you and he did a face plant on the dock," Betsy explained, raising her voice to be heard over the baby's earsplitting shrieks and the boisterous sounds coming from a group farther down the slip. A bevy of women's voices were calling out, "Bravo, bravo, speech, speech."

Betsy struggled to hold on to Maxwell's twin, Oliver, who was now screeching in sympathy with his brother and holding out beseeching arms to Janelle.

"C'mere, then, you jealous toad. You're lucky

I've got two hips." Janelle hoisted the second baby and kissed each fat little cheek. The boys quieted, thumbs plugging into mouths, heads turning toward the clapping and cheering and loud wolf whistles coming from the celebrants.

"What's going on over there, Betsy?"

"Oh, it's the Boston Harbor Sailing Club," Betsy explained, gathering up plastic toys and stuffing them into the giant red diaper bag. "That sailboat just won the race, I heard two women saying that this is the second in a row for the skipper."

As Janelle watched, the tall skipper hopped off the daysailer, doffed his cap with a graceful gesture, and bowed low to his admiring fans, most of whom were female. He then uncorked a bottle of champagne and held it up over his head, letting the foaming wine roll down one muscular arm. The other was hooked around a tousle-haired blonde whose generous breasts all but spilled out of her black bikini top.

"He must have his own harem," Janelle said.

Betsy laughed. "With a boat like that he can probably afford one."

"What's the name of the boat?"

"I didn't look, I was too busy keeping the gang from leaping off the wharf."

Curious, Janelle took a few steps closer to the rowdy group and squinted at the name on the boat's prow.

"Webbsite." Something dangerous in Janelle's voice made Betsy stop what she was doing and stare at her friend.

"Webbsite," Janelle repeated. "You know who that is, don't you?"

"Oh, lordie. Janelle, now don't do anything crazy here." Betsy reached out a cautionary hand, but Janelle shook it off. She was already striding across the wooden dock, babies bouncing on her hips, heading straight for the revelers.

"Here's to victory!" Richard Webb took a long swallow from the champagne bottle, pulled Sunny close and gave her a long, passionate kiss, which brought a round of applause and several catcalls from his exuberant friends. He'd just won his second skipper's trophy in a row, and he was feeling better than fine. Sunny returned the kiss with interest and he teased her, letting out a lascivious growl and bending her back over his arm.

"Richard Webb."

The voice was husky, loud and female, but it wasn't friendly.

Richard started and pulled Sunny upright.

The crowd went quiet as the tall redhead in the skintight scuba suit shouldered her way through and came to a standstill two feet away. She was glaring at him as if she'd take great pleasure in harming him, but she had kids hanging from each slender hip instead of pistols. The babies' huge blue eyes were identically round and innocent, but the woman was giving him a look that could have ignited asbestos.

"Yeah, I'm Richard Webb," he acknowledged with a puzzled frown. He could swear he'd never seen her before in his life.

"Who are you?" Maybe she was a sore loser, married to one of the skippers he'd bested in today's race.

Whoever she was, she had amazing eyes, large and thick lashed and pure aqua green. In fact, she was amazing, period. She was at least six feet tall, and the scuba suit fit like a second skin over a long-legged curvaceous body any Victoria's Secret model would have envied.

She hoisted the kids higher on her hips and in a carrying voice she said, "Boys, meet Richard Webb. He's a bottom feeder, and he happens to be your daddy."

Stunned, Richard gaped at her. Then he shook

his head and stammered, "Hey, hey, look, lady, you got the wrong guy here—"

But she shook her head harder. Her wild mop of wet red curls whipped from side to side, and her voice was like a razor.

"Not a chance in hell, Richard Webb. These babies are *yours,* you rotten philandering lowlife." She gave him one last scathing look, turned on her heel and marched off.

It took him several shocked moments to react. Sunny was clinging to his right arm with both hands, and he had to peel her off. The rest of the crowd was staring at him as if he'd suddenly grown an extra nose or something.

"It's a mistake," he said with as much conviction as he could muster. He shoved the champagne at Sunny. "Here, drinks all round, I'll be right back."

He took off at a fast jog down the dock. By the time he reached the parking lot, the woman was climbing into a robin's-egg-blue Sedan. Richard broke into a run.

"Hey, you. Lady, wait just a damned minute here—"

The redhead was in the driver's seat. There was another woman on the passenger side, kneeling on the seat and fastening the twins into car seats. He knew they saw him; a six-foot-three-inch man running toward them waving his arms was hard to miss.

The redhead looked straight ahead, and she didn't so much as glance his way as she swung the vehicle around in a tight turn and accelerated out of the lot.

He was probably lucky she hadn't decided to run over him.

Cursing and puffing, Richard sprinted for his white Corvette.

Thankfully the keys were in the zippered pocket of his shorts. He dragged them out and was in the car and out of the lot just as the other car pulled away from a traffic light.

Richard stepped on the accelerator and shifted up, shooting through the intersection on the tail end of an amber light. He dodged between cars, keeping the Sedan in view and trying to read the plate number. He was just committing it to memory when the siren sounded and red lights flashed behind him.

He swore and smacked the steering wheel, then pulled over. The uniformed policeman took his time getting out of the patrol car. Richard knew he was running the license plate on the Corvette through the computer, and he breathed a silent prayer of thanks. He'd paid seven out-standing speeding tickets just a week before, so he was in the clear, but now he'd lost his quarry.

Repeating the license number over and over so he wouldn't forget it, he handed the cop his registration and driver's license without being asked.

"Mister Webb, I thought it was you. Now where are you off to in such a hurry?"

Richard opened his mouth to explain about the woman and the twins and the accusations she'd made, but he closed it again.

His grandfather, Lawrence Webb, had a saying that used to drive Richard nuts. "Discretion is the better part of valor," the old man would pronounce in stentorian tones, reprimanding Richard for some misdeed.

For the first time in his life, Richard understood exactly what Gramps meant. All during the all-too-familiar process of getting yet another speeding ticket, he kept his mouth shut and concentrated on remembering that blasted plate number.

CHAPTER TWO

THAT EVENING, Richard ducked out of the victory party early and alone, and drove home. The redhead in the scuba suit had lodged herself in his brain, and try as he would, he couldn't dislodge her.

He was certain he'd never seen her before, but she'd been so sure of herself, so positive. She'd known his name. Could he have been drunk enough to have had sex and then forget all about it?

He wanted to deny it, but the simple truth was it was remotely possible, considering the parties he'd given and gone to and the number of women he'd known over the past several years, in what Gramps would call the biblical sense. Well, longer, actually. He was thirty, and he'd been carousing around since his teens.

As always, his cocker spaniel, Freddy, was watching for him through the front window of his Back Bay condo. Freddy was one of the reasons he'd bought the condo; tired of the commute from the small house he owned forty miles out of Boston, Richard had searched for something to rent in the heart of town, only to find that in most rentals animals were frowned upon.

The condo had a minute backyard, and Richard had optimistically put a doghouse there, but Freddy didn't spend much time in it. He preferred the living room. Richard had tried a million times to discourage the dog from standing on the sofa and pressing his nose against the window, but it was hopeless.

As he unlocked the door, he could hear Freddy giving his usual excited yelps. Stepping inside, Richard waited.

Freddy was entirely predictable. He crouched and launched himself at Richard, whining ecstatically, hell-bent on licking his boss to death.

"Down, you maniac." But for once, the dog's antics didn't make him laugh the way they usually did. "Let's go for a walk. Where's your leash?" Freddy went charging off, appearing a moment later with the leather leash in his mouth.

For the next hour, Richard walked down historic gaslit streets, but his mind wasn't on the downtown ambience.

He tried to convince himself that the redhead

was a nutcase who regularly accused men of fathering her twins, but it didn't stick. There'd been keen intelligence in those angry green eyes, and a kind of dignity that shone through the anger. She seemed too genuine to be pulling a con, which meant she believed what she'd said.

And that meant Richard was going to have to find her, for his own peace of mind, but also because there was just a chance she'd somehow locate his grandfather, Lawrence Webb, and repeat what she'd said about him being a father.

Gramps would be furious and outraged if he thought Richard had children and wasn't supporting or acknowledging them. But it wasn't Lawrence Webb's anger that Richard wanted to avoid. It was the fact that he knew his grandfather would be disappointed in him, and he'd already disappointed the old man enough.

Lawrence had wanted Richard to take over Webb Worldwide, the internationally successful family business. He'd wanted his grandson to marry a suitable woman and start a family.

As he'd done his entire life, Richard had rebelled. He preferred the challenge and downright fun of developing computer games for kids. He and his college buddy, Peter Butler, had started their own company, Childsplay, and it was doing so well that even Gramps was reluctantly impressed.

But Richard's lifestyle was another thing altogether. He and Lawrence had had many heated arguments about it. Lawrence had accused him of being a playboy and a rogue, irresponsible and careless. Richard couldn't deny the accusations outright, but they stung.

The fact was he had his own moral code and stuck to it religiously. Granted, it was liberal, but it absolutely didn't include getting women pregnant. He had a stock of condoms that would rival any drugstore, and he was meticulous about using them.

Which brought him back to the woman with the twins.

He had a friend on the Boston P.D., and when he got back from his walk, he phoned him.

Getting an address from the license plate number ended up expensive. Richard had to promise to set up Jackson's new computer and design a web page for his wife, who had her own line of maternity wear.

"I design computer games for kids, I know zilch about maternity stuff," Richard protested, but Jackson didn't get the difference.

"So? I'm a detective, not a traffic cop," he

responded. "If I can do license plates, you can do maternity."

Richard gave in, and it was worth it, because Jackson called back late Monday afternoon. The woman's name was Betsy Clagman. She was a solicitor, which brought up a whole new set of questions.

Why hadn't she taken legal action, if she believed what she'd said? Determined to get to the bottom of the puzzle, after work Richard drove to the South End address and pulled up in front of an older apartment building.

Chances were good the redhead wouldn't let him in if he buzzed, so he waited until a young couple loaded down with groceries came along. He held the door for them, and then took the steps two at a time.

He knocked and waited, figuring out exactly what he'd say. He'd decided to demand a blood test. That would settle the thing once and for all.

"Hello?"

"Betsy Clagman, please." The woman standing at the door wasn't the redhead. This one was short and dark and plump, with round spectacles perched on an upturned nose.

He hadn't gotten a close look at the other woman in the sedan, but this was probably her.

Her wide smile faded the instant she laid eyes on Richard. She started to shut the door. He put his hand on the knob and resisted.

"Look, I really need to speak to Betsy Clagman."

"Do you mind?" Color was flooding her cheeks. "You're intruding. How did you get in here anyway?"

"Could you just get Betsy Clagman for me, please?"

"*I'm* Betsy Clagman. And I don't know you. If you don't leave this minute I'm gonna call the cops."

"*You're—?*" Damn. The Sedan didn't belong to the redhead. Richard felt like banging his head against the door. "Please, just listen for a minute. I really need to find the woman with the kids, the redhead who was with you at the dock yesterday. I need to talk to her, if you'd just give me her name—"

"Get out of here. I've got nothing to say to you."

"*Please,* Ms. Clagman, just a phone number, a name, anything—"

"I'm calling the cops. Let go of the door."

He did, and she slammed it. He heard the security bolts snip into place. There was nothing to do but leave unless he wanted a harassment charge on top of the latest speeding ticket, and there was only so much Jackson could do to keep him out of the slammer.

Richard hurried down the stairs and jumped in the car, keeping a wary eye out for the cops as he drove away.

Now what? The whole thing was out of hand. He was starting to feel desperate.

It was Monday night, and he and Peter had a long established routine on Monday nights. It had started as a therapy session of sorts, and eventually turned into a ritual. They met at Donovan's, a hole in the wall pub that served Guinness on tap and had the best Irish stew going.

Peter was divorced and he'd had his kid all weekend. Sunday night he dropped her back with her mother, Leona. By Monday, he was crazy again with missing them both. Usually, Richard listened, but tonight he was going to reverse the roles. If he didn't confide in someone he'd explode.

Over a pitcher of Guinness, he laid the whole incredible story on Peter, but Peter's reaction wasn't all that Richard had hoped for.

"I told you those one-night stands would backfire on you."

Sanctimonious bastard. Richard wanted to say that affairs could backfire just as easily, but he held his tongue because it was such a sore point with Pete.

Peter had married Leona, his high school sweetheart, five years ago. Three years later, after Abby was born, Peter had gone nuts and had an affair with some bombshell he met in a drugstore, and three months after that Leona found out and divorced him.

Now, Peter saw Abby on weekends. The bombshell was history; she had no time for a kid. Peter had told Richard that one morning he'd climbed out of bed in the bachelor pad he was renting and just started bawling, because he realized how badly he'd screwed up. He still loved Leona, he hated not being able to live with her and his daughter.

"She wasn't a one-night stand, Pete. She wasn't *any* kind of a stand. I swear I never saw that woman before in my life."

"What did the twins look like?"

"Twins." Richard thought about it. "Babies, big babies. Blond curls. I wasn't paying much attention to them. Blue eyes, I remember they had these really blue eyes."

Peter studied Richard's really blue eyes and

shook his head. "Didn't you tell me once that your mother was a twin?"

He had. Richard thought about that, and it didn't make him feel comfortable, but he wasn't about to admit it.

"Cut the bull, Pete. Half the population of Boston has blue eyes. And twins, they're a dime a dozen these days what with fertility drugs. The question is, what do I do now?"

They brainstormed through two pitchers of beer. The only solution they came up with was that Richard could do surveillance on Betsy Clagman, hoping that she'd lead him to the red-head, but what with work and the dog and the need to eat and sleep, Richard didn't have time for it. Besides, if she spotted him she'd sure as hell charge him with stalking.

Richard finally staggered home. He fell into bed, slept two hours, and woke up sweating from a dream in which faceless women chased him naked through a tunnel. He tossed and turned for another hour, but he couldn't get to sleep again. Finally, he got up, found a soda in the fridge and shoved a resentful Freddy to one side of the sofa, then turned on the tube.

There were old and new movies, talking heads discussing the beautification project that had disrupted Boston for years, and two shopping channels. He stayed with one for a few minutes because they were selling exercise equipment that seemed to come with a lascivious blonde in a thong.

The station went to a commercial for bath oil. He was about to click the remote, but there was a shot of a tub filled with bubbles and a redhead artfully exposing one endless, slender leg and the tops of rounded breasts. "Bodysoft, the only bath oil that will leave your skin feeling like silk," crooned the voiceover.

It was her. It was the redhead.

CHAPTER THREE

RICHARD'S SHOUT brought Freddy off the couch and into a barking fit. The fur on his neck and back lifted, and he tore around the room, searching for the bad guys.

Richard fell to his hands and knees, his face inches from the set. There she was, in living color, waving those incredible legs and giving him a sensual, why-don't-you-join-me look.

Over the next hour, he saw the commercial twice more, and by dawn he'd figured out a way to find her. It meant waking up a lady he hadn't dated for several months, who was less than polite when she learned all he wanted was the name of the talent agency for whom she modeled.

Fortunately, it opened early. Fortunately, too, it had connections with other agencies, and when he explained to the starstruck receptionist that he was a talent scout looking for a specific model to star in a big budget movie, she was more than helpful.

By seven-thirty Richard knew the model's name was Janelle Jamison. She was thirty-one, and she hadn't modeled for some time, but they had a phone number nonetheless.

By quarter past eight, he was pulling up in front of a modest condo. Like Betsy Clagman, she lived in the South End, but not in one of the fashionable areas close to the restaurants and specialty shops. The condo was on an obscure side street that had somehow escaped gentrification. It was one of four, all with minuscule fenced front yards littered with bicycles and baby carriages.

Just as he stepped out of the car, the front door of Janelle's unit swung open. The sounds of frantic screams accompanied her as she backed out. She was wearing navy jogging shorts. *Short* jogging shorts. In a loud voice, over the din she was saying, "Be good boys, Mommy will be back in thirty minutes."

She closed the door and turned, and her eyes went wide when she saw him.

Janelle was feeling even more frazzled than usual. The twins had recently started howling the moment they thought she was going to be out of their sight. It made it difficult to enjoy her usual morning jog. It made it impossible to even go to the toilet with the door closed.

Janelle's neighbor and baby-sitter, motherly Gwen Little, had assured her that this was a passing stage, and the boys would get over it when they understood that every time she left, she came back. So far, that hadn't dawned on them, and the cacophony of brokenhearted sobs and tiny fingers clutching her bare legs made Janelle want to just give in and give up on fitness until the boys were teenagers.

And now the sight of Richard Webb climbing out of his gleaming white Corvette right in front of her gate made her say a word she'd vowed to stop using before the kids learned it. It also made her heart pound with anxiety.

How had he found her? And why, oh why, had she confronted him in the first place? But she knew the answer to that one. What had driven her insane was stumbling onto a scene that graphically illustrated the difference between her own hectic, harried, money-pinching lifestyle and his lavish, carefree existence.

He'd obviously spent the day sailing in his fancy sloop, and he was kissing blondes and drinking champagne and celebrating. She'd spent the same day working hard when she longed to be with the twins.

Her boss had offered her a commercial diving

project that would substantially boost the amount she had saved to replace her battered old van, which had so many things wrong with it the mechanic just shook his head and rolled his eyes whenever she took it in. The problem was, the project had to be completed on Sunday, and Gwen spent that day with her grandkids.

Betsy, dear friend that she was, had offered to baby-sit. She'd also ended up chauffeuring Janelle and the twins when the cranky old Volkswagen refused to start.

When Janelle climbed out of the water after four solid hours of diving, she'd been exhausted, and she knew that the day's work was far from over. The babies needed to be fed, bathed, played with, put to bed. She had loads of laundry still to do, and she was going to have to ask Betsy to stop so she could buy groceries.

Richard Webb, their biological father, was as free as air.

It had suddenly been more than she could stomach.

But lordie, now she was going to pay for those few moments of furious satisfaction. Her gut tightened into a knot.

"Janelle Jamison, I need to talk to you." He

sounded furious as he came barreling through the gate and into the toy-strewn yard.

Janelle panicked and bolted. She dodged past him and took off down the road. It led to a make-shift jogging path that wound through alleys and along tree-lined streets. All she could think of as she tore along was that maybe she could lose him long enough to figure out what she ought to do next.

She ran hard. She'd seen enough to know he wasn't dressed for running, but he was doing it anyhow.

"Those kids aren't mine, lady," he shouted, and a glance over her shoulder confirmed the awful fact that he wasn't too far behind her. His brown sport jacket billowed out around him. He had on leather shoes and dress pants.

Dismayed, she lengthened her stride.

He pulled up beside her.

"Just exactly—where and when—did we get together—long enough—*to start them?*"

He was puffing but he was keeping up, even when she quickened the pace still more. She was getting a stitch in her side.

"I did—cross-country—in college," he puffed out. "Don't think—you'll lose me—this way."

And right then Janelle knew it was hopeless.

No matter how far or how fast she ran, he'd still be there, plaguing her. He knew her name, he knew where she lived. Why, oh why, had she complicated her already difficult life by being so stupid?

She stopped and turned to face him, hands on her hips, puffing.

"You do—remember—the Flamingo Lounge?" Sarcasm dripped from every word. "Well, on that day—almost two years ago—you'd lost the boat race." She stopped to catch her breath.

"As usual, you were drinking champagne, and rather a lot of it. There was piano music, slow dancing." She pinned him with a caustic glare. "You suggested a midnight cruise on your yacht, but the boat didn't move from its moorings." She swallowed and tried to ignore the way her heart was hammering. "There were navy-blue sheets on your bunk and sandalwood soap in your bathroom, Webb." Venom dripped from her voice.

"Oh, and don't forget the monogrammed navy towels to match the sheets. The terry robe was brown, but it didn't stay on long afterward. You made it clear you wanted to be alone. It was pretty humiliating, and very obvious that all you'd wanted was a quickie. You called a cab.

And that, *Richard,* is how the twins were conceived. Does that answer your question?''

He was staring at her. He was in good shape, she'd give him that much. His breathing had steadied almost as quickly as her own, but he was sweating, and his sandy brown hair stuck to his forehead.

She was painfully familiar with the ocean blue of his eyes. Oliver and Maxwell had his eyes— their color, shape, obscenely long, curling lashes. At times, even their little faces wore the same puzzled expression his was wearing now.

She knew he couldn't deny the details she'd supplied. The description of the yacht was exact.

He gave his head a shake as if to clear it. ''You missed one thing,'' he finally said. ''And it's a big one, Ms. Jamison. No matter how drunk, no matter how carried away I was, I would have used protection. I *always* use protection, it's a hard and fast rule with me.''

''You wore a condom.'' She gave him a withering look. ''Condoms have about a six percent failure rate, or hadn't you heard? The twins are a result of that six percent. Maybe you oughta think about a vasectomy if you're serious about not having any more kids.''

That got his temper going again. It gave her a

feeling of smug satisfaction to see his eyes narrow and his jaw tighten.

"What about you, Janelle? Don't you have some responsibility here? Or haven't you heard about the Pill?"

It was all Janelle could do not to lift a fist and clout him a good one. She felt herself begin to shake, and she clenched her hands and tried to draw in a deep breath. Her stomach felt sick.

"Members of my family are subject to blood clots," she snapped at him. "Birth control pills are not an option. Got that?"

He frowned at her. "What are you getting so riled up about? It was a perfectly logical comment. And anyway, arguing about this isn't getting us anywhere. I want a paternity test."

"No. Absolutely not. I don't want anything from you, Webb, except that you disappear and stay gone. Do you think for one minute I'd allow a—a *jerk* like you to be around my sons? You may be related biologically, but that sure as heck doesn't make you a father."

His eyes narrowed. "You're lying. For some twisted reason of your own, you've set out to ruin my reputation, just because your own is ruined. How do I know how many men you've pulled this on before me? You're a psycho, lady. I've got a good mind to charge you with defamation of character."

The unfairness of it, the knowledge that he could well afford a lengthy court case, drove her over the edge.

"You want a court case?" she screamed at him. "There's a DNA lab that does paternity testing on Brookline Avenue. My friend Ruby works there, she'll get us in on short notice. You meet me there at noon, and we'll see who has the potential for a court case."

Janelle didn't wait for his response. She turned and ran, hardly able to see the path for the tears that poured down her cheeks. She was furious, with herself for letting him goad her into the blood test, with Webb for denying his paternity. But most of all she was afraid, terribly afraid.

He had money.

She came from blue-collar working stock. Her father was a bus driver, and she'd always been proud of him. She'd worked hard all during high school and college, supporting herself and doing whatever she could to help her baby sister, Tracy.

When he found out he was the father of her beautiful children, would Webb try to take the babies away from her?

With every frenzied step, she berated herself for being a fool, not once, but twice.

CHAPTER FOUR

RICHARD WATCHED HER GO. She was graceful and fast, like a big, flame-topped cat running along the path and disappearing into the trees. She had a world-class backside, and those legs were showgirl quality. And she had a temper, which he'd just used to his advantage.

He didn't feel victorious at besting her, though, he actually felt a little sick in his gut. There was an innate decency about her that made him ashamed of what he'd just done.

You had no choice, he assured himself. *She's mistaken, God alone knows how. You've got to prove it once and for all.*

He turned and made his way back to the car, pondering the words they'd fired like bullets at one another.

She'd surprised him with her accurate description of the boat. And when she described the scene, he vaguely remembered being picked up by a woman in the Flamingo. He'd been pretty wasted, and she'd been a blonde, but that didn't prove anything. He'd taken her back to the *Webbsite*, he did remember that much. The most troubling part was that he couldn't believe he'd totally forget making love with a stunning woman like Janelle Jamison. She was no bimbo out for a good time, that was obvious.

Maybe Gramps had a point about his lifestyle. If he was starting to forget whole episodes that ought to have been memorable, maybe it was time to rethink the way he was living.

He was still pretty certain about one thing, though.

Those kids weren't his. They couldn't be. He liked kids, hell, he made his living designing games for them, but he wasn't planning on having any of his own, not for a good long time.

Being a father meant taking on responsibility, and he was the first to admit that that wasn't one of his strong points. He managed to keep Freddy fed and watered, but Freddy was a dog. A couple of kids? No way.

He drove to the office, feeling anxious and keeping well within the speed limit all the way.

WHEN RICHARD WALKED IN, the waiting room at the DNA lab was filled with men, women and

babies. None of the adults looked very happy to
be there. Who would have believed there'd be
this many people needing confirmation of paternity?

Richard sat down, and the two women nearest
him gave him accusing glances, moved to seats
farther away, and then went on with their dis-
cussion of court orders and support and deadbeat
dads. He picked up a magazine and tried to concentrate on foreign stock prices.

Janelle arrived ten minutes late, but it didn't
look as if their names were going to be called
anytime soon anyhow. She was wearing tan pants
that hugged every curve, and a navy T-shirt. On
each hip she had a shiny clean, sturdy baby. Because the women had moved, the only available
seat was now beside Richard, and he could tell
by her expression how reluctant she was to take
it.

"Hi," he said with an attempt at a smile. "I'm
glad you could make it." Damn, that sounded
sarcastic and he didn't mean it that way. He was
nervous.

She didn't answer. She set the boys down and
they stood side by side for a moment, surveying
the faces that smiled at them, the coffee table
filled with magazines, the other babies.

They looked too small to be walking, but Richard noticed that they were already surefooted in their little red trainers. They were also fast, going off at high speed, in opposite directions. The door to the clinic opened on a hallway, and one of them wheeled out of it and disappeared.

Janelle hurried after him, and the other baby plopped down and began to howl, but he stopped in midscream when Janelle reappeared. He gave her a tearful toothy grin when she picked him up.

"He's pretty attached to you." Richard didn't know what to say. He'd never come across any etiquette guide for this particular situation.

"I'm his mother." She shot him a disparaging look. "I suspect even *you* were attached to your mother when you were a kid."

"Could have been. I don't remember much about her, though. She and my father died when I was four. He was a musician, there was a fire." It wasn't something he really thought about much anymore. He had when he was a little kid, though. He'd spent a long time waiting for his mother and father to come back from wherever they'd gone.

Janelle stopped one baby from tearing pages from a magazine and pulled the other out from under the table where he was spitting on the carpet and then licking it. When she sat down again, she said without looking at him, "I'm so sorry. I wasn't aware of that. So who raised you?"

"My maternal grandparents. They adopted me and my two sisters. Hey, ooops, kid, you're gonna—" One of the babies, the one with the fastest grin, had climbed up on the coffee table. One small trainer slipped on a shiny magazine just as Richard grabbed him, using a technique he'd learned as a wide receiver in football games. The little body felt solid and warm in his arms, the baby's bones terrifyingly fragile. The kid grinned at him and wriggled to get down, not at all fazed by his near mishap.

"His name's Oliver, not kid." Her voice was haughty.

"There you go, Oliver." Richard set the boy on his feet and watched him do the four-forty after his brother, who was disappearing behind the reception desk. Janelle retrieved them both again.

"So that's Oliver and this is—?" Richard poked a gentle finger into the other baby's fat middle. The boy solemnly grabbed it, guided it to his mouth and sank his sharp teeth in.

"Owww. Those are some choppers you got there, ki—, boy."

"Maxwell, you know biting's not allowed," Janelle chided, but Richard could see a tiny smile of satisfaction come and go.

The baby grinned at her and babbled out a string of vowels.

"Maxwell and Oliver, huh?" Richard liked the names. "Those are good names for boys. There's nothing wimpy about Maxwell and Oliver." Nothing wrong with their chompers, either.

Janelle sniffed and said in a defensive tone, "I wanted them to have names they could grow into."

"Absolutely." Maxwell was now trying to scale Richard's leg. *The kid sure had blue eyes.* He was trying to reach the silver pen Richard carried in his shirt pocket, so Richard pulled it out and offered it to him, illustrating the button that moved the top in and out.

Maxwell studied it a moment and after three abortive tries he did it himself. Oliver came to investigate, and Maxwell showed him how to push the button.

"Smart kids." Richard caught the deadly glance Janelle gave him. "Um, smart *sons* you have."

"*We* have," she purred, retrieving the pen and handing it back to him.

A technician appeared before he could think of a rejoinder. "Ms. Jamison? Mr. Webb? And this must be Oliver and Maxwell. Come with me, please."

The moment of truth was at hand. Richard's heart gave a thump and for a moment he couldn't breathe.

CHAPTER FIVE

DONOVAN'S FELT different, probably because it wasn't Monday night, Richard decided. He'd put in a panicked call to Peter and been pathetically grateful when he agreed to meet.

"You knew in three hours? I didn't know they could get the results of a paternity test that fast," Peter mused.

"Yeah, well it wasn't the speed that knocked me on my ass, it was the results." Richard stared into his mug of Guinness. It was off, it had to be. It didn't taste right. But then neither did the Irish stew. He'd eaten two mouthfuls. Peter was cleaning off his plate.

"They're over a year old, and I didn't even know they existed, Pete. They've got my eyes, and now I think of it, they're gonna have my hands, too. Their thumbs are the exact same shape." He flattened his palms on the table and looked at his thumbs as if he'd never seen them before. "Gramps used to call them hammer tops."

"When you gonna tell him?" Peter had a knack for the jugular.

Richard's throat was dry. "Soon. The minute I get my own mind around it." The awe he felt reflected in his voice. "They're my *sons,* Peter. They've got my genes. And they're so damned cute and smart, you wouldn't believe it."

Peter grinned. "I know the feeling. I still figure Abby's the most beautiful, intelligent kid in the entire universe."

Richard barely heard him. "They're identical twins, but they're easy to tell apart, Maxwell's more outgoing, Oliver's more thoughtful. Max has a different grin than Ollie, wicked and wide-open. Ollie's is sort of trusting and sweet."

"Not like his daddy, then. If you're not gonna eat this—" Peter grabbed Richard's plate. "So did their mommy say I told you so?"

"She just gave me one withering look, and then she grabbed the twins and hotfooted it out of there. I tried to help her with the door and the car and stuff, but she told me to get lost."

"She sounds like one independent lady."

"She is." She was also blazingly beautiful when she was mad, but then he hadn't really seen her any other way just yet. What would happen if she ever aimed the tender smile she gave the twins at him, Richard wondered?

"Her being so bloody proud and self-reliant is gonna present a real problem, because she keeps saying she doesn't want a thing from me, and I can't accept that. I want to *support* my kids, Peter. I want to make sure they get a decent start. And lord above, Pete, you should see the car she's driving." Richard shuddered. "It's an old van that should have hit the wrecker's ten years ago. I can't believe she can even get insurance for it, it's such a bucket of bolts." He scowled. "Damn, I hate to think of her driving my kids around in a heap like that."

Peter was methodically decimating the stew, but he was also watching Richard with a bemused expression. "I can't believe I'm hearing this. I never thought the day would come when you'd be talking like a father."

"I *am* a father." The admission was terrifying. It gave him an odd feeling in the pit of his stomach. He took a long, determined swallow of his beer, hoping it would help.

"So what are you gonna do about it? Unless she agrees, you won't be around them much." Peter's face was somber. "Believe me, I know.

I'm Abby's daddy, but I only see her every other weekend."

"Somehow I've got to convince her I'm serious about having an active role in raising those boys. I have to find a way around her."

"It won't be around her, buddy. It'll only be *through* her."

Richard thought about that and had to agree. "That could be tough. She thinks I'm a bozo, a real lightweight. She figures all I think about are boats and women."

Pete raised his eyebrows. "Wonder where she ever got that idea?"

Richard shot him a dirty look, but he had a point. "So what am I gonna do to change the way she thinks?"

They brainstormed through another pitcher of Guinness, and by the time it was finished, Richard had come up with a plan.

THE PHONE RANG five minutes after Janelle had finally gotten the twins to settle for the night. She snatched it up before it could ring a second time and wake them.

"Please don't hang up."

She recognized his voice instantly and tensed.

"I wondered if you and the boys would come

on a picnic on Saturday with me and my dog, Freddy.''

If he hadn't included the dog, she'd have refused point-blank. But then he'd have called again, and she had the feeling he wasn't the type to give up when he wanted something. She had to figure out a way to discourage him.

"Is the dog used to young children?"

"He's grown up getting mauled by my partner's little girl. He doesn't always like it, but he's long-suffering.''

She took her time thinking it over, letting the silence stretch.

"What kind of dog?"

"Cocker spaniel. I want to get to know you and the boys, Janelle. I want you to get to know me. And Freddy too, of course.''

The humility was an act, she knew that. A devious plan started to formulate in her brain.

"I want to learn how to be a father to Oliver and Maxwell, Janelle.''

She blew a raspberry. "Father, as in diapers?" This was going to be amusing. He'd last maybe an hour, two at the most. "You want to learn how to feed them, chase them, clean them up, listen to them howl?''

"All of the above. If you'll let me.''

"Okay. Pick us up at seven-thirty."

"In the morning?" He sounded taken aback.

She gave a feral grin. It was starting already. "Is that a problem?"

"Nope. No problem at all."

"The boys are up at six. By seven-thirty, they've eaten and they're dressed and raring to go. That's the time we go out if we're going," she snapped.

"Gotcha. I'll be there."

And by noon you'll be hustling us home and disappearing back into your comfortable life, Richard Webb.

Which was just what she wanted. When he found out what being around the twins really entailed, he'd gladly leave her alone.

CHAPTER SIX

IN SPITE OF HER resolve, Janelle got more and more nervous as Saturday approached. She prayed for rain, and got blazing sunshine. Neither of the boys had the slightest rash or the faintest trace of fever. She'd decided that if he was even five minutes late, she'd load the boys in the car and vanish. Then she remembered that he had a sports car. The twins needed car seats, and they'd never fit in the Corvette. So they wouldn't be able to go.

Relief filled her, but at 7:35, a shiny new red van pulled up and Richard got out and knocked on the door. He was wearing white shorts and a deep-blue shirt that matched his eyes and emphasized his deep tan. It was impossible not to notice how handsome he looked.

She opened the door and shoved Oliver into his arms.

"Maxwell's messed his diaper, I'll be back in a minute." She knew perfectly well that Ollie would scream bloody murder the minute she was out of sight. Might as well start Richard's initiation right away.

She sponged Max's bottom and took her time replacing his diaper and playsuit, puzzled by the silence from the other room. She was getting worried by the time she'd washed her hands and rubbed lip balm on her mouth.

When she hurried outside with Max on her hip and a loaded diaper bag over her shoulder, she saw why Ollie was so quiet.

Richard had given him his cell phone and introduced him to the golden-haired cocker spaniel. Ollie was sitting on the grass with the dog beside him. The baby was happily punching numbers, holding the phone to the dog's ear and babbling. The dog was wagging his short stubby tail and looking nervous.

Janelle grudgingly gave Richard one mark for ingenuity. "Here's the keys to my van, Richard. You'll have to get their car seats."

"No need, I took care of that." He opened the van's door. It was new, and the leathery smell was intoxicating. So were the state-of-the-art baby seats he'd attached in the back.

The dog climbed in and scurried to the very back. Janelle had Max firmly belted in while

Richard was still trying to get Ollie's chubby legs into the proper holes. She took over, and far too quickly, she was sitting in the soft leather bucket seat beside him as they drove through the deserted early-morning streets.

"Where are we going?"

"There's this place I know about that's off the beaten track. It's quiet and private, my grandmother used to take us kids there when we were little. It's not far from where I grew up."

He maneuvered with expert precision through downtown streets and then turned onto the freeway.

"What sort of work do you do, Janelle?"

The twins were quiet, occupied with toys she'd brought for them. She was beginning to relax a little. "I'm a marine oceanographer. I work at Woods Hole Oceanographic Institution. I'm currently doing research on the reproductive patterns of whales."

She could see by his expression that he was surprised. She gave him a cynical look. "What, you figured I was a barmaid?"

His ears turned red and he looked guilty. "No. I didn't know at all what you did. I just—" he pulled up to a stoplight and rested his forehead on the wheel. "Oh, hell. Am I ever off to a bad start here. When you said we met at a bar, I guess I sort of— Look, can we cancel this and start over?''

She wanted to laugh, because he was so obviously embarrassed. She decided to let him off the hook.

"Okay, let's. What do *you* do, Richard?'' She already knew he had a computer company. Not that he needed to work. One look at the boat, the Corvette, the quality of his clothes, would tell anyone he had unlimited access to old money.

"I started a business with a guy I met in college, it's called Childsplay. Peter and I design and manufacture computer games for kids. We started out on a shoestring, we worked out of my apartment at first, but now we have office space. It's been a tough grind, and for a while it was touch-and-go, but in the last four years it's really taken off.''

It was Janelle's turn to be surprised. So maybe he actually knew what work was. There was another question that had been nagging at her.

"How did you find me? I know Betsy didn't tell you where I lived.'' Betsy would undergo torture without divulging a word.

He shot her a look and then returned his attention to the highway. She'd noticed how carefully he was driving, staying well within the speed limit and a good distance behind the vehicle ahead. She appreciated it. The twins were precious cargo.

"I saw you doing an ad for bath oil on late-night TV."

"Oh." She'd thought maybe a private detective. "I didn't think they were even running that ad anymore."

"It's really good." He grinned at her, a hint of mischief in his blue gaze. *"The only bath oil that will leave your skin feeling like silk,"* he quoted. "Is that just hype, or is there some truth to it?"

"Who knows? The boys dumped my last complimentary bottle of the stuff into their toy box. I don't know about soft skin, but it sure has staying power where plastic is concerned, their toys are still slippery from it." She thought over what he'd said. "But how did you get my address from an ad?"

He looked a little abashed. "Well, I got hold of the talent agency that handled you and talked them into giving me your phone number. From there I got your address. I wasn't entirely honest, but it worked. Was that the only ad you did, or are there more I should know about?"

Janelle refused to be embarrassed or apologetic. "That ad and a couple of others helped pay my way through university."

They'd done more than that. They'd helped pay some of her mother's medical expenses when she was diagnosed with Parkinson's. If they were in use again, she'd get residuals and they might even pay for diapers until the twins finally got trained. If that day ever came.

"Did you grow up in Boston, Janelle?"

"Yeah, I did. My dad drove city buses until he retired last year. He and my mom still live in the apartment where I grew up. And you?" She was certain she knew the answer, but she asked anyway. She'd done some research on Richard Webb.

"I grew up in Dover. My two sisters and I went to live there with my grandfather and grandmother when my parents died. I was four. I have a cottage of my own nearby, on the Charles River."

Janelle knew that the Webb estate was called Oak Meadow. She'd seen photos of it in a home and garden magazine. And Richard's *cottage* was probably much bigger than the apartment where she and her sister had grown up.

"I go up there on weekends," he added. "But

I recently bought another place in the city, a small condo. It's a good investment, and I don't have to worry about the neighbors complaining about Freddy barking in the hallway.''

"Where'd you get him?" A glance back made her smile. The little dog was standing on the back seat, nose pressed against the window, tail wagging. The twins had their heads turned, mesmerized by him.

Richard took an exit off the freeway, and soon they were driving through lush green countryside.

"Believe it or not, I saw him in the window of a pet store, with his nose pushed up against the window, just like he's doing now. He looked so pathetic, and I thought he was doing it because he'd fallen for me, but I know now he's just a voyeur."

Janelle laughed. Richard grinned and pulled into a parking area beside a small park. There were only two other cars, and when she opened the door, she could hear birds singing and the ripple of water nearby.

He'd thought to bring a tartan blanket. He also had a huge picnic basket and a cooler. It took several trips, but they were finally settled underneath a dogwood tree—for all of three minutes, until Oliver headed at a dead run for the nearby stream.

Before Janelle could make a move, Richard sprinted after him, grabbing the baby up and making a game of running in circles and then heading back to the blanket. Janelle caught herself admiring his butt and forced herself to concentrate instead on keeping Max from sucking on Freddy's ears.

"I brought some stuff for them to eat." He unloaded the picnic basket. "I wasn't sure what they'd like."

It looked as if he'd bought out a convenience store.

Janelle studied the assortment. "They can't eat popcorn, they choke on it. And the candy bars are out, they go nuts when they get too much sugar. But the apple juice is great, and the bananas are, too— Ollie, no."

Oliver grinned at her and put another stone in his mouth.

"Oh, my God, he'll choke." Richard sounded panicked. "Here, tiger, give me—owww." He stuck a finger in Oliver's mouth and the baby's eight sharp teeth sank into his flesh.

"Ollie, let go." They'd be heading back to Boston before another hour had passed, Janelle speculated. "This is the best way to get stuff out of their mouths." She demonstrated sliding a finger in behind the teeth and dislodging the stones as well as loosening Oliver's death grip on Richard's finger. She didn't let her amusement show.

"Sorry, they're bad for biting. It has something to do with teething, the pediatrician says." She glanced up just in time to see Maxwell wade into the stream. "Ooops."

Again, Richard got there ahead of her. His white shorts were dirty and soaked through when he returned with Max, dripping wet, muddy, and crowing with delight.

"He fell before I could get him," Richard said in an apologetic tone. "I guess you wouldn't happen to have any spare clothes for him?"

Again, the situation amused her. "I never go anywhere without at least two sets of extras for each of them." She pulled minuscule shorts and a T-shirt out of the bag, along with a diaper, and deliberately handed them to Richard.

CHAPTER SEVEN

JANELLE WATCHED as he knelt on the blanket and clumsily wrestled Max out of shorts, T-shirt and sodden diaper, with Max doing his best to escape.

"That's backward," she prompted as Richard struggled with the diaper. "The thick part goes to the front."

"I did take anatomy, why didn't I figure that out?" Tongue between his teeth, he reversed the diaper.

She had to admit he did pretty well for a virgin attempt. Dressing the twins was what she imagined wrestling greased piglets might be like. He was sweating by the time he pulled Max's shorts up, but he also sported a triumphant grin.

"No wonder you're in such fantastic shape," he said, sinking back on his haunches and swiping his forehead with the tail of his shirt.

So was he in good shape. She couldn't help noticing that he had a flat, brown belly and what she'd heard referred to as a six-pack of abdominal muscle.

"I brought iced tea, want some?"

They sipped the tea in between rescuing Freddy from the twins' onslaughts, stopping them from tasting goose droppings and heading off several more determined attempts at drowning in the stream.

Janelle kept expecting Richard to give up and take them home, but he seemed to be enjoying himself. He was even beginning to understand the boys' garbled attempts at words, and he picked up quickly on the way she repeated what they said.

Before she knew it, it was lunchtime. Richard helped her feed the boys, spooning the contents of containers of vegetables and fruit into eager mouths. The twins were tired, and when they began to fuss, Janelle settled them in the shade with blankets and bottles. Their eyelids gradually grew heavy and Janelle rubbed their backs as they went to sleep.

Richard watched and then gently took over with Max while she stroked Ollie's small spine. It was companionable. Janelle had never shared these moments, and she found it a novelty to exchange glances with him as the boys resisted and then at last succumbed to sleep.

Janelle covered them lightly, and she and Richard sat on a bench a short distance away so as not to disturb them while they ate the ham-and-cheese sandwiches he'd brought. There was even a bottle of wine, and as she sipped her wine, Janelle relaxed fully for the first time all morning.

She closed her eyes and leaned back, letting the sun bathe her face and body. She tried to ignore the fact that Richard was barely a foot away, and she sensed that he was watching her.

"God, they're such amazing kids," he sighed. "They're incredibly smart, aren't they? And you're doing such a good job with them, you never seem to lose your cool. How'd you learn to be such a good parent? Are there courses a person can take?"

The praise was so genuine, Janelle's heart swelled with gratitude. She still had nights when she couldn't sleep, worrying over how she was parenting the boys. "No courses that I know about. It's pretty much common sense and trial and error."

He asked questions about their diet, nap times, daily routines. It was obvious he hadn't had much to do with babies, but he was both honest and humble about his ignorance. And it amazed her that he seemed so touchingly eager to learn.

A new and terrifying thought came, and a shudder of fear ran down her spine. Janelle knew she had to ask him straight out. She sat up and looked him in the eye.

"Do you—are you going to try to take the boys away from me, Richard?"

The shocked amazement on his face was answer enough.

"God, no. I wouldn't do that, not ever. I mean, I might if they were in danger or not being properly cared for, but I've just told you, I don't think they could have a better mom than you." He was quiet for a moment. "I figure kids are always best off being raised by their natural parents," he added. "My sisters and I were lucky my grandparents adopted us. They were wonderful to us, but I don't think it was the same as growing up with our own mom and dad would have been." He gave a rueful smile. "Gramps was strict, and he was already old when we came along, so there was one heck of a generation gap. Not that he's out of touch, but he is old-fashioned. He's also a powerful man, and he's used to having every-

GET 2

HOW TO GET YOUR
2 FREE BOOKS AND FREE GIFT!

1. Peel off the MIRA sticker on the front cover. Place it in the space provided at right. This automatically entitles you to receive two free books and an exciting surprise gift.

2. Send back this card and you'll get 2 "The Best of the Best™" novels. These books have a combined cover price of $11.98 or more in the U.S. and $13.98 or more in Canada, but they are yours to keep absolutely FREE!

3. There's <u>no</u> catch. You're under <u>no</u> obligation to buy anything. We charge nothing – ZERO – for your first shipment. And you don't have to make any minimum number of purchases – not even one!

4. We call this line "The Best of the Best" because each month you'll receive the best books by some of today's most popular authors. These authors show up time and time again on all the major bestseller lists and their books sell out as soon as they hit the stores. You'll like the convenience of getting them delivered to your home at our special discount prices . . . and you'll love your *Heart to Heart* subscriber newsletter featuring author news, horoscopes, recipes, book reviews and much more!

5. We hope that after receiving your free books you'll want to remain a subscriber. But the choice is yours – to continue or cancel, anytime at all! So why not take us up on our invitation, with no risk of any kind. You'll be glad you did!

6. And remember...we'll send you a surprise gift ABSOLUTELY FREE just for giving "The Best of the Best" a try.

SPECIAL FREE GIFT!

We'll send you a fabulous surprise gift, absolutely FREE, simply for accepting our no-risk offer!

Visit us online at
www.mirabooks.com

® and TM are trademarks of Harlequin Enterprises Limited.

thing his own way. From the time I was a kid, he and I have butted heads a lot of the time.''

''What about your sisters? Do they get along with him?'' Janelle couldn't help but be intrigued by these unknown strangers who were her son's blood relations.

''One of my sisters, Diana, is a total rebel. My other sister, Sally, is the angel. She's Gramps's social secretary, she bends over backward to keep peace in the family. So it's two to one.''

Janelle thought of her own sister, Tracy. Maybe every family had its rebel and its peacemaker.

She didn't say so, though.

He refilled her plastic glass with wine and changed the subject.

''How did you happen to study oceanography, Janelle?''

''Oh, it seemed the natural thing for me to do. I loved biology, and I got a summer job my senior year for Mass Bay Lines, on the whale-watching cruises. I learned how to dive that summer, and it was addictive. I wanted to know about the forms of life in the sea, I wanted to know how humans impact on that environment.''

He watched her closely as she answered. ''Having the twins must have had a major impact on your work. You wouldn't have been able to dive while you were pregnant. And I know oceanographers have to travel a fair bit. You're not as free to go away on assignments as you were, right?''

He was astute. She'd had to turn down a promotion because it would have meant longer hours and less time with her babies.

"It's my choice, and I've never regretted it for an instant.''

"I can see that, but I'd like to help out financially—''

"Absolutely not. No.'' She cut him off before he could get any further. "And if you're going to make an issue about that, you can take us home right now.''

"But they're my sons, Janelle. I want to feel I have a part in their lives.''

"So find some way other than financial.'' Her voice hardened. "Money's easy for you, Richard. It would just be a cheap way of buying off your conscience.''

Richard's temper flared at her sarcastic tone, but when he thought it over, he had to admit there was a grain of truth in what she said.

Her eyes were closed again, and she'd put on sunglasses. She was slumped back on the bench, her long, elegant body draped carelessly, soaking in the sunshine. The cups of wine rested between them, and every now and then she'd languidly reach for hers and take a slow, appreciative sip.

She was wearing hiking shorts and a close-fitting green T-shirt. She had a beautiful, sexy body. Her legs and arms were long and sculpted, her breasts high and round. It was an athlete's body, and there wasn't a spare ounce of flesh on her graceful frame. He tried to imagine what she'd looked like pregnant, and failed entirely.

All day, he'd spent moments trying to remember how she looked naked. He'd made love to her, and how he could forget the details of that body was beyond him, but somehow he'd managed. He felt disgusted with himself.

He'd been trying to figure out a tactful way of asking her something that was nagging at him. Finally, he just swallowed hard and came out with it.

"Are you seeing anyone, Janelle?"

Her head came up and she slipped her glasses down her nose and peered at him.

"As in, dating?"

"Yeah. Dating. I mean, I know you must date, but I just wondered. If...there's anybody special?"

She tipped her head back and laughed, full and easy. The line of her throat was breathtaking. He longed to press his lips there and feel the pulse beat.

She shook her head. "You just don't get it, do you? Exactly one guy has asked me out since the twins came along. They both got roseola that day, so I couldn't go. He never asked again. Tell me, Richard, how many times have you dated a woman with twin babies?"

"Once." He dared to wink at her. "Today. And I hope the lady will let me do it soon again, because I'm having a great time."

Her challenging look turned to confusion, and her cheeks went crimson. He decided he liked catching her off guard.

"Today is just so that you could get to know the twins." Her tone was dismissive.

"And you," he corrected. "God knows where my head was the night we made love, Janelle. I know it's too little too late, but I'd like to apologize. I was an idiot, and worse."

She gave him a long, sad look and then nodded. "Yeah. You were."

"One thing bothers me. When you knew you were pregnant, why didn't you get in touch with me?"

Her laugh was harsh. "According to your secretary you were away for several months on a business trip to Canada. When you returned, you weren't answering calls from women who claimed they were pregnant."

His face burned. He knew now exactly what had happened. While he was away, he'd gotten mixed up with a woman who was mentally unstable. She'd followed him back to Boston, and she'd pulled every trick in the book to get him to see her. She'd found out where he lived, she'd followed him for weeks, she'd scratched up his car with her keys and threatened him with a knife. She was now in the Fairhaven Mental Health Facility. He'd instructed his secretary to ignore all calls from women during that period.

It was humiliating, telling Janelle about her, but he did it.

"I'm so sorry," he said again. He'd never meant it this much in his life.

She shrugged, turning her head away to look over at the twins, still sleeping underneath the tree.

"You're a playboy, Richard. Things like that are bound to happen."

He'd heard the accusation before, but this was

the first time it made him cringe. He'd have given anything to be able to deny it, but he couldn't. All he could do was make a fervent, silent vow that from this moment on, he'd change.

CHAPTER EIGHT

THE TWINS SLEPT for over two hours. When they woke, Richard had his first experience with changing Oliver's messy diaper.

Janelle, who was performing a similar task with Maxwell, couldn't seem to stop giggling each time she looked at him. He tried not to gag, but he didn't quite succeed.

After that challenge, they took the boys walking, Maxwell on Janelle's hip, Oliver on Richard's. A few more people had arrived with picnic baskets. Kids of all ages were paddling in the stream and playing on the swings hung from the giant trees.

"My, those babies sure do favor their daddy," one man remarked.

Richard could feel his chest expand with pride, and he couldn't seem to stop grinning. It was incredible. He'd always been so certain he wasn't ready to have kids, and now he wanted the world to know that these beautiful babies belonged to him.

Janelle had brought balloons, and they tied them to a mortified Freddy's collar after the boys accidentally let them go for the third time.

He was disappointed when she insisted it was time to go home. "Can I take you out for an early dinner?" He didn't want the day to end.

Again, she laughed. "You've obviously never dined with boys this age. It's fairly primitive, they spill, throw food and spit out what they don't like. Fast-food establishments are the only ones that don't faint when they see us coming, and I don't like to give them that type of food often. So we eat at home, but I don't even try to eat with them. I feed them first and grab something after they're in bed."

It took courage, but he asked anyway. "Do you think I could help you put them to bed? Maybe?"

She shot him an assessing glance. "I'd have thought you'd have had more than enough of us by now."

"Nope. I'm having the time of my life."

"You are truly warped, Mr. Webb." But she smiled when she said it, and when Richard helped her into the house with the twins and their paraphernalia, she didn't ask him to leave.

JANELLE LET HIM HELP her feed them supper and then, at his request, bathe the twins.

She showed him how much water to put in the tub, how to test it with his wrist, which shampoo and soap belonged to the boys, where their bath toys were, and then she closed the bathroom door and left him to it. She trusted him, which surprised her. He'd proven to be responsible, once he knew the rules. And he was eager, which astounded her.

Even more amazing was the fact that the boys didn't howl when she left them alone with him in the bathroom. They liked him, and she wasn't sure yet how she felt about that. They called him something that sounded like *itchy,* and it wasn't far from the way she felt around him.

Was she setting them up for disappointment when he disappeared from their lives?

Today he'd told perfect strangers the boys were his sons. She'd had mixed feelings about that, and she'd had to remind herself that after all, it was only the truth.

Instead of getting annoyed and impatient as the

day progressed, Richard had seemed to take sincere pleasure in being with the babies, and honesty forced her to admit that she'd enjoyed being with him.

It shocked her to realize that if things had been different, if he was a stranger she was dating, she'd probably be halfway in love with him by now. As the day progressed she'd had to constantly remind herself that this was Richard Webb, unscrupulous user of women, and not the nice guy he appeared to be.

"Freddy, come on out from under there, the demons are safely in the bathtub." Janelle knelt and coaxed the patient little dog from under her bed, where he'd taken refuge after the twins made one too many explorations of his ears and nose.

"Come and have some water, and I'll see if your boss will let you have a leftover burger."

Janelle walked to the bathroom and she opened the door, and her heart skipped a beat. The room was filled with steam. The boys were splashing in the tub, and just as usual, the bathroom floor was awash.

Richard had taken his shirt off, and he was kneeling on a sodden mat, soaping Oliver.

His back was broad and brown, the skin stretched smoothly over firm muscle. One huge hand held Oliver's small arm, and the contrast between the small boy's fragile shoulder and the man's strength was dramatic.

He turned, and she couldn't help but admire the muscular definition of his chest, the thick mat of chest hair, the dramatic way his torso tapered to a trim waist and narrow hips.

There was a blob of soap on his nose, and without thought she reached out and brushed it away. His grin faded and the look in his eyes changed in a blink from humor to heat.

Her throat felt constricted and she had to clear it. "Can Freddy have some leftover burgers?"

"Sure. He isn't on any special diet."

"Mummum." Both boys gave her toothy smiles and their clutched-fist wave. They were obviously enjoying themselves.

"Have fun," she croaked. When she closed the bathroom door again she leaned against the wall for a moment with her eyes closed. Her knees felt weak. It had been far too long since she'd been around a half-clothed adult male.

"Remember who and what he is," she reminded herself forcefully. "Hormones, think hormones. That's all this is."

He emerged half an hour later with shiny clean, naked babies, one in each arm, and she managed not to look anywhere except in his eyes.

"Don't go in there until I have a chance to mop it up," he warned. "We got a little carried away with the shower spray."

She led the way into the twins' bedroom, and he wrestled Maxwell into diaper and pajamas while she did Oliver. Their cribs were side by side.

"They hold one another's hands before they go to sleep," she explained, and his face softened.

When the boys were ready for bed, he sat down with them in the rocking chair and read them *Goodnight Moon*. Janelle went to the kitchen to get their bottles, but she could hear his deep baritone, giving the story a different slant than she did. He read well.

When the story was over, she kissed each boy and told him she loved him, as she always did, but tonight she was conscious of Richard, standing quietly by the door, watching and listening.

He cleaned up the bathroom, just as he'd

promised. When he came out with a load of wet towels and soiled clothing, she put a load in the washer, again conscious of him watching her.

"How about I go out and pick us up a pizza and some beer, Janelle?"

This had nothing to do with the boys. She ought to refuse. But she thought of another long evening spent alone, reading work-related material and watching something dumb on television.

The toughest part of raising babies alone was the longing for adult conversation.

"Okay. I'll make a salad."

She grabbed a quick shower while he was gone, pleased with the scrubbed clean look of the bathroom. He'd wiped down the walls and mopped up the floor, and put the baby's toys and soaps back where they belonged. It was a luxury for her to be able to step into the shower without first doing a major cleanup.

She pulled on sweats and a fresh T-shirt, deliberately leaving her face clean of makeup and her hair wet, just the way she would have done had she been alone.

As she chopped lettuce and cut up avocado, she assured herself that she had no desire whatsoever to impress Richard. She set the table in the kitchen, just the way she would have for her-self.

But sitting across from him, relishing the veg-etarian pizza he'd chosen without her prompting, talking to him about the candidates for mayor and when and if the city would ever finish the Big Dig, a part of her recognized that for the first time in months, she was having fun with an adult male.

They each had a beer with their meal, but she noticed that he refused a second.

"I have to drive home. And the last thing I need is an impairment charge."

That reminded her of something she'd won-dered about earlier. "Where'd the van come from? I thought you drove a Corvette."

"Oh, I rented it for the day. The car seats wouldn't fit in the Corvette."

"It came with car seats?"

"No, I got my friend Peter to tell me which ones were suitable. I bought them."

"You bought car seats for a one-day excur-sion?"

"I guess maybe I was hoping we could do it again soon?"

"We'll see." *We'll see what happens when*

you go back to your everyday life, Mr. Webb. Maybe this is just a little diversion, and you'll get bored with it real fast.

He helped her load the dishwasher, and he noticed when she yawned for the second time.

"I guess you go to bed pretty early."

"They wake up at dawn. I'm usually in bed by ten."

It was twenty past nine.

"I should be going." He sounded reluctant, and to her surprise, she felt the same way. It was hard to remember that he was the enemy.

"I really enjoyed the day, Janelle. Thanks for letting me share it with you and the boys."

"I enjoyed it, too." Something prompted her to be honest. "I didn't think I would, but I did."

He winked at her. "Surprise is a good thing." He dug in his shorts pocket for his keys and whistled for Freddy.

She tensed, waiting for him to make a move on her. When he didn't, she couldn't figure out whether she was pleased or disappointed.

"Can I call you?"

"Sure." She watched from the window as he and Freddy climbed in the van and drove away.

Don't think for a moment you'll see him again,

she warned herself. *He might have gotten a charge out of playing daddy for a day, but forget about him being around for the long haul. You know his reputation.*

She also knew why he was like honey to bees where women were concerned. Richard Webb was a dangerously attractive man.

CHAPTER NINE

RICHARD RETURNED the van and collected the Corvette. He was tired, but it was a good, physical tiredness. Hefting those boys all day long was as good as a workout with free weights at the gym. Janelle had the figure to prove it, slender, extraordinarily strong, and so sensual it blew him away.

Being with her today had brought on surges of powerful physical desire, but it wasn't just the way she looked that turned him on. It was also the easy conversation they'd enjoyed, the laughter, her quick wit, and their shared responsibility for two little lives.

The women he dated played fast and loose, and serious conversation wasn't their strong point. Like him, all they wanted was a good time—lots of laughs, lots of wine, great sex. Today Janelle had shown him how much was missing from that formula, aspects he'd never have thought of if it hadn't been for the twins.

He thought of Oliver and Maxwell, sprawled in their cribs, small hands intertwined, and he had to swipe a fist across the moisture in his eyes.

He'd fallen head over heels in love with his sons today.

Tonight, he had to call his grandfather and tell him about them, and that conversation was going to be tough. Lawrence Webb was a stickler for honor, and he'd be sure to point out the many ways in which Richard had been less than honorable in this situation. He'd be dead right, too. Richard seldom felt ashamed of his actions, but he did this time, mortally ashamed. Telling Gramps was going to be a lesson in humility.

But even that scenario couldn't diminish the overwhelming pride he felt when he thought about his sons. Bathing them, holding them, seeing them smile and even hearing them howl had amazed and intrigued him as few things ever had. Two living, breathing small human beings carried his blood, his genetic makeup. Amazing.

He couldn't wait to see them again.

Let's be dead honest here, Webb. You can't wait to see their mother again, either. So get creative and figure out how best to go about it.

The first step was to buy a van, and first thing Monday morning, he did—a top-of-the-line, cherry-red Windstar. The next challenge was to figure out how to get Janelle to accept it.

"HE'S CALLED every single day for fourteen days?" Betsy whistled, and she and Janelle laughed when first Oliver and then Maxwell pursed their lips and tried to copy her.

They were sitting on plastic lawn chairs sipping cans of beer in Janelle's minuscule front yard, where she'd blown up and filled a plastic pool for Oliver and Maxwell. It was Thursday evening, and Betsy had brought take-out Chinese to celebrate winning a trial that had dragged on for weeks.

"Every day since that first day in the park, he's been in touch," Janelle confirmed. "He's been over as often as I've let him come."

"Which would be—?"

Janelle shrugged and avoided Betsy's eyes. "Oh, three or four times."

Betsy lifted a skeptical eyebrow. "Seems like he's been here every time I've called, and that's more than three or four times."

"Well, maybe it's been a bit more often." Janelle felt her face redden.

"Uh-huh. And what sort of things do the four of you do?"

"Oh, just ordinary stuff."

"For instance?"

Janelle knew by Betsy's expression she wasn't about to get away without going into detail. "Well, last weekend he took us out on the boat for the day. Then he wandered around behind me in the supermarket with the kids so I could do my shopping. Then we went to a kid-friendly burger place for dinner. He's coming over later today to put them to bed so I can go to the library—there's some research I want to do."

"Sounds like he's hooked, Janey."

Janelle shook her head and frowned. "I keep waiting for the novelty to wear off. I keep thinking I'm making a huge mistake letting him be around the twins so much. They call him Itchy, and they're getting attached to him. It's gonna be a big letdown when he gets bored and disappears."

Betsy considered that. "Maybe he will. But then again, maybe he won't. Maybe he'll stick around. He *is* their father. You oughta think positively here."

Janelle sighed. "I don't know what positive is anymore. I figured that he'd be long gone by now. I've tried to discourage him, but the guy is so persistent, he wears me down. And he's also diabolically clever at thinking up things that I actually want to do, things that the twins enjoy. He brought over jogging strollers and we took them running the other day. I always wanted to do that, but with two of them—''

"And what about the two of *you?* How do you feel about him now?''

Betsy knew all too well what Janelle's opinion of Richard had been before.

Janelle thought it over. The whole issue was troubling. "I trust him with the boys. He's careful with them. He's a male presence in their life, which they desperately need. My dad's too busy taking care of mom to spend much time with them.''

Betsy gave her an appraising look. "Sounds as if you could get awfully used to having him around. You two get along, or he wouldn't be asking you to go with him and the kids all the time, and you wouldn't be accepting. He'd be at my office trying to get visiting rights that didn't include you. And I think you're nuts refusing to let him pay you support, by the way. It's the kids' birthright, to have a father financially support them.''

"I will not let myself rely on him, and I will not fall for him, either,'' Janelle said forcefully.

"This is *not* Mr. Responsibility we're talking about here, Bets. This guy's track record with women would make Casanova blush."

Betsy shrugged and shoved her glasses up her nose. "People do change, I've heard it happens. None of the guys I've ever met have managed it, but hey, that's not a huge segment to base any conclusions on. Has he kissed you yet?"

"Never even tried. Not that I'd let him. So cancel out those rosy fantasies about mommy and daddy and babies all living happily ever after. It just ain't gonna happen, counselor."

Betsy sighed. "I wish just for once life would mimic fiction."

"You read too many romance novels."

Betsy shook her head. "I have too many ugly files that deal with divorce and custody. I'd like to know just one happily married couple."

Janelle thought about it. "There's a woman at work who seems happy. She's been married twelve years and has three kids."

"Bravo." Betsy's arm shot up in a salute. "I knew there had to be one around somewhere." She took a sip of beer and got serious. "In spite of everything, I still believe in marriage and family. Don't you ever dream of meeting the right guy and getting married?"

"I used to." Janelle knew she sounded wistful. "But since the twins, no. I wouldn't be just choosing someone for me, I'd be finding them a stepfather, and that's scary, Bets. I figure I'll just raise them by myself and then when they're grown find a really rich old guy with bad eyes who adores me."

"Hell, I'd settle for him right now," Betsy growled, and they laughed.

Betsy left, and shortly afterward Richard drove up. He'd bought a red van, and Janelle had noticed but not commented. If he wanted to collect cars, that was his own business. She wasn't about to assume responsibility for his reasons.

"Hi, Janelle." He grinned at her and sat down in the lawn chair Betsy had vacated. It looked too fragile to support him. Freddy crawled underneath it, a veteran of too many ear tugs and tail pulls.

"Hey, tigers, how ya doin'?"

The boys trotted over to Richard, vying with one another to jabber the loudest. Ignoring the fact they were naked and soaking wet, he hoisted them up, one on each knee, planting kisses on sun-kissed cheeks.

Something inside of Janelle shifted as she

looked at them. The longing she'd been careful to ignore suddenly caught her by surprise.

Why couldn't there be a happy ending, just like Betsy said?

She rejected the idea the moment it registered and shot to her feet.

"I'll go now. They've had dinner, they should have some fruit and yogurt before bed, but I'll be back by then."

"Take your time. I'm not on any time clock."

"Okay." Why not take advantage, if he was offering? "Their pajamas are on the dresser, you know where the diapers are. See you later." She smacked a kiss on each twin, noted with a tiny, regretful pang that they didn't even seem to notice that she was leaving, and hurried toward her car, hoping it would start.

"Why not take the van?" Before she could refuse, he flipped her the keys.

Why not? Apart from stubborn pride, she couldn't think of a single reason. She thanked him and then headed for the shiny new vehicle.

It was a dream to drive. She took the long way to the library, enjoying the ease and power as well as the heady feeling of being free to do much needed research for a couple of hours.

She tried to ignore the tiny voice that whispered that in spite of what she'd told Betsy, she was already becoming far too dependent on Richard Webb.

WHEN JANELLE walked in the house two hours later, the sound of excited squeals and laughter greeted her.

Richard was flat on his back on the floor of the living room, and the twins, freshly bathed and wearing only diapers, were wrestling with him. They launched themselves like rockets, landing on top of him, and he growled and blew raspberries on their round tummies.

''Mummum.'' Oliver spotted Janelle and ran over to her, dragging her into the melee. Richard caught her arm and gave her a tug so that she lost her balance and landed half on top of him. She was laughing, and the twins instantly threw themselves on her back so she couldn't get up.

The physical contact with him unnerved her. He was wearing a T-shirt, but she could feel the heat of his skin, searing her own where their bodies touched. Before she could move, he reached up and snagged a hand around her neck, under her hair, holding her still, looking up at her with a question in his blue eyes.

She meant to shove him away the instant she

saw what was in his eyes. Afterward she wasn't sure, whether she had lowered her head by herself, or whether he had pulled her down.

She only knew that when their lips met, incredible singing pleasure surged through every pore of her body, like a geyser she couldn't control.

The kiss didn't last long. It couldn't, because the small boys were wriggling over and around them like eager puppies. Janelle pulled away and scrambled to her feet, feeling for a desolate instant as if she were leaving everything in the universe that she'd ever wanted.

"Time for bed." She covered her discomfiture with busy activity, wrestling Max into pajamas, and finding a book to read to the twins before she and Richard tucked them into their cribs.

The time came all too soon when the boys were asleep and they were alone. She half hoped he wouldn't say anything, that he'd ignore what had happened and they'd go on as before. But of course, he didn't. It was like trying to ignore a rhinoceroses who'd taken up residence in the living room.

"Janelle, I won't apologize." He sighed and shoved his hair back with his fingers. "I've wanted to kiss you since that first morning when you ran away from me. I want to kiss you right now. It's getting harder and harder to keep my hands off you whenever we're together. I'm powerfully attracted to you."

Shaken, she took refuge in cruel sarcasm. "You're powerfully attracted to any woman you're around for longer than five minutes," she said in a scathing tone. "You're not trustworthy when it comes to relationships, Webb. That kiss was a mistake. You caught me off guard," she lied. "You can bet it won't happen again."

She saw anger and hurt flare like quicksilver in his eyes, and she told herself she was relieved when he snatched the keys to the van off the table where she'd left them. He stalked out without another word.

She sank down on the couch, aware that she was trembling. So that was the end of it, then. It would be ridiculous to think for one moment Richard Webb could be relied on or trusted with her feelings, with her heart. She wouldn't even consider it.

She was glad he was gone, she assured herself stoutly. She was glad the boys were so young; they'd forget about him in the space of a few days.

As for herself, it was time to get back to the realities of her life. There was no reason whatsoever for her throat to close up this way, as if she were holding back tears.

CHAPTER TEN

BEFORE HE'D GONE three blocks, Richard's temper subsided and regret twisted his gut into a knot.

For a brief moment, she'd responded to him with all the incredible passion he'd sensed was in her. Just for a moment, she'd let her guard down and Richard had seen how it could have been between them—if he hadn't been such a prize idiot the first time he'd been with her.

Trying to remember that night in detail had taken up more than one sleepless night, and he knew it would go on bothering him.

Why didn't he remember kissing her? He must have, more than once, that first night, but he had no memory of it at all. How could that be, when the kiss they'd shared tonight was so explosive it had sent hot need thundering through his body?

Heavy guilt had niggled at him over the past weeks, as he learned the intricate patterns of his son's personalities, heard the sound of their mother's husky, full-out laughter, noticed the way her hair fell in a thick, flaming mass over her ears when she bent over to pick up one of their children.

Tonight guilt and remorse were no longer manageable emotions. They were ferocious and gut-wrenching, painful beyond belief. He thought of what his grandfather had said when Richard told him about Janelle and the twins.

At first, predictably, Lawrence had been furious with Richard, raging at him about responsibility and honor and reckless disregard. But after the stinging lecture, he'd surprised Richard.

You can't change the past, son, Lawrence Webb had declared with a protracted sigh. *All you can do is learn from it and make sure you do better the next time around.*

The accusations Janelle had tossed at him tonight were a direct and justifiable result of the callous way he'd treated her when she was pregnant, when she needed him and he hadn't bothered to even return her frantic phone calls. He deserved the sharp side of her tongue, and more.

But for that one moment, when he was kissing her, he'd felt her arousal, her instinctive response. She was just as attracted to him as he was to her, but she was afraid to admit it.

He'd make it up to her; he vowed on his life that he would. He'd court her, prove to her that he was a changed man. Richard never wanted a woman the way he wanted Janelle. He'd never felt this way about any woman before.

He'd fallen head over heels in love with his twins, and he was beginning to suspect he'd done the same thing with their mother.

Richard had never tried to charm a woman before; he'd never had to. He'd have to give it some thought, but he was determined to do a top rate job of it.

THE PACKAGE ARRIVED by courier, just as Janelle was leaving for work. Puzzled, she tore it open.

It was a gigantic bottle of Bodysoft, the wickedly expensive bath oil she'd done the ads for. The card read, "Ollie and Max may have spilled the stuff, but I'm the one who keeps falling flat on my face. Forgive me? Richard."

Janelle sniffed with disdain and stuck the package on top of a bureau, where the twins couldn't reach it. She'd bundle it up and send it back when she got home from work. But the note was funny all the same and she had to give him reluctant marks for creativity.

She couldn't keep from smiling as she kissed

the wailing twins, called goodbye to Gwen and headed out the door.

When the balloons arrived that afternoon, she'd been home only half an hour. There were so many helium-filled globes in rainbow colors, they half filled the living room. The twins were beside themselves with glee. There was no question of returning them. Within half an hour, dozens were broken, and the rest were stuck to the ceilings and walls, giving the condo a reckless, party atmosphere.

The note read, "I'm deflated and I promise I'm empty of hot air. Forgive me? Richard."

When the florist's van arrived at eight the following morning with four dozen of the extravagant Gerbera daisies she loved, Janelle didn't even consider sending them back. They were arranged with a ton of greenery in an old-fashioned copper washtub, the kind mothers used to use to bathe their babies. She'd admired it one day when she and Richard were out walking with the twins.

She tore open the envelope. This time the note read, "I've cleaned up my act. Could our friendship flower again?"

Damn him. How did he know exactly what would charm her?

And then on Saturday afternoon, Betsy arrived unannounced, her coal-dark eyes sparkling. She crouched down to the twins' level.

"Guess what, my pretty rogues? You guys are gonna stay with Auntie Betsy tonight, because Mommy's got a heavy date. Auntie's gonna feed you and put you to bed, and then have a sleep-over so Mommy doesn't have to hurry home."

"I don't have any date." Janelle was folding clothes and the twins were unfolding them.

"I beg to differ. Your chariot will arrive at seven this evening complete with Prince Webb, and you are going out for dinner and dancing at that new swish club on Columbus Avenue. And don't go all huffy because he didn't call and ask you. I told him not to because you'd just turn him down flat."

She gave Janelle's cutoffs and the beet stains on her T-shirt an appraising look. "You'd better start getting ready now, because you have your work cut out for you—Migod, look at those nails. Go have a bath in that heavenly oil he sent. I'll spoon tins of God-knows-what into these guys and then we'll watch *Law and Order* on the telly."

Janelle scowled at her friend. "Whose side are

you on, anyway? I told you I was relieved when he stormed out. I don't want to see him again."

"As your lawyer, I have to advise you that you're making a mistake here. The guy sincerely cares about the kids and, unless I miss my guess by a country mile, he cares about you as well, Janey. What you said to him was true, but it was also pretty harsh. And he's apologized for slamming the door, so quit being so mule-headed and go soak in the tub and do something about that hair."

Janelle shook her head. "I haven't got anything—"

"—to wear." Betsy finished the sentence and tossed a carrier bag at her. "Your birthday is next week, so don't go all stiff-necked on me."

The dress was a scant handful of bias cut jersey, the same aqua green as Janelle's eyes. "And don't say a word about it being too short," Betsy warned. "I'd kill for those legs of yours. When you've got it, flaunt it."

Janelle caressed the dress for a moment, thrilled by its seductive texture. She hadn't worn anything this sexy or pretty for what seemed half a lifetime. She met Betsy's eyes and saw affection and caring there, and without any more argument, she headed for the bathroom.

CHAPTER ELEVEN

"YOU LOOK RAVISHING." His voice sounded as stunned as he felt. If Richard had any doubts about his feelings, they were gone the instant he first saw Janelle that evening.

She was breathtaking. She had on something green and snug and short, that clung to her body like the wisps of a lascivious dream. She'd gathered her fiery hair up and back. Tendrils curled against the tender pale skin of her throat, living flame against creamy satin.

"Thank you, Richard. You're not half bad yourself." There was a teasing note in her husky voice, and relief spilled through him.

She'd forgiven him for storming out.

The evening lay before them, a rare gift of hours uninterrupted by the demands of the twins. It would be the first time they were entirely alone together, apart from that first fatal encounter.

He handed her into the newly washed and polished Corvette like the royalty she resembled.

The longing to touch her, to hold her in his arms, to make love to her, was nearly overwhelming, but he'd vowed to himself that he wouldn't make a single move tonight unless she invited it. He had to instill trust, and it was going to take time. Time, nerves of steel, and maybe a generous dose of saltpeter. *Steady, Webb. Don't blow this all over again.*

He slid behind the wheel, pushed a CD into the player, and the evening began.

IT WAS PAST one in the morning, and Janelle knew she should ask him to take her home, but the hot wind on her face and the sky filled with stars overhead kept her delaying.

She rested her head back against the fragrant leather and warbled along with the song.

Richard joined in, their voices blending with the music on the car stereo, and Janelle laughed at the sheer lunacy of driving through the sleeping city in this sleek luxurious car cocoon, singing along with the sixties hits.

Dinner had been spectacular. They'd sipped wine that probably cost more than her monthly rent, and afterward he'd taken her to a club where they danced to a smoky blues band, the angles of his body meshing perfectly with her curves.

And all the while they talked, easy, amusing conversation that seemed to flow as freely as the wine.

Each confided stories about their childhood. He spoke of his love for sailing, and Janelle found herself telling him how much she wanted to learn to fly someday. That surprised her, because she'd never confided that particular fantasy to anyone before.

When they'd both had enough of the club atmosphere, they got back in the car and Richard slipped another CD into the player, a collection of rockabilly hits and crooning love ballads, songs Janelle had listened to as a girl and half forgotten.

The music was more powerful than the wine had been, she mused. Or maybe it was the combination of the two. Whatever it was soaked into her pores, and she felt carefree and reckless as he drove aimlessly, through busy downtown streets and quiet burbs, along the waterfront, through the park.

All evening, she'd wondered when he was going to make a move on her. *Now,* she kept thinking. Now he'd park, slip an arm around her, try to kiss her, and with waning enthusiasm she rehearsed the refusal she'd prepared. She may be enjoying herself, but she wasn't about to end the evening in Richard's arms, she kept reminding herself.

It was far too risky, too dangerous. There was an animal magnetism about him that roused her every female hormone, and she had to be on guard against it.

"You want a coffee, Janelle? Dessert? Wine? There's a little place I know of—"

She shook her head. "Thanks, but no." She sighed with reluctance. "I really should be getting home now."

Betsy might be staying over, but Janelle knew from past experience that her friend was next to useless until ten in the morning. Janelle would be getting up with the twins, not Betsy.

"I hate the evening to end." All the same, he turned at the next intersection, heading back toward her house.

When the car glided to a stop in front of her darkened condo, Janelle's heartbeat accelerated.

Now. Now, he'd try to kiss her.

But instead he got out and opened her door for her, extending a hand and then holding hers as they walked to her door, releasing it as she dug in her handbag for her key.

"I had a wonderful time, Richard." Her stomach tightened and her breathing grew erratic.

Now, he'd—

But all he did was lean forward and press his lips against her forehead. "So, lovely lady, will you come out with me again?" His voice sounded strained.

She hesitated, but only for an instant. "Yes. I will."

He expelled a long, relieved breath, and they both laughed. "I'll call you in the morning, if that's okay? I'd love to drop by and see the twins, maybe go for a walk with the three of you?"

"Sure." She nodded, and he gave her a little salute and headed back for his car.

Dazed, Janelle opened the door and went inside. The house was silent. A night-light glowed in the hallway, and she tiptoed down to the twins' room and went in.

She stood still, breathing in the familiar sweet scent of her sleeping babies, trying to figure out what it was she was feeling about their father's exemplary behavior. It couldn't possibly be disappointment, could it?

WATCHING HIM roughhouse with the twins the following afternoon, Janelle remembered the confused mix of feelings that had kept her tossing and turning half the night.

They'd just come back from a long walk, and the boys were full of fresh air and mischief. Richard was down on all fours on the floor, pretending to be a horse, and they were clambering on and off his back.

It was impossible not to admire the way he looked, his sandy hair tousled and bleached by the sun, his blue eyes shining with pleasure as he pretended to rear and buck, one big hand holding Maxwell steady.

"Ollie, get down," Janelle ordered. Oliver was climbing on the sofa, obviously intending to leap from it onto Richard's back.

She was across the room from him, and when she saw what was about to happen, she moved as fast as she could to intercept him.

Ollie saw her coming, squealed and climbed still faster up on the sofa's high back.

"Ollie—" Janelle saw him teeter. She leaped to catch him, but she was an instant too late. He fell sideways and hard, striking his forehead on the sharp corner of the fireplace.

"Ollie, oh, my God—" Janelle gathered him, limp and silent, into her arms, and absolute terror overcame her. The baby's forehead was split open, the gash so wide and deep that white bone showed beneath the pooling blood.

"Oh, Ollie— Richard, he's not crying—"

Ollie's blue eyes, dazed and empty, slowly focused on her face, and finally he began to cry, but it wasn't the hurt cry Janelle was accustomed to. This was weak, wavering, and it scared her so much she could hardly breathe. Her insides were shaking, and for an instant she thought she was about to faint.

CHAPTER TWELVE

IT WAS RICHARD who found the first-aid kit in the bathroom. He placed a sterile dressing over the cut. He swept Maxwell into his arms and snatched a blanket from the chair, wrapping it around Ollie.

"Out to the van, quick," he ordered. "He needs to go to the hospital and driving him will be faster than calling 911."

"We need the diaper bag." Janelle's voice trembled.

"I'll get it. Just go on out, it's going to be okay."

Within moments, they were on their way. The drive was tense. Janelle cradled Ollie and did her best to soothe Maxwell, who understood that something was very wrong and wailed at the top of his lungs from his car seat.

Ollie cried only intermittently, which was terrifying for Janelle. She wished with all her being that he'd roar and thrash around the way he usually did when he was hurt.

"It's gonna be fine," Richard kept assuring her, but Janelle could tell by the tautness of the muscles in his neck and jaw, the harsh constriction in his voice, that he was as scared as she.

At the hospital's emergency department, Richard again took charge, dealing with the seemingly endless paperwork while Janelle was conducted to a curtained cubicle.

"Hi. I'm Dr. Norman." The young woman had a sympathetic smile and weary eyes. She had Janelle lay Ollie on the examining table, and Janelle felt sick all over again when the baby didn't scream or protest at all. He lay on his back, his limbs flaccid. His eyes were open, but he still looked dazed.

Dr. Norman talked to Ollie in a gentle, reassuring fashion as she conducted a thorough examination.

Maxwell watched from the safety of Richard's arms, sucking his thumb. Janelle's heart was thundering, and she could taste bile in her throat. Her entire body was trembling.

"I suspect all he has is a mild concussion," the doctor concluded. "We're going to take X rays and do a CAT scan just to make certain there's no skull fracture. Unless there's a fracture, I won't admit him, but I do want you to watch him closely for the rest of the night and for the next twenty-four hours. I'd like you to wake him up every hour during the night. If he starts to vomit, if the pupils of his eyes appear unequal, or if he seems listless and confused, bring him back in immediately. In the meantime, we'll get these tests underway.''

For the next two hours, they trailed from one area to another and then spent what felt like forever waiting for the various tests to be performed.

Richard took Maxwell on long ambling walks down the corridors, and dealt with several diaper changes. He found a cafeteria and brought Janelle hot chocolate and refilled Maxwell's bottles with milk.

To Janelle's intense relief, Ollie soon got over his listlessness, and by the time the tests were over, he was alternately howling and struggling to be set free.

With a smile, Dr. Norman assured them there was no fracture. She stitched and dressed the wound on Ollie's head, a procedure that had Janelle feeling light-headed all over again.

Richard noticed, handed Maxwell to her, and

gently restrained Ollie while the stitches were being done.

Reminding them again to watch Ollie closely, the doctor sent them home.

With Richard's help, Janelle bathed the twins. Ollie seemed his usual cheerful, busy self, and he enlisted Maxwell's help in trying to remove the bandage the doctor had applied.

Richard distracted them both with a toy that squirted water.

Janelle managed to help dry them off, but it was Richard who got them into diapers and pajamas.

He was the one who read them *Goodnight Moon.*

Janelle rubbed Ollie's back, Richard rubbed Maxwell's, and the boys fell asleep right away, hands clasped as usual through the bars of the cribs.

"You're exhausted. I'll order us in a Chinese dinner, and then you go and sleep," Richard suggested when they were back in the kitchen. "I'll check on him every hour, don't worry."

Janelle started to thank him, and then all of a sudden she was sobbing and couldn't stop. Blindly, she reached for him, and when his arms closed around her, she collapsed against him. The panic she'd been holding back for hours turned to hurtful sobs that tore from her throat, and for long, harsh moments she couldn't speak. She could barely stand up.

"Easy, honey. It's okay, he's fine." He put a hand on her head and pressed her cheek against his neck. With the other hand, he stroked her back, big, slow, comforting circles, just the way he stroked the twins.

"I—was—so—*scared.*" Her nose was running.

"So was I." He reached in his pants pocket and drew out a tissue, using it to mop at her face. "I was as terrified as I've ever been in my life. I've never felt that helpless before." There was misery in his voice. "I'm so bloody sorry, Janelle. It was my fault, I should've been watching him closer."

She gave him an astonished look, and then took the tissue and blew her nose. "That's totally ridiculous. One thing I've learned with kids, you can't blame yourself for everything that happens with them. They're rowdy little boys, and they're bound to get banged up every now and then. It wasn't anyone's fault."

She drew a shuddering breath. "I don't know what I'd have done without you, Richard. I sort of went to pieces there, I couldn't think what to do. And at the hospital, I could never have managed Max as well as Ollie." She wrapped her arms around him to give him a grateful hug. "Thank you, more than I can say."

For the first second, a hug was all it was. And then his arms came around her, and the way his body reacted to her nearness set off explosives in her. The tape in her head that always cautioned her against him suddenly broke, and with a deep sigh she gave herself up to him and the feelings singing inside of her. She closed her eyes and tipped her head up for his kiss.

The urgency of his lips and mouth fanned the desire rushing through her like a flash flood. His tongue probed and hers answered in a feverish, wordless message.

She could feel him trembling. Her breath was coming in gasps as wave after wave of frantic need rolled over her. She could feel his heart, thudding against her rib cage. The pulses in her wrists and throat throbbed in response.

"Love me," she begged in an urgent whisper. "Please, Richard, make love to me."

"I want to, more than anything." His voice was ragged. "Are you sure?"

The only thing she was sure of at this moment

was that she'd die if he didn't. She drew him
toward her, moved against him, and felt the last
shred of caution melt away in the heat that ra-
diated from him to her and back again.

Greed for each other overwhelmed them, and
although they moved toward the sofa, they didn't
make it. Shedding clothes as fast as they could
tear them off, they tumbled to the floor.

He kissed her mouth, her neck, found the front
fastener of her bra and released it. His mouth on
her nipples brought her hips surging upward,
searching for him.

"Hurry," she urged, shivering with the fire
that threatened to consume her. "Please, Richard,
hurry."

He was the one who remembered the condom.

For just a fleeting instant she felt a stab of
anger, knowing he had one with him all the time,
just in case—but the emotion was gone the instant he thrust into her.

All thought was gone, replaced by feeling so
intense she was certain her body would tear apart
and fly away when the final moment came.

CHAPTER THIRTEEN

WHEN HE COULD breathe and think again, Richard knew with absolute certainty he'd never made love to Janelle before, but he also knew that was impossible; he was the father of the twins sleeping in the upstairs bedroom.

Shaken to the core and more confused than he'd ever been, he propped himself on an elbow and looked at every inch of her, searching for clues.

Her eyes were closed. Her long, slender body was close to perfect, breasts full and high, creamy skin stretched without a single blemish across a taut, concave belly. There were no stretch marks, no scars, no indications whatsoever that she'd ever been pregnant, much less with twins. Wouldn't it show?

"Janelle?" Her eyes opened, slow and languorous.

He longed to lean over and kiss her, drown his doubts in the taste of her mouth, the lure of her body. But a demon was driving him now, and he had to know.

"Janelle, I know we've never been together like this before. This is the first time I've ever made love to you. So what's really going on here?"

Her green eyes widened. She was still for a moment and then she scrambled away, propping her back against the sofa and hunching her knees up, grabbing the blanket he'd used to wrap Ollie in and winding it around herself like a protective cocoon. Her head was bent, her hair spilling forward so he couldn't see her face.

"Janelle?" The tone of his voice reflected the confusion he felt. "Honey, please talk to me here, I honest to God don't know what's going on."

She lifted her head, and he saw that tears were coursing down her cheeks all over again. She swallowed and her voice was a whisper he had to strain to hear.

"It was Tracy. It was my sister Tracy you had sex with that night."

"Tracy? Who the hell is Tracy? You never mentioned you had a sister." Incomprehension was fast becoming fierce anger. Her *sister*.

They'd played some elaborate trick on him. But why?

"So just where the hell is this sister of yours?"

"Dead. She's dead."

He felt frozen with shock as she looked at him, green eyes cloudy with tears and misery. "She had the twins by cesarian section, and a week later she died from a blood clot that traveled to her brain."

"Oh, God." Horror and a painful twist of sadness ripped through him for the woman he'd really never known, the woman who'd borne his sons. He had to know more, all of it. "Tell me about her, please, Janelle. Tell me all of it."

She drew a shuddering breath and when she spoke her voice was a monotone. "She was three years younger than I was. She wasn't like me, wanting to do well in school, wanting a career. Tracy was always like some wild bird trapped in a cage. She drank, and she went from man to man, never settling on any one. I think she was scared of caring for anyone, in case they didn't care back. She had a tender heart, although she hid it well. When she found out she was pregnant, there was never any question of abortion.

She wanted her babies, wanted to try to make a new life for herself and them.''

Richard swallowed hard against the bitterness of bile. ''Did she—did she try to get in touch with me when she knew about the twins?'' He was trying to assimilate what Janelle was telling him now with what she'd told him before.

Janelle nodded. ''I told you how it happened.'' Tears were rolling down her cheeks and she absentmindedly swiped them away with the palm of her hand.

''Over and over, she tried at first. I know, because she was living with me. She told me every detail of the night she'd spent with you so many times I knew it off by heart.'' Her voice hardened. ''It hurt me, it made me furious, hearing her call your office over and over again. Betsy wanted to hit you with a paternity suit, but Tracy wouldn't hear of it. She was still so naive, in spite of her lifestyle.'' A bitter facsimile of a smile came and went.

''I think she wanted you to be glad about the babies, just as she was. I was the one who told her to forget about you, that you weren't worthy of having children. I promised if she did we'd raise the twins together, that I'd help her financially.''

Richard felt as if he were being pummeled. He'd thought he couldn't feel any worse about his actions, but he found there was a whole new depth of shame he hadn't dreamed existed.

"So you adopted them." Mixed with the desolation was a kind of relief, a renewed faith in his own reactions.

He'd known all along he hadn't made love to Janelle that night.

"I buried Tracy, and Betsy dealt with the adoption for me," she said with a hitch in her voice that broke his heart. "I was there when they were born, and I loved the babies with all my heart and soul. They were all I had left of my sister, and I wanted it absolutely legal, so there'd be no way *anyone* could take them from me."

"Anyone being me." It wasn't a question.

Her glance was tortured. "I thought I hated you, Richard." She gave a painful attempt at a laugh. "My life changed so drastically, and it was all because of you. The guy I'd been seeing for two years, the one I thought I was in love with, dumped me when he found out I was adopting the twins. I couldn't take the promotion I was in line for because it would mean traveling. Financially it was devastating, physically it was exhausting. They had colic for three full months. Emotionally I was grieving for my little sister, but there wasn't even time for that. And then— that day on the wharf, when I saw you without a care in the world, something snapped inside of me.''

He tried for a smile that didn't work. ''I don't blame you.'' He felt stunned and stupid, filled with remorse. But in the midst of it, there was a solid core of intense emotion that he needed to tell her about.

''Janelle, I'm sorry, more so than I can ever say. Apologies are useless considering all that you've gone through because of me. I wish I could go back and redo everything, but like my grandfather once said, no one can change the past.'' He reached out a tentative hand to touch her, but she jerked away and his heart sank. ''The thing is, Janelle, we've got a future, you and I and the twins. I care about them, but I also care about you. Making love to you just now—Janelle, it's never been that way for me before.''

''Don't.'' It was a wail, and she covered her ears with her hands. ''Don't say any more. It's over, Richard.'' She was shaking her head from side to side, and he wanted to grab her, kiss her, force her to stop reacting and see reason.

But after a moment she quieted, and her face was closed, her expression hard. "What happened between us just now was a huge mistake, *my* mistake. As to what went on before that, I can't just forget and forgive." Her voice rose. "Don't you see? I feel I'm betraying my sister by being with you. I feel I *have* already betrayed her, in the very worst way." She wasn't crying now. Her eyes were burning into him.

"Go away, Richard. I'll agree to whatever visitation rights you want, but I won't see you again. Betsy will do the legal stuff, talk to her about it, but right now, go, please. *Just leave me alone.*"

An edge of hysteria crept into her voice. She had shadows under her eyes, and her face was pale with fatigue, drawn so that the lovely bones stood out in prominent relief.

He choked back the anger he felt at the unfairness of it all. This was no time to argue with her; he could see that she was exhausted. So without another word he got up and put his clothes on.

He went up and checked Ollie. The baby woke readily when Richard stroked his head and pressed a kiss on his cheek. Ollie sat up for a moment and gave his father an insulted stare before he plopped down, plugged his thumb in his mouth, and went back to sleep.

"Oliver woke up right away, he seems okay," he told Janelle when he came down. "I'm going now, but I won't easily accept not seeing you again. We'll talk about it in the morning."

"*Don't.*"

The single, fierce word was like a projectile, and it hurt. On his way home, Richard stopped at a pay phone and dialed Betsy. When she answered, he explained quickly and concisely what had happened to Oliver. He told her he knew about Tracy, adding, "Janelle's exhausted and upset, she won't let me stay and help her tonight. Do you think—"

"Absolutely. I'm on my way."

It was all he could think of to do. The frustration and helplessness he felt were overwhelming, and there was a burning need to be with her and his sons.

But he assured himself for the rest of the sleepless night that now that the worst was over, now that he knew the truth, Janelle would admit that it was senseless for them to be apart. She'd see that, she was an intelligent woman. Their lovemaking had been as profound for her as it had for him, he was convinced of that.

At some point he admitted he'd fallen in love with her, and the realization hit him like a bolt of lightning. He'd been feeling it all along, he just hadn't known what the hell it was.

He'd never understood being in love, but now that he did, he understood as well all that went with it. He wanted to marry Janelle. He *would* marry Janelle, and they'd raise the twins together. More than anything in his entire life, he wanted her. Being together was so right, she couldn't possibly not realize and accept it.

Could she?

CHAPTER FOURTEEN

SHE REFUSED to answer his phone calls, so he drove to Woods Hole and asked to see her.

She had the security guard order him off the premises. He tried three times, and three times he was told to leave.

He went to the condo when he knew she'd be home and leaned on the doorbell. He could hear one of the twins crying, but she didn't answer. Rage flared. He wanted to drive his fist through the door, break it down, kidnap her and his sons. He had to get her to listen to him.

"Janelle, open this damned door." He could hear other doors opening in the complex, glimpse curious faces staring at him.

"I'm calling the police, Richard." Her voice was like ice.

Sick at heart, he got in the car and drove home, and that evening, Betsy phoned him.

"Janelle doesn't want to see you, Richard. If

you keep on bothering her, she's instructed me to get a restraining order.''

It took every ounce of control to keep from revealing how desperately miserable he felt. ''That won't be necessary, Betsy. The last thing I want is to cause Janelle any more trouble. I'll leave her alone from now on—on one condition.''

''What's that?''

''I know it's her birthday this week. The van is hers—it's registered in her name. She accepts it and I back off. Those are my conditions and they're not negotiable.''

Betsy was silent for a moment. Then she gave a long sigh and said, ''I'll do my best. God knows she needs it in the worst way. She's said that she'll agree to whatever visitation rights you want with the boys. Within reason, of course.''

He couldn't bear to think about that, not now.

''I'll let you know. I've set up a trust fund for the boys, all the paperwork will be on your desk tomorrow afternoon.''

''This is the most ridiculous case I've ever had, and I've told her so,'' Betsy snapped. ''I'm her solicitor, but between you and me, I don't agree with one single damned thing she's doing.'' Betsy slammed the phone down.

SOMEHOW THE WEEK PASSED. Friday rolled around, and Peter whistled as he looked Richard up and down. "I know about casual Fridays, but you've gone way overboard, pal. You must be going for the whiskery-mean-hombre look."

Richard had caught a glimpse of himself in the rest room mirror. His eyes were bloodshot because he hadn't been sleeping well, and shaving was the farthest thing from his mind. For the first time since he was twelve, he'd started pulling on the same clothes he'd worn the day before.

"Peter, I'm gonna take a week or so off as soon as these orders are processed. I'm going to Dover, do some fishing. Call me there if you need me."

Richard had told Peter the whole miserable story. Peter had listened, although it was obvious his attention wasn't fully on Richard's problems.

"No luck with the lady yet, huh?"

"Nope." It hurt like hell to admit it. "I've pretty much decided not to see the twins again. It's just too painful." He cleared his throat against the thickness there. "She'll meet somebody else, she's so damned beautiful, and then I'd have to hurt him if I saw them together." His pathetic attempt at levity fell flat. "I just couldn't stand it, Pete. I *can't* stand it. So it's better for all of us if I just butt out."

Peter squinted at him through his smudged glasses. "I think you're making a big mistake. Don't give up, Richard. No matter what, don't give up." Leona had finally agreed to give Peter another chance, and the reuniting of his family was all he could think about.

Richard didn't blame him. For the first time, he absolutely understood how miserable his friend had been feeling all these months.

"I never thought I'd say this, but I want to talk this whole thing over with Gramps," Richard said. "Maybe the old man'll have some useful suggestions. For the first time in my life, I'd welcome his advice."

"I've never heard you say that before, but if it feels right, do it. Why don't you take the rest of the day off? Don't worry about stuff here, I'll see to it."

Richard took him at his word. He was on his way out the office door when a tall, muscular man stepped in front of him.

"Are you Richard Webb?"

"I am." Richard was impatient to get going. "I'm in a hurry just now, my partner, Peter, will be able to help you with whatever—"

The man shook his head. "It's you I need to speak to, Mr. Webb. My name is Mark Solomon. I'm a private detective." He held out a manila envelope. "My client has asked me to hand deliver this directly to you."

Richard's first thought was that it had something to do with Janelle and the twins. He snatched it from the man's hand and studied the return address.

Warren Cooper, it read. *Twin Oaks, Cooper's Corner, Massachusetts.*

It had nothing to do with Janelle. Richard lost interest. "I don't know this person." He tried to hand the envelope back to the detective. "You've got the wrong guy."

The man shook his head and stepped back. "I recognize you from the photo I was given. You're the right man." He smiled and gave Richard a small salute. "Goodbye. Good luck to you."

He stepped out the door and was gone.

Photo? The guy had a *photo* of him? Whatever this was, Richard decided, it had to be bad, because that was the direction his life was heading. Well, it could damn well wait.

He loped out to the car and tossed the envelope carelessly on the seat. He drove home and picked up Freddy, then started for Dover. Just for half an hour, he wasn't going to think about Janelle or the twins or his own misery, he vowed. He was going to enjoy the drive.

He cranked the stereo up high, shoved in the Springsteen CD, and managed to collect two speeding tickets on the forty-mile drive. And all his good intentions blew away on the breeze, because the tickets reminded him of Janelle.

They were the first he'd gotten since he met her; he'd been far too conscious of the twins on-board to do anything rash like speed. Misery settled back down on him like a shroud.

As he neared Oak Meadows, his spirits sank lower and lower. The thought of seeing his grandfather, of explaining this whole new scenario, exhausted him, and he changed his mind about going to Oak Meadows.

He'd spend today alone at the bungalow, he decided. Maybe he'd do some fishing, like he told Peter. There'd be plenty of time tomorrow to speak to Lawrence Webb. He stopped at a market to pick up some supplies, and then headed for his house.

But for the first time, his comfortable home seemed empty rather than restful. He was unloading groceries when he spied the brown envelope on the car seat. He took it inside, and when he had things stowed away in cupboards and fridge, he fed Freddy, opened a beer and turned on the television. Without much interest, he tore the envelope open.

Yellowed news clippings tumbled out, and Richard frowned at them, at a loss to explain why anyone would have saved the old accounts of his graduation from both high school and college. There were several clippings from business magazines that had noted the increasing success of Childsplay over the past couple years.

There were other, more personal mementos. There was a photo of him beside his boat, sunburned and grinning, after he'd won his first skipper's trophy. There was even a picture he'd forgotten about, taken when he was ten and had just won the junior riding trophy at the local gymkhana.

Stunned, Richard studied the assortment. It documented portions of his life, important events, like key pieces in a jigsaw puzzle. Who'd done this? How had they managed to get such material? And why had they wanted it?

He reached into the envelope again and withdrew a letter on two pieces of watermarked stationery. He unfolded it and read, *My dear grandson, Richard.*

Puzzled, Richard flipped to the second page, the end of the letter. It said, *With all my love, your grandfather, Warren Cooper.*

There was some huge mistake here, he assured himself. He'd never heard of any Warren Cooper. Why would a stranger sign a letter that way? But his heart was banging against his rib cage and a cold shudder ran down his spine as he went back to the beginning and began to read.

CHAPTER FIFTEEN

My DEAR grandson Richard,

By the time you receive this letter, Richard, I'll have passed on. I've had a long life. In many ways it's been lonely, and I'm not sorry to go. My only regret is never having had the chance to know you and your sisters.

Richard shook his head, more confused and puzzled than ever. He sank back in the worn cushions, beer and television forgotten as he deciphered the spidery handwriting.

Your grandmother, Helen Aster, grew up next door to me. I fell in love with her at ten, and I've loved her steadfastly all my life. I should have courted her when the time came, but I had a crooked leg, the result of an accident when I was a teen, and the physical deformity and a shy nature kept me from telling Helen how I felt. When she married Lawrence Webb, I thought my heart would break. He was a serviceman. I was denied

*even the chance to fight for my country because
of my leg.*

*Helen came home to Cooper's Corner when
Lawrence was shipped overseas, and word came
that he had been killed in battle. In her grief, she
turned to me. It was wrong of me, to take advantage when she was most vulnerable, but as a
man, Richard, perhaps you can understand the
overpowering desire I felt for her. I adored her,
I wanted to marry her, and she promised to think
about it. She needed time. For six short weeks,
we were lovers, and then we learned that
Lawrence was alive. It was the most agonizing
moment of my life, hearing her say she must return to her husband. She begged me not ever to
reveal what had been between us, and of course
I promised. I would have died for Helen, had she
asked it of me.*

God, he knew that feeling. It was the way he
felt about Janelle and his sons. He'd die protect-
ing them. Richard's hands were trembling. He'd
already guessed what this old man was going to
say, but still the words mesmerized him as he
read on.

*The twins she carried, your mother Donna and
her sister Diana, were born seven months later,
and I knew they were mine. Twins run in the*

Cooper family. I marked their birth the only way I could, with twin oaks planted on either side of my driveway. My heart broke when Diana died in infancy, and yet again when your mother died in the fire. Lawrence Webb took you and your sisters. I knew it was the right thing, but it was hard not to claim the three of you as my beloved grandchildren. I'd promised Helen, though, and I kept that promise. But now she's gone, and before I die I must tell you the truth. Your mother was my daughter. You are my beloved grandson. Know that not a day has passed since your birth but what I thought of you and wished you well. My legacy to you is the blood that flows in your veins and the love I carry with me to the grave and beyond. The twin oaks I planted at their birth are tall and strong. They stand steadfast through every storm. May you do the same, dear Richard.

There was no one to witness the tears that trickled down his cheeks as he read and then re-read the letter and pondered the message that lay beneath the words.

He felt frustration and a degree of anger at Warren Cooper, he realized, mixed with the poignant sadness. What was so obvious was that Warren could have chosen differently. He could have come forward, shared in some way in his offspring's lives.

Sure, he'd promised Gram he never would, but the loss had been not his alone; three grandchildren could have had another adult in their lives, benefited from his advice, his love. Instead, Warren had lived and died a lonely man.

On the other hand, Lawrence Webb had raised not only Warren's daughter, but also his grandchildren, proving himself to be their parent not only by his words, but by his actions. No matter how stern, how strict he'd been, he was like a rock to which they were all anchored. He'd been there for them all their lives. He was there now, and would be as long as he lived.

As Janelle was for her nephews. The analogy was clear in Richard's mind. Whether she'd given birth to them or not, she was and would always be their parent, their mother.

As he was their father. It seemed to Richard that suddenly two choices were clear to him. He could follow in Warren's footsteps, surreptitiously watching his sons from afar, longing for the love that he hadn't been bold enough to claim, living a small and lonely life, dying with regrets.

Or—

He leaped up and found paper and a pen. Warren's words were powerful, because they came from the depths of his heart.

When Richard finished the letter to Janelle, he knew that his words, too, conveyed truth, passion and promise. He'd poured out his heart, telling her again how sorry he was for the way he'd treated Tracy. But, he wrote, two wrongs didn't make a right. He loved Janelle with all his heart and soul, and he loved their babies. He wanted them all to be a family. He would ask her to marry him, he declared with bold and certain strokes of the pen.

He would go on asking until he no longer had breath in his body, if that's what it took. The only way she could get rid of him was to tell him honestly that she didn't love him and never would.

When he was done, he went into the bathroom and showered and shaved. He found clean clothes and put them on. He took Freddy for a walk, and then he locked the door of the bungalow, loaded the dog back in the car, and drove back to Boston. It was just past noon.

There was no desperate haste in him now, so he didn't get a single ticket. He was calm and very clear in his purpose, and he didn't for an instant allow himself to consider failure.

He hired a courier to hand deliver the letter to Janelle, and then he methodically visited the finest jewelry stores in the city, until he found the engagement ring that seemed most like her.

It was a solitaire, square cut, strong and dramatic, utterly beautiful in its simplicity. Aquagreen fire flashed in its depths, the same color and intensity as her eyes.

It was late afternoon by the time he pocketed the small black velvet box and drove to her house.

Betsy's car was parked in front. There was no sign of the new van. He got out and walked to the door.

"Richard." Betsy stood there, drying her hands on a towel. She had tomato soup on the front of her blouse, and from somewhere behind her he could hear the twins, gabbling to one another. "I'm feeding them dinner," she said in answer to his unspoken question. "What are you doing here, Richard?"

"Waiting for Janelle." It seemed to make perfect sense. He'd wait the rest of his life if he had to.

"She's gone on a dive, I'm not sure how long

she'll be. Gwen had to leave early, so I'm filling in." Betsy looked sympathetic. "Janelle told me about the letter you wrote her. She said it made her cry."

He'd thought he was pretty calm, but the way his heart lurched told him otherwise. "Do you think that's a good sign? That she cried?"

"Who knows with Janey? She's been doing a lot of crying lately."

They both flinched as something breakable crashed to the floor inside the house. "Look, Richard, I've gotta go before they wreck the joint. I can't ask you in, since the last I heard you weren't welcome here, but when the boys finish eating I know they'll want to come out and play in the wading pool, and it would be nice if you could watch them while I clean up the kitchen. Then I think I need to go to the drugstore, if you could mind them for me?"

"Thanks, Betsy."

Several moments later, his sons came barreling out the door and straight into his arms. Their hands were sticky, their faces smeared with tomato soup. Their exuberant joy at seeing him and the way they mangled his name brought a choking fullness to Richard's chest.

Usually he brought them some little treat, but

this time he'd been too preoccupied to remember. To make up for it, he fished the ring box out of his pocket and snapped it open. The solitaire caught the last rays of the sun and reflected it in a breathtaking shower of rainbows. The twins blue eyes widened, and four pudgy hands reached for the ring.

He showed Ollie how to snap the velvet box open and shut, and he let Maxwell slide the glinting diamond onto his fat thumb.

"I'm gonna marry your mommy, fellas," Richard confided. "You'll have to practice saying *daddy*. Say *daddy*."

"Dada." They grinned at him.

He was as nervous as he'd ever been, and it was comforting to talk to his sons, even though he knew they couldn't possibly understand.

CHAPTER SIXTEEN

JANELLE STOWED her diving gear in the back of
the van and climbed wearily behind the wheel.
Being under the water was always meditative for
her, and today was no exception.

No matter how many times she went down,
that eerie green underwater world remained a
place of silence and mystery, a world with which
she was familiar and where she was totally alone.

Today she'd felt not only alone, but lonely
down there, the soul deep, utterly bereft loneli-
ness she'd been feeling ever since she'd sent
Richard away.

She tried to concentrate on the task at hand,
but her mind kept straying to him, to the letter
she'd received just before she left to go on the
dive.

He'd written that the only way she'd ever get
rid of him would be to tell him she didn't love
him and never could, and it was the one thing

she couldn't force herself to say, because it would be the biggest lie she'd ever told.

Diving today into that mysterious underwater world had seemed a metaphor for digging into her own subconscious, to the place where truth was all that existed. She could go on letting the past determine the future. She could allow old pain to ruin not only her own life, but Max and Ollie's lives as well.

Would Tracy want her to do that?

Her sister had been a creature of the moment. Even when the twins were born, Janelle recalled, she hadn't blamed Richard for the pain she endured. Instead she'd rejoiced in her beautiful, healthy babies.

Tracy's voice seemed to echo in her head as Janelle kicked for the surface. *Do whatever will make all of you happy. In the end, love is all that matters.*

She'd call him the moment she got home.

Her heart slammed against her chest when she saw the Corvette. There was no sign of Betsy's car.

He was playing with the twins on the front lawn. Janelle pulled the van to a standstill, blew out the breath she was holding, and with it let go of the past.

"Richard." His name was sweet on her lips. She saw the emotions that swirled in the blueness of his eyes, the hope and also the fear as she came through the gate—and kept walking straight into his arms.

She felt the tension drain from him when she lifted her head for his kiss. Another sort of tension gripped them both as their lips met and the taste of him sent heat spiraling through her.

And then he drew back, dropped to one knee on the grass, and looked up at her with his hopes for their future blazing in the blueness of his eyes.

"I love you. Will you marry me, Janelle?"

She was aware of the twins clamoring for her attention, and she thought how right it was that they were here at this moment.

"Yes, I will. I love you too." Ollie was trying to show her something, pulling at her shorts. "We'll all three marry you."

Richard was fumbling in his pocket, and she glanced down at Ollie. He was holding a black velvet ring box. Richard took it from him, but when he snapped it open it was empty.

"Max." Richard's shout was an instant too late.

Janelle saw the diamond ring Maxwell held refract the last of the sunlight. She watched him chortle and pop it in his mouth just as Richard lunged for him.

It was the purest coincidence that Dr. Norman was on duty again when they arrived in Emergency. She assured them that there was nothing to do but wait and watch. The ring would eventually reappear. All that was needed was patience, and faith.

Mixed with love, it was a powerful prescription.

Dear Reader,

Please accept my invitation to join in the weddings of some very special couples here in Twin Oaks. It was great fun to keep Diana and Mark together long enough for them to realize they had more in common than one passionate night.

I admit I'm in the mood for a wedding. I have four grown children of marriageable age whom I lie to all the time when I say, "Of course I'm not ready to be a grandmother yet."

I am ready for an excuse to throw a party, buy a fancy dress and go on a diet. I want to send invitations, wrap presents with big silver and white bows and weep gently into a lace-edged handkerchief while a grown child says, "I do."

Speaking of tears, let me confess one more thing: I've begun collecting silk wedding handkerchiefs. They are fragile squares of ivory, delicately monogrammed and oh, so lovely. I like to think the brides who carried them were deliriously happy. I'm sure their mothers were!

Kristine Rolofson

A NIGHT TO REMEMBER

Kristine Rolofson

CHAPTER ONE

MARK SOLOMON SHARED the Tuesday afternoon ferry to Nantucket with packs of noisy tourists, bored commuters content to read newspapers in the snack area and a host of delivery trucks. He'd never been to the island before, though the place intrigued him. Not because of the many millionaires who called it home in the summers, or the picturesque New England coastal architecture, but because a distant ancestor had once captained a whaling ship from the island's famous port.

He wondered how that particular ancestor felt coming home to his family, especially on a warm August afternoon like this one when the wind whipped across the bow of the ferry and the island appeared in the distance. Would his wife and children have been standing on the dock? Would he have greeted an infant for the first time, learned news that loved ones had died, that friends had moved on?

Mark took a long drink of soda, then tossed

the can into the garbage. He was ready to go home himself, only home was hours away, on another island. The job was almost done. He would hand over the last letter from the late Warren Cooper, an old man who wanted nothing else before his death but to communicate with the three grandchildren he'd never met.

Mark supposed that was one way to find everlasting peace, but he preferred conversation to the written word. Since the last two envelopes he'd delivered to the Webb siblings appeared to have come as a surprise to the recipients, Mark had reason to believe that this delivery would follow suit.

This Diana Webb was in for a surprise. And Mark Solomon, a private investigator ready for some time off, was about to give it to her. He hoped she'd take the news okay, but that part wasn't his problem or part of his job. If he was younger or not quite so burned out, he might have given more thought to what the woman would look like. Her sister had been pretty damn attractive, in that casual way some women carried off so well, as if they never looked in the mirror.

But Mark had decided he'd head home first thing in the morning, show up at his nephew's birthday party and meet his sister's neighbor, a divorcée with two young boys and, according to Jess, an easygoing personality and a pretty face.

Mark went over to the railing and watched the island loom larger and larger as they headed toward the harbor. Maybe he was ready to settle down, eat some meat loaf and go to Little League games. Maybe it was time to have an uncomplicated life.

And to finally stop searching for the perfect woman.

EVEN WITH ONE arm in a cast, Diana managed to assemble a blender full of strawberries, rum and a frozen can of margarita mix, diluted with water. She couldn't paint, she could no longer fix the shingles on the ancient roof of her ancient cottage, but she could still sit in the middle of her tiny patio and sip something frozen, fruity and filled with rum while she felt sorry for herself.

She turned the dial of the blender to high and pushed the ON button.

Maybe later she would walk down to the Rose and Crown for dinner—which would be finger food, of course, since she wasn't too coordinated with her left hand yet. Diana thought of fried shrimp and French fries dipped in tartar sauce and, later, she might stand in line with the tourists and stop to buy a creamy cube of peanut butter fudge. She would eventually become a chubby recluse, Diana decided as she poured herself a strawberry margarita, but there were worse lifestyles. She put the blender pitcher in the refrigerator, grabbed her sunglasses and her drink, and padded barefoot through French doors to her brick patio.

Sometimes she would sit quietly and, separated by a chest-high hedge of boxwood, listen to the tourists from the bed-and-breakfast next door chatter about the island, how quaint the houses were or how crowded the sidewalks, how beautiful the gardens.

This afternoon as she stretched out on the chaise longue and rested her aching wrist on a pillow, she never expected to hear her name.

"—Diana Webb," a low male voice said, as its owner must have stepped onto the adjoining patio. "Which house is hers?"

Someone, Silas perhaps, must have pointed to her gray-shingled home as he said something too low for Diana to hear. She should have stood, peered over the hedge and identified herself, but she was too comfortable. Too lazy and much too content being surrounded by roses to talk to someone who probably wanted to buy one of her paintings. Sometimes the gallery told its customers to contact her if they wanted to view all of her work, not just the ones Capizzo's Gallery displayed.

She took a large swallow of strawberry ice and closed her eyes behind her sunglasses. *Go away,* she thought, willing the man to leave her alone. He could knock on her door and there would be no answer, he could leave a message on her answering machine if she had remembered to turn it on or he could—

"Miss Webb?"

Or—obviously—he could walk over to the hedge and interrupt her attempt to self-medicate with rum. Diana didn't open her eyes. She lay very still and hoped the man would assume she was sleeping.

"I'm going to tuck my business card here in the hedge." There was a slightly amused tone in his voice, as if he knew she wasn't napping. She pictured him middle-aged, wearing an expensive polo shirt that would be white or the Nantucket shade of faded red that mirrored the clothing of the summer visitors. He would most likely be short and paunchy, confident and extremely rich.

"Please contact me at your earliest convenience. I'm staying here at the bed-and-breakfast next door.''

Well, good for him. Diana didn't want to speak to him. But what she wished for was the ache in her wrist to ease and wondered if she could hold a spoon in her left hand in order to eat a bowl of clam chowder. She also wanted another sip of her drink, which would mean risking the intruder realizing that she was available for conversation.

She didn't move until she heard murmured conversation and a door shut, and then Diana opened her eyes and reached for her drink. She sipped, then turned toward the hedge. Sure enough, a white card sat in the hedge as if it were a card in the middle of a flower arrangement.

Diana chose to ignore it, as she did most things she didn't want to deal with. In the past few years she'd managed to ignore quite a few things— such as telephones, men and, most of all, memories.

The embarrassing ones especially.

IT WAS ALMOST DARK when Mark knocked on the blue-painted door. He'd seen Diana Webb's lights come on in the front room of the cottage a few minutes ago. He hadn't minded waiting for the woman to return home, since he'd already planned on spending the night on the island. This business needed to be concluded, though, as soon as possible. He'd been paid generously for this simple assignment and he owed the dead man a job well done.

When the door opened, Mark was confronted by the tall, slim dark-haired woman he'd thought he'd never see again. She wore a sleeveless blouse a shade of bluish-green that matched her eyes and khaki shorts. He tried not to look at her legs, but the glimpse he took showed they were tanned and shapely, the same legs that had wrapped around his naked body and pulled him deeper inside her a million years ago.

"Yes?" was all she said, but there was a brief flicker of recognition in those green eyes that made Mark certain he wasn't wrong. It *was* her.

"I'm looking for Diana Webb," he managed to say.

"May I ask why?"

"I spoke to you earlier," Mark said, wondering if somehow he could be mistaken. But her mouth, and that stubborn chin belonged to a woman he'd known before. Intimately known. "I left my card in the hedge."

"It's still there," she said. "I forgot—"

"To give me your name all those years ago."

"We agreed names weren't important."

A stupid agreement, Mark knew. But he'd respected her privacy then, as he would now. "It's been a long time."

"Years." She didn't open the door wider or step back to let him in.

"Four years." She stood there, beautiful and calm, and looked at him, waiting for him to explain his presence on her quaint cobblestone doorstep. "I'm here on business," he said, when he finally remembered that fact himself. "If your name is Diana Webb, I have a package for you."

Her gaze dropped to the thick envelope tucked under his left arm. "What is this about?"

"*Are* you Diana Webb?" Just because every nerve in his body was on high alert didn't mean he couldn't act professional. She hesitated, broadcasting loud and clear that she really was the woman he'd been sent to meet.

"Yes," she said, not sounding at all pleased with the fact. The look she gave him was one of annoyance instead of fear, but she moved aside nonetheless and opened the door wider. "Come in."

He saw the fresh white cast on her arm. "What happened?"

"I fell off the roof."

Mark realized she wasn't kidding. And from the look of the cast, the injury was recent. He didn't like the feeling of protectiveness that surged through him, so he frowned. "Are you all right?"

"I broke my wrist, but it's getting better." With her left hand she gestured toward a white love seat positioned in front of a stone fireplace. In fact, the entire room was white, or shades of white with brief splashes of pale blue. The only other color came from the paintings displayed against the textured walls. He remembered the paintings. Yes, he was in the right place. He'd know her work anywhere.

"And you're right-handed."

"Unfortunately." She perched on the arm of a fat ivory chair and watched as Mark sat down on the sofa and placed the thick package of information on the glass-topped coffee table.

"What have you brought?"

"Do you know a man by the name of Warren Cooper?" Of course she didn't, but Mark wanted to stall for time. This woman, the woman he'd made love to on a beach in the Bahamas four years ago, was as composed as if she were about to discuss car insurance. He wasn't often rattled and resented her for causing it.

"No."

"I didn't think so." He pushed the package toward her. "He hired me to deliver this to you."

Diana leaned forward and took the package, then sat down in the chair as if she were resigned to having to put up with company. She didn't open it, but she did turn that green-eyed gaze to Mark. "I don't like surprises."

"I think Mr. Cooper explains everything in his letter. Your sister and brother received similar packages."

Her eyebrows rose as if doubting his words. "They would have called me."

"Warren—Mr. Cooper—preferred you each learn in your own way. In fact, he insisted that the packages be hand delivered to each one of you." Which was a pretty damn big coincidence as far as Mark was concerned.

"I don't think I can do this," Diana muttered, the package in her lap, the plaster cast resting on the arm of the chair. Her long fingers looked fragile; she wore no rings and her fingernails were short and unpainted.

"Warren wouldn't hurt you," Mark assured her. "I'm sure once you—"

"I meant," she said, her embarrassed smile charming him before it disappeared, "I don't think I can open this. It's sealed quite well and my wrist is aching.'' With her left hand she set the package on the coffee table and gave it an awkward shove back towards Mark. ''Will you do it for me?''

''Of course.'' He was still attracted to her, but he was four years older and a hell of a lot wiser, and he knew better than to want what he couldn't have. She probably owned cats and fussed over her white furniture and was too eccentric for her own good. There were reasons why beautiful women like her lived alone on islands and if he could keep a rational thought in his head, he would open the package and then run for the door.

CHAPTER TWO

IT OCCURRED TO Diana that she still didn't know this man's name. She resisted the urge to fidget in her chair and forced herself to remain perfectly still, as if old lovers knocked on her Nantucket door every evening. As if his presence didn't embarrass and shock her.

He didn't look any older. If anything, the lines of tension had disappeared from his face. He looked tired and a bit sunburned, but his dark eyes were free of pain. He had most likely married again, perhaps had a child or two, though he wore no wedding ring. Many men didn't, for all sorts of reasons.

"There," he said, having made short work of ripping tape from the package's flap. It was one of those oversize padded bags, she noted, and it was stuffed with papers. Whoever this Warren Cooper was, he had much to send her. And she didn't want it, for she knew that the man seated only a few feet away from her meant trouble enough. "I'm sure there's a letter in here for you."

"Could you find it for me?" She ignored his surprised expression. The fingers on her right hand felt swollen and achy. She didn't want him to see how clumsy she was with her left hand. She would read the letter and then decide if the rest of the contents of the package interested her.

"This is very private," he said. "And none of my business."

"But you know it anyway," she said, watching him retrieve a white business-size envelope from the package.

"Some of the story, yes." He flicked the glued flap open with his thumb, then withdrew the folded pages of white paper. "I'm sure this will explain everything. Mr. Cooper knew what he wanted."

Diana took the letter with her left hand. The handwriting that filled the thick parchment paper was wavering but dark, a man's writing in blue ink. *My Dearest Diana,* it began. *How long I have waited to tell you who I am and how much I have loved you.*

She looked up, toward her visitor. "Is this some kind of joke?"

"No." He stood, looking for all the world as if he couldn't wait to escape.

"Who are you?"

"A private detective." He still didn't tell her his name. She supposed he wanted her to ask; damn him. He wanted her to be curious *now,* four years later? It was as if her frustration was amusing to him.

"And," she lifted the letter. "This man?"

"Can't—and won't—hurt you," he said. "I'm sure you'd like to be alone, so—"

"No," she heard herself say. She didn't want to be alone, that much was true, but asking this man to stay didn't make any sense at all. Except she knew she could trust him, had trusted him a long time ago and had not regretted it. "You can help yourself to a drink." She pointed to the tall armoire in the corner. "Everything's in there but the ice, and the kitchen is through that door. Please, make yourself comfortable."

"And you? Can I fix you something?"

She shook her head. "No."

"Read it, Diana," her guest told her. "The man loved you very much."

She took a deep breath and turned back to the letter in her hand. *I am your grandfather,* he wrote, *though circumstances made it impossible for us to meet. Your grandmother Helen was my first—and only—love. Now that she has passed on and I am about to join her, I am free to tell you and Richard and Sally the truth. I was a shy young man, in love with the girl next door in Cooper's Corner and too shy to tell her so. It broke my heart when she went to Boston to visit a relative, and met and married your grandfather, Lawrence Webb, before he went off to fight in World War II. I thought I would never get over the disappointment. She was the only girl for me, you see.*

Diana tried to picture her grandmother as a young woman, but failed, though once she'd been told that she had her grandmother's eyes. Helen Webb had been a sweet and loving grandmother, but she couldn't help her oldest granddaughter. And she couldn't bridge the gap between her husband and Diana, no matter how hard she had tried.

Helen returned to our town after her husband was shipped overseas. I had a crooked leg and couldn't enlist, though I tried my darndest. My brother was killed in the war, and then Helen found out her husband was, too. It was a hard time back then, my dear, and I hope you never have to know such heartache. My Helen turned to me for comfort and, in the midst of the war, we were happy.

Diana wondered what *we were happy* meant. Had her grandmother had an affair with this man? And—obviously—Lawrence Webb wasn't killed in the war. He was as alive and stubborn as ever, though Diana hadn't spoken to him in years. She heard her visitor open a tray of ice cubes in the kitchen, wondered at the strange sound of having another person walking around her house, then returned to reading Warren Cooper's story.

But of course Lawrence Webb—a man for whom I came to have great respect—was alive after all and my Helen knew her place was with her husband. The twin girls she gave birth to months later were mine, though I promised Helen I would always keep our secret from the rest of the world. I planted twin oaks along the driveway of my farmhouse in honor of my little daughters, one of whom was your mother. I feel all of you with me when I stand under those trees.

My own life is slipping away now, but I wanted you to know that you are part of me, my blood, my life. You are loved and always have been. You have had a privileged life, but I know you have had your share of heartaches, too. I hope you will never forget what I have written to you, that you know my love for you doesn't end because my life is ending. My love for my grandchildren is forever, as is my love for their grandmother.

Love, your grandfather, Warren Cooper.

Diana blinked back tears, unwilling to let teardrops mar the letter she held in her lap. Her wrist ached and so did her head, but she had never felt better. Lighter, somehow. Free. Lawrence Webb was not her grandfather, not really. No wonder their relationship had been such a difficult one. Her sweet and patient grandmother had loved another man. A man Diana needed to go to. She raised her head to see the private detective looking at her with sympathy.

"Please tell me he's still alive," she whispered.

"I'm sorry, Diana." He shook his head. "The truth couldn't be told until both he and Helen were gone. That was a promise he made to her."

"And he kept his promise." What a concept, she thought. A man keeping his promises.

"Yes." He set his drink on the coffee table. "He seemed to be a very sincere man."

"Did you know—my grandfather well?" *My grandfather. How odd.*

"No, unfortunately. He hired me to deliver the

letters. He was very...particular about how he wanted this done, and in what order. As soon as we were finished, he died.''

She had the overwhelming urge to burst into sobs, but Diana pressed her lips together and took a deep breath. She had lost something of unimaginable value before she'd known she possessed it. She'd had another grandfather who loved her, not one who demanded obedience and dispensed criticism at every opportunity. ''It doesn't seem fair, does it?''

''No.'' He surprised her by leaning forward and covering her left hand with his own. His skin was cool, his long fingers curving over hers and grazing her thigh with the lightest touch imaginable. Maybe she imagined the jolt of awareness that shot through her, but she didn't think so. Whatever physical attraction that had brought them together four years ago on a beach in the Bahamas was still there, and she thought he must have felt it, too, because he withdrew his hand and then quickly stood up.

''I'd better get going,'' he said, not looking at her, but at the painting above the fireplace. ''I imagine you want to be alone.''

''Yes.'' An automatic reply, but not necessarily the truth. What she wanted was to be held, to have someone tell her that she wasn't alone, that she could cry.

That someone understood how the love of a man she'd never met could break her heart. When she looked up, her visitor was gone.

THAT WAS THAT, Mark decided. By the time he hit the sidewalk and took the few strides to the neighboring brick walk, he'd resigned himself to never seeing Diana Webb again. Of course, he told himself, he was happy about that. And he'd been through this particular situation four years before, when he'd wakened after a night of the most astounding sex he'd ever experienced, only to find the woman gone. The sheets, indented from her body, had been cool when he'd smoothed his hands across the cotton. He'd somehow hoped to feel her, but he'd been a fool. Two strangers had found each other, comforted each other, made love to each other in the dark exotic night.

Mark didn't take time to admire the brick steps to the front door of what was to be his home for the night. He barely glanced at the plaque stating the name of the sea captain who'd built the yellow house. He pushed open the navy-painted door and walked directly up the stairs to his small room under the east eaves. The twin beds were covered in blue quilts and there were vintage maps of Nantucket framed over the white iron headboards. A ship model encased in a glass box sat on top of a thick pine dresser. It was all very neat and very nautical, and Mark could smell the sea coming in on the breeze from the open window. From that single window he could look down on Diana's home, but Mark resisted torturing himself any longer. He would be on the first ferry out of Nantucket harbor tomorrow morning. He would not look back.

He had found her, but he'd brought her upsetting news. This time she was the one in pain and he could only stand by helplessly and watch.

Damn.

CHAPTER THREE

IT DIDN'T TAKE Diana all night to decide what to do, but she had to wait until dawn to put her plan into action. She ignored her aching wrist, drank two pots of black coffee and waited for the sun and her ride to Cooper's Corner. Diana would hire the private detective to take her there, and she would hide her embarrassment over having made love with him. And she would ignore the fact that he was one of the most attractive men she'd ever met.

In other words, she would continue to put her past behind her and live for the moment.

At six, the private detective walked down the steps of Silas and Lydia's house. He wore a lightweight jacket and gray slacks; a black leather bag was slung over his shoulder. The morning was cool, with the promise of warmth, and patchy fog blocked whatever sunlight might have appeared.

Diana, perched on her front step, waited until

he was in front of her home before calling to him. "Mark?"

He stopped and turned, and for a split second she thought he was going to smile. "You finally got my business card out of the hedge."

"It was right where you left it. Mark Solomon," she quoted from memory. "Investigative Services. Serving New England from Newport, Rhode Island."

He nodded. "At your service."

"Exactly." Diana stood, awkwardly lifting herself from the step with her one good arm. She'd packed a small bag of overnight things, along with a change of clothes and makeup. Used to traveling at a moment's notice—she'd been a corporate wunderkind for too many years—Diana could make do with what she carried in an oversize ebony leather tote and a small carry-on bag.

"You're going somewhere?" Mark Solomon—what a pleasant name, she thought—didn't seem enthused about whatever travel plans she had in mind.

"Excellent deduction." She slung the handbag strap over her shoulder and wheeled the little bag behind her as she headed toward him. "You must be very good at this detective stuff."

He didn't smile. "Are you sure you're up to it? That wrist—"

"Is going to ache no matter what I do," she interrupted, giving the suitcase an extra yank when it stalled on a bumpy cobblestone. She tried not to wince as the movement sent a jolt of pain to her broken arm, making her glad she'd decided to wear the sling today.

"You're up early."

"I never went to bed. I tried, but I kept thinking of my grandfather." She joined him on the sidewalk and he took the rolling suitcase from her and set it aside. "I had a feeling you'd take the six-thirty ferry and I didn't want to miss you." Diana started walking down the street, and Mark hauled her small case behind him. "I decided calling your cell phone was silly."

"Why?"

"Because you were sure to walk past the house this morning and—"

"No," he said. "Why did you want to see me?"

"To hire you, of course." Diana glanced toward him and saw that he was still frowning. "I can't drive right now and I don't want to wait."

"Wait for what?"

"To see my grandfather's home. His grave.

The oak trees. And where he and my grandmother grew up. I need to hire you to drive me
there.''

"To Cooper's Corner," Mark said, as they
rounded the bend and a view of the harbor appeared in the distance.

"Exactly."

"Today."

"Yes. I thought about it all night."

"I see," was all Mark said, which was enough
for now. If he couldn't be hired to take her to the
other end of Massachusetts, she would either
have to call one of her siblings or hire a limousine, and neither option appealed to her in the
least. The simplest solution, since Mark already
knew where her grandfather had lived, was to
have him drive her there. She could easily continue to pretend that she barely remembered having made love with him, of course.

They were almost to the end of Broad Street,
past the brick Whaling Museum and its neighboring gift shop, before Mark spoke again.
"What about your brother and sister? Wouldn't
you rather make the trip with one of them?"

"Sally would think she was being disloyal to
Lawrence Webb, since she works for him. And
if Richard couldn't *sail* to Cooper's Corner—or

if there wasn't a Red Sox game being played there—then he wouldn't go.'' She loved her brother and sister, but they hadn't bothered to contact her about this mysterious grandfather and his letters. Unfortunately, she'd no idea what went on in her siblings' lives. Her three closest friends were pregnant, in France or hiking in Wyoming. It clearly wasn't a good time to need help.

"And if I can't take you," Mark asked. "What then?"

"I'll pay double—no, *triple*—your daily rate. I checked the map," Diana informed him. "I think Cooper's Corner is about a five-hour drive from Hyannis."

"That depends on the traffic." Mark followed her toward the ferry ticket kiosk at the beginning of the wharf.

"We're getting an early enough start to do it in one day," she pointed out. "One *long* day, but we have a good start."

"I appreciate the offer of a job," he said, not sounding interested at all. "But I have plans for this afternoon."

"Plans?" Which meant he had a date. Which meant he might be married, though she didn't think so. Once or twice she'd sensed the strong physical awareness between them, which wouldn't be there if he was committed to someone else. Diana bought a one-way ticket to Hyannis anyway. And stood aside while he did, too.

"A birthday party," Mark said, pocketing his ticket in his inside jacket pocket. "My nephew's turning nine and I promised I'd be there."

"And I don't suppose he lives anywhere near the Berkshires," Diana guessed, hiding a tinge of envy. She'd love to have a nephew—or a niece. Sally was planning a wedding, but her sister was also involved in the family business and devoted to her career. Diana didn't dare hope that Sally would have a houseful of children.

"No. He lives next door to me, in Newport." He still held her suitcase in one hand as they walked onto the ramp that led to the ferry's deck. He didn't stop until they reached the door to the snack area, when Diana caught a whiff of fresh coffee and cinnamon rolls. Mark set her suitcase down next to her foot. "So you'll either have to go back home or figure out something else. I can't take you where you want to go."

Diana watched as he headed to the bow of the ferry, where other early travelers sat on the benches and had a foggy view of the harbor. She wouldn't go home, not now. She was on a mission, broken wrist or no broken wrist. She'd have to drink another cup of coffee and, because she had a cell phone, credit cards and a stubborn streak, she'd figure out how to come up with Plan B.

MARK'S SISTER told him that he drank too much coffee and slept too little, that he spent too much time alone and neglected his social life. She was right. He knew too many cops and not enough women and at the ripe age of thirty-six, he felt twice his age. He preferred cold beer in summer and fine whiskey the rest of the year. He didn't smoke, didn't sleep around—much—and once owned a mongrel dog named Hank, after his father. It was meant to be a compliment to the old man, who had died three years ago this month. Hank had died last winter.

Mark sat alone along the edge of the large ferry and watched the harbor disappear from view as the boat moved away from the island and chugged steadily across the Nantucket Sound to Hyannis Harbor. His old man would have thought his son was half-crazy, turning down a chance to help a beautiful woman. *They don't come along like that every day, son,* Hank Solomon would have said.

No, not every day. Only every four years. The

first time he'd been raw with pain, suffering from the senseless death of his young wife and still shaking from the revenge he'd sought—and won—with the death of the criminal who'd murdered his young bride. As a result, his promising career as a homicide detective in Boston was over, his actions conveniently ruled as "self-defense." His resignation surprised no one and relieved his bosses. He drifted for months, drinking too much and hoping to die. He'd ended up— he still didn't remember why or how—in the Bahamas, on one of those beachfront resorts with the little cabins facing the sea. He'd watched the long-haired woman paint, dismissed her as a silly tourist until one morning he'd walked closer, curious to see what she looked like under the broad brim of her straw hat. For three days she'd worn the gauzy white outfit, which he later realized was a very expensive sundress. He'd been prepared to see an older woman painting sweet seascapes, but instead he'd found a younger stranger. He'd been shocked by her beauty and the raw pain and anguish that emanated from the ocean onto her canvas. To this day he didn't know why she'd allowed him to sit near her and watch her paint. She'd let him talk—*made* him talk—and he'd told her everything, how he and

Janice had met in college. The small outdoor wedding that had been postponed due to a hurricane. Her murder. His revenge.

And after the dark-haired artist put down her brush and he'd wiped the tears from her face, they walked down the beach to his little house and made love. She'd had her own demons, he knew, pain she wouldn't discuss. It was enough, though, for him to know that somehow they'd found each other for a brief period of time, that they'd removed some of the pain and replaced it with the kind of intimate pleasure that only lovemaking could provide.

It had been more than great sex. He'd never experienced anything even close to that kind of passion since. And now he'd found her again, on another island, and she acted as if they'd met over a game of cards years before.

Well, he'd probably exaggerated the physical attraction each time he'd taken out that particular memory and replayed it in his mind. He should practice self-preservation more these days. Or so he told himself, knowing that fifty feet away he would find Diana and hot coffee. It was a good morning for coffee. It was not a good morning for rescuing an old lover with a broken wrist and a broken heart and a sensual appeal that made him want to find a secluded place under a tarp and make love to her while the fog hid them in its mist.

One hour and fifteen minutes later, when the ferry docked at its wharf in Hyannis, Mark stood, stretched and slung his bag over his shoulder. He would put Diana out of his mind. He would meet the divorced mother of two this afternoon and he would consider asking her to dinner and taking her to bed. He was ready to get on with his life and spend less time by himself.

Yes, he vowed, as the sun broke through the fog and lit up the wharf. He had a birthday party to go to, a gift to purchase, a woman to meet. He would forget Diana Webb and the troubling sadness in her sea-green eyes, even though he saw Diana walking toward the exit, a lanky college-aged kid beside her, his baseball cap on backward and Diana's overnight bag in his grip.

Hell. Warren Cooper wouldn't want his granddaughter paying some pimply college kid with more muscles than brains to help her out. The dying old man had paid Mark well, had expected his instructions would be carried out. "Take extra care with Diana," he had whispered, and Mark had shaken the man's callused hand, a silent promise to do as he'd been ordered.

Mark grimaced, his plans for a peaceful after-noon forgotten, and hurried toward the exit ramp. Tourists, eager to make the trip to Nantucket, were bunched together on the other side of the dock awaiting their turn on the ferry. He'd made a vow to an old man and maybe he even owed Diana a favor, too. He would not get himself caught up with wanting a woman he couldn't have. He wouldn't have to do anything more than drive her to a small town in the country, and he could damn well resist wanting to make love to her.

And if that oversexed teenager put his meaty fingers on Diana's bare shoulder again, he would toss him into the water like an empty clam shell.

"GET IN."

Diana, her cell phone against her ear, turned to see Mark Solomon standing next to the opened door of a silver Mazda sedan. "Really?"

"Hurry up before I change my mind," he said, but he reached over and took her suitcase, then opened the back door and tossed it on the seat.

"Never mind," she told the limousine booking agent. "I'm all set." She pushed the End button on the phone and smiled at her handsome private detective. "You changed your mind. Thanks."

"Where's the kid?"

"Who?" She slid onto the leather bucket seat and, after turning off the cell phone and tossing it in her tote, placed the bag at her feet. Mark shut her door, then went around the back of the car and got in on the driver's side. After fastening the seat belt, he donned a pair of dark sunglasses and answered her question.

"College Boy."

"Dartmouth, to be exact. His name is Tim and he offered me a ride to Boston." She put on her own sunglasses, but snapping her seat belt into place was another matter. Mark looked down and put his right hand over hers.

"Stop," he said. "I'll do it."

She should have thanked him, but Diana's pride kept her silent.

"So," Mark said, once his hands quit brushing her thigh and were back to doing things like turning the key in the ignition and putting the gear shift in reverse so they could leave the parking spot. "You didn't want to go to Boston? You could have hired a plane there."

"I'm not wild about small planes *or* younger men."

He shot her a curious glance, and then had to stop and pay the parking attendant, which gave

Diana a few moments to ease her arm out of the sling and set it in her lap. Her neck was already sore from the unaccustomed strain.

"There are a few conditions," Mark stated, not looking at her.

"Of course." She closed her eyes for a moment, knowing that whatever the conditions were, it didn't matter, as long as she could lay her arm in a somewhat comfortable position and get some relief.

"You'll have to find a place to stay in Newport tonight," he said, once they were out of the parking lot. With easy skill he negotiated the summer traffic north through Hyannis until they were on Route 6, the fastest road west and off the Cape.

"That's fine." A soft bed sounded especially wonderful now, when her lack of sleep seemed to be catching up with her. Diana hid a yawn behind her left hand and turned to face her detective. *Her detective.* She liked the sound of that, especially when Mark sounded so stern and, yet, was taking her where she wanted to go. She'd forgotten how handsome he was, too, and had the surprising urge to lay her head on his shoulder and smell his skin. She remembered his scent, a combination of ocean breezes and the faint tang of mint aftershave.

"We won't leave for Cooper's Corner until tomorrow," he was saying. "And then we'll head out first thing in the morning."

"That's fine." It was more than fine, a thousand times better than waiting at the ferry terminal for hours while she tried to find a limousine to hire for two days. And the driver would be a stranger, not the man who had met her grandfather and knew the way to his former home and whose skin she wanted to smell, just to see if she had remembered the scent correctly. Diana fought to remain professional and impersonal. "Do I pay by the day or will you bill me?"

He swore under his breath. "Go to sleep, Diana. God knows you look like you need the rest."

"You have to stop giving me compliments," she managed to say, though she yawned again and closed her eyes. She heard him fiddle with the stereo system on the dashboard until the soft sounds of the blues filled the car. Her last conscious thought before drifting off to sleep was that she was in exactly the right place at exactly the right time...for a change.

CHAPTER FOUR

"UNCLE MARK, why's there a lady in your car?"

"Shhh," Mark told his nephew. He stepped out of the Mazda and shut the door behind him as quietly as he could. His passenger was either asleep or dead, and when he thought about the trouble she was going to cause him for the next couple of days he had mixed feelings about which he'd prefer. But right now Toby was bouncing up and down with birthday excitement, so he took his nephew by his skinny shoulders and moved him toward the back door of his house. "She's sleeping," Mark told the kid. "She's really tired."

Jess eyed her brother as she opened the screen door to usher them into her kitchen. "And why, precisely, is the lady so tired, Mark?"

He grinned. Jess had ears like a cat. "It's not what you think."

"What's that?" the boy asked, looking from his mother to his uncle. When he received no answer he moved on to his favorite topic of conversation. "Mom made a chocolate cake for my birthday."

"Mom *bought* a chocolate cake for your birthday," Jess said, laughing. "Six layers, no less."

"Cool, huh?"

"Very cool," Mark agreed, glancing back toward the car to see that his passenger hadn't moved.

"Don't go home yet," the boy said. "I've got to show you something." He ran out of the kitchen and Mark heard him run up the stairs. He turned to his sister. "What time does this party begin?"

"At four," his sister answered, peering out the door to see his car parked in the driveway they shared. "Is your lady friend joining us?"

"Yes."

"Mark, for heaven's sake," Jess blustered. "I told you I had someone I wanted you to meet. You said you were okay with that, remember? You said you wanted to start dating and thinking about settling down now that you're thirty-six and time is running out and—"

"She's a client," he said, cutting off Jess's scold.

"You've never brought clients home before." Leave it to his older sister to point that out.

"I have to take her to the Berkshires tomorrow."

"The Cooper business with the grandfather who never met his grandchildren?" Jess, who worked for his company, never forgot a case. "No kidding. Which one is she?"

"Diana, the final delivery. And don't worry, she's not staying with me. I'm taking her to a hotel." He looked out the screen door again and then felt ridiculous. Diana Webb was not the kind of woman who would wake up and panic because she was in a strange place. "She has a broken wrist, so be nice."

Jess lowered her voice and looked concerned. "Abuse?"

"A roof."

"And I'll bet she's single, beautiful and thinks private detectives are sexy."

"Of course, Jessie," Mark said. "She thinks I'm so exciting that she's been asleep all the way from Hyannis."

"She's awake now," his sister informed him. "You'd better go rescue her."

Somebody had better rescue him instead, Mark

thought, as he saw Diana's long legs emerge from the car. "Can I bring her in?"

"Will she mind the mess?"

He thought of Diana's white, spotless home. "Of course not."

"Yeah, right. Didn't you say the Webbs were multimillionaires, from old Boston money?" Jess picked up a mound of papers and magazines and shoved them in the oven. Mark opened the kitchen door and waved to Diana, who smiled at him in a sleepy way that made him wish he could tuck her into bed. His bed. He was insane, Mark reminded himself, as Diana stepped across the lawn.

"Uncle Mark, look!" Toby ran into the kitchen and held up a small brown gerbil. "His name is Sam and Mom got him for my birthday. I got to pick him out at the pet store and everything."

Mark stroked the animal's head with his index finger. "He seems like a nice little guy. Do you keep him in your room?"

"Yeah. I got a cage and stuff. Wanna see?"

"I sure do, but say hi to my friend Miss Webb first." He opened the door for Diana and introduced her to his family. She said hello and smiled as if she really was happy to meet them.

"Hi," the boy said, giving Diana's sling a curious look. "Did you have a good nap?"

"Yes. Happy Birthday."

"Thanks. I'm *nine* now," he informed her proudly.

Mark leaned over and spoke into Toby's ear. "Do you have the list?"

"Yeah." He started to hand his new pet to his mother, but Jess was busy setting dishes into the sink. So he gave the gerbil to Diana, who let it nestle in her sling before she turned to wink at Mark. Then Toby dug a wad of paper from the pocket of his shorts which he handed to his uncle. "Here."

"Thanks." Mark tucked the paper in his pants pocket. "I guess I'd better get shopping." His nephew grinned up at him, which tickled Mark to no end, then tried to take his gerbil back from its hiding place. Diana laughed and bent down to make it easier.

"I guess you don't mind animals," Jess said, looking more at ease.

"We never had pets when we were children," Diana confided, her voice soft. "But my best friend's family had dogs, cats, gerbils, parakeets and rabbits. It was great fun to visit."

"Cool," Toby said. "My best friend Tommy's

grandma has a dog that's so little she carries it around in a purse. Tommy says sometimes he bites.''

"I don't blame him," Diana said. "I might bite too if I was stuck in a handbag."

"Put Sam back upstairs before he gets loose," Jess said. She turned to Diana. "Would you like some coffee or iced tea or anything?"

"Later," Mark answered. "We've got errands to do."

"Don't spend too much," Jess said. "I mean it, Mark."

"Don't worry," he laughed, and ushered Diana out into the sun. He lowered his voice once the door slammed shut behind them. "Jess says I spoil the boy, but I don't think so. Toby's father hasn't been around for years, not since the divorce."

"And you live here together?" She turned to look at the colonial house, a familiar style in the historic section of Newport called The Point. Many of the homes had dated plaques beside their front doors and steps directly on the sidewalk, similar to the architecture of Nantucket. He'd give her a tour once they were back from the store.

"It's actually a duplex," he explained, pointing to the south side of the two-story shingled home. "One of the first in the area. My parents bought it when they got married and rented the other half. Jess and I decided to keep it in the family. We share the backyard and the brick patio."

"That's really nice," she said. "How—"

"Mark?" Jess opened the door and leaned out. "I forgot to buy ice cream. Can you—"

"What kind?"

"Chocolate chip." She grinned. "You won't forget?"

"I'll remind him," Diana promised.

"Thanks."

Mark didn't want to like this woman. It was bad enough that he wanted to make love to her. And here she'd hired him to drive her around, like he was her Boston grandfather's chauffeur. She was beautiful and rich and she didn't fit into his life at all. Desire was one thing, lifestyle was another. He should deposit Diana Webb at the Marriott and let her fend for herself. And he would try to remember to be very nice to Jess's divorced friend this afternoon. If Diana could pretend she barely remembered that night in his bed, then so could he.

"THERE IS NO way in hell," Mark declared, "that I'm going to ask that woman out." He rummaged through a kitchen drawer until he found a tie for the garbage bag.

"She's really nice. Her kids—"

"—are spoiled rotten," Mark finished for her.

"Mark, that's unkind." But his sister chuckled anyway.

"It's true." He grinned and picked up the heavy trash bag and twisted the tie around the top. The party had lasted until after seven and no one was happier than he was to see the end of it. Toby had loved it all and was so wound up Mark didn't know how the kid would ever go to bed.

"I thought you wanted me to fix you up with someone."

"I did. I do. Just not her." He set the bag by the back door and looked outside to see Diana helping Toby clean off the picnic table. She held an oversize trash bag in one hand while the boy filled it with used gift wrap and unwanted boxes.

"What about Diana?"

He turned away and pretended he didn't know what his sister was getting at. "What about her?"

"There's something going on and you're not telling me what it is." Jess turned from the sink and dried her hands on a dish towel. "So what is it?"

"I met her a few years ago. Briefly." He leaned against the wall and crossed his arms in front of his chest.

Jess waited for him to continue.

"It was after—well, we knew each other once. Leave it at that."

"She's lovely."

"Yes."

"Very polite."

"Yes. Her manners are impeccable. And she's good with children."

He shrugged. "Want to share a beer?"

"Don't try to change the subject. You can't take your eyes off her."

"That's ridiculous." Damn. Now he couldn't take the garbage out to the shed without Jess thinking he had the hots for a client.

It was Jess's turn to shrug. And then she threw the sponge at him, but he caught it before it smacked him in the chin. "She can stay in the guest room."

"Yours or mine?"

"Mine, you poor idiot." She grinned at him.

"You're calling a highly trained, professional, sharpshooting genius private detective *names?*"

He sent the sponge whizzing back across the room, but Jess ducked. The sponge bounced off the window and splashed into the sink. "I can take care of myself where—" He stopped in mid-sentence when he heard Diana and Toby approach the back door.

Jess only laughed and turned back to the sink. She'd always known when he was bluffing.

CHAPTER FIVE

"I PROMISE not to fall asleep this morning." Diana waved goodbye to Jess and Toby and then helped Mark fasten her seat belt. Soon they were on their way down the street and Diana gazed out the window at the colonial homes that lined the sidewalk.

"You can sleep if you like," Mark said, guiding the car out of The Point and onto a busy street that ran parallel to the waterfront. "We're going to be on the road for close to four hours, depending on the traffic."

"I don't want to miss anything." She'd forgotten how beautiful the town of Newport was, with its restored buildings and its busy waterfront. Across the street a large white-steepled church rose from a wide lawn of green grass. The aching in her arm had stopped, she'd slept for ten hours in a four-poster bed decorated with carved pineapples that Jess confided she'd bought at a neighbor's yard sale, and Toby's birthday excitement had been contagious. She didn't remember laughing so much as she had yesterday and she didn't remember ever feeling as comfortable anywhere before.

"You've never been to Newport?" He sounded surprised. "I assumed you'd traveled everywhere."

"I was here one weekend, when I was in college," she said. "Several of us came for the Jazz Festival."

"I thought you'd be part of the yachting set." He waved toward an array of expensive-looking boats tied to long wharves. "Like those."

"No, thanks. I'll stick with the Nantucket ferry. My brother's the sailor in the family. I'd rather drive. Or fly."

Mark turned the car around at the next light and headed in the opposite direction. Soon they were crossing a long bridge. "Check out the view," Mark said. "We've got great weather."

She saw blue water, small rocky islands, sailboats and even an abandoned lighthouse. Then she leaned back and rested her cast outside of the sling. She was actually having an adventure, something she'd avoided for years. At one point she'd done some corporate work advising growing companies with marketing and financial strategies, but she'd discovered that her true passion was in art, something her grandfather—Lawrence Webb—had always discouraged. He'd insisted she major in business management in preparation for taking over the family businesses some day, but she'd secretly added art courses to her schedule each semester.

She'd ended up turning her back on everything Lawrence wanted. She'd spent a large chunk of her trust fund buying the cottage in Nantucket and no one was more surprised when her paintings actually sold for sums that guaranteed her a comfortable living.

A comfortable living, she repeated to herself. Yesterday she'd poured fruit punch for noisy boys, helped grill hot dogs and rescued a gerbil from the clutches of a screaming little girl. She'd helped Toby find the lost piece to a Lego set and he'd showed her how to play a handheld video game. She'd made friends with Jess Saunders after the party was over and they sat on the patio and drank wine. Jess was a woman who was as protective of her younger brother as she was of her son,

"I like your sister," she told Mark. He had a strong profile, she noted. She didn't think he smiled often, except around his nephew. He passed a truck and returned to the right lane before answering.

"Jess is okay. She does a lot of computer work for my company." Mark turned on the radio and found an oldies rock station. He didn't seem to want to talk, so Diana took in the scenery along the Rhode Island coast as they headed south toward Connecticut. She took a New England road map out of her tote and managed to unfold enough of it so she could see when they should leave the coast and begin the diagonal crossing of Connecticut that would take them to the Berkshires.

To her grandfather's house.

MARK DIDN'T STOP until they were just west of Springfield, Massachusetts, on the Massachusetts Turnpike, and then only because it was time for lunch. He figured the brief visit to Dunkin' Donuts for coffee didn't count because he'd used the drive-up window. But now it was after twelve and there was no putting off getting something to eat, even if his preference was to get through this day as quickly as possible, before he did something foolish, like kiss her. For the past three hours, while Diana looked at scenery and checked the map spread open on her lap, he'd pretended to listen to the radio and concentrated on getting through the occasional traffic jam. But he'd actually been trying to reconcile the mysterious woman in his bed four years ago with the one who had laughed at Toby's knock-knock jokes and charmed Jess, who was no fool when it came to people. And why did she live alone like a hermit on Nantucket when she obviously enjoyed backyard barbecues and road trips?

"We should eat," was all he said, when he pulled off the interstate and into the large parking lot of a roadside restaurant. "Does this look all right to you?"

"It's fine," she said, sounding pleased with the suggestion of food. Once they were seated inside, across from each other in a blue vinyl booth, Mark glanced at the plastic-coated menu and then his watch. They were making good time, and if the visit to Warren Cooper's farm was uneventful, he could take the turnpike back through Massachusetts and then the 495 freeway to Hyannis, dropping Diana at the ferry wharf and out of his life before the last boat left for the island.

"I have to thank you again," Diana said, smiling at him. She really was a beautiful woman. And he was a sucker for green eyes and dark hair, he reminded himself. There was no reason to stare at her mouth and wonder what it would be like to kiss her again.

"We're not there yet," he felt obligated to point out. "You could be disappointed at what you find."

"That's not what I meant."

"No?"

"I'm trying to thank you for yesterday, for inviting me to Toby's birthday party. I had a wonderful time."

"Good. Toby did, too." The waitress came over and took their order—hamburgers, fries and iced tea times two—giving Mark a few extra minutes to think about what to say next, but Diana had her own questions.

"Are you going to ask that woman out—the one with the two little boys? I think she wants you to. She was pretty obvious about it."

"I don't think she's my type."

"You don't have to look so grumpy about it," she said, smiling in a way that made him realize she was teasing him and enjoying it. "What exactly is your type?"

"Is this topic of conversation necessary?"

"No. But since you haven't spoken three sentences since we crossed the Newport Bridge, I figured we'd talk while waiting for our lunch to arrive.'' Yes, he realized, she was definitely teasing him.

"My type," he drawled, as if he were giving it all of his concentration. "Well, I don't go for ex-cons, married women, college girls or cops. No real thin women—they don't eat and won't go out to dinner. No smokers. No heavy drinkers. I don't hang out in bars but I'm not looking for an instant family either, although if the perfect woman came along I wouldn't toss her aside because she already had children."

"That doesn't sound too unreasonable."

"What about you?"

"What about me?"

"Your type is—?"

"Oh. I'm not sure anymore. I seem to choose the most terrible men," she confessed, looking as if she were telling the truth and not happy about the revelation. "So I don't date at all."

"Yeah, right." He didn't believe the men in Nantucket were that stupid—or lazy. Or blind.

"It's true," she insisted. "I'm better off that way. Really."

"How?"

"I don't run the risk of making mistakes."

"Is that what *I* was? A mistake?" He wasn't

pleased with himself for asking the question, but Mark figured he might as well know the truth.

"I'm not proud of having a one-night stand with a strange man I met on the beach. And I don't do that kind of thing anymore."

He was glad to hear it. If she made love with anyone it should be with him, but he didn't like that night being referred to as a "one-night stand." "So that's all it was, casual sex?"

"What else would you call it?" She didn't look at him again, and when the waitress arrived with their lunch, Diana busied herself with her knife. It took a minute for Mark to realize she was trying to cut her hamburger in half.

"Here," he said, moving his plate aside and pulling hers toward him. "Let me help."

"I can't get used to only having one working hand," she confessed. The rest of their lunch together consisted of conversation about the nice weather and what little Mark remembered of Cooper's Corner.

When they returned to the car he kissed her, just to get it out of the way. To get it out of his system, because it wouldn't matter once they reached their destination. This woman, who so recently returned to his life, could decide to stay at her grandfather's home for a while. She could wave her private detective goodbye with a fat check and a sweet smile of thanks and that would be that.

So Mark took her by the shoulders and turned her away from the Mazda's open door. She lifted her chin as if she expected him to kiss her—or if she intended to protest or maybe voice her surprise. But she said nothing as those green eyes of hers studied him, softened and closed when he touched her mouth with his. Her lips were cool and soft, her left hand touched his forearm, a light erotic touch because her fingers seemed to be burning through the thin cotton of his shirt.

He slanted his mouth across hers, deepening the kiss, sensing her arousal when her lips parted and their tongues touched and teased and tangled together. He shifted away from her body when he would have moved closer, careful not to press on the casted arm in the sling across her chest. A car honked and he heard the low murmur of conversation and then laughter. He released her mouth, though he could have stood there all day under the shade of the only tree at the edge of the parking lot, kissing her.

"Will you look at that!" someone exclaimed, and Mark dropped his hands from Diana's shoulders and frowned.

"You'd think they never saw anyone—"

"They're not looking at us," Diana said, laughter coloring her words as she gazed past him. "Turn around."

When he did, he saw the large Lincoln sedan parked next to him, also taking advantage of the shade. Through the closed, tinted windows of the car, he saw a fuzzy white poodle looking back at him.

"I'll call the police," Mark muttered, reaching into his pocket for his cell phone. "It's too hot to leave a dog in a car like that, with the windows closed and—"

"Mark." Diana interrupted him again, and this time she really laughed. "The car is running. The owner left the air-conditioning on."

Sure enough, the little poodle looked completely content. It wasn't even panting and the little fluffy knot on the top of its head blew backward, as if the dog had positioned itself in front of the air vent. "Some detective I am," he said.

"You can't know everything," Diana reassured him. "I saw the other people's reactions before you did."

He opened the car door for her and waited until she got in. "And here I thought they were shocked because I was kissing you."

"No," Diana said. "I think I was the only shocked person in the parking lot."

He bent over, his arm resting on the car door. "Because I kissed you?"

She shook her head. "No. Because I liked it."

CHAPTER SIX

IN LESS THAN an hour they drove into Cooper's Corner, a quaint town on Route 7, south of Williamstown. Mark drove slowly along Main Street while Diana stared out the window, entranced by the Victorian-style buildings.

"It's beautiful up here," she said, not realizing she had spoken aloud until Mark answered.

"Yes. The town was named for a farmer who settled the land in the early 1800's. I've read a little bit about the town."

"I wish I had my paints." She caught a glimpse of what must be the village green. "I'd even try painting with my left hand, just to preserve this."

He slowed the car and parked in front of a store that looked as if it sold just about anything anyone could need. "Wait here," he said.

Diana didn't have time to ask where he was going before he was out of the car and down the sidewalk. She wished she knew how she felt about everything that had happened in the past two days. Since she'd received the letter from Warren Cooper—*her grandfather*—her life had changed. She found herself doing things she never would have done before. It was as if she'd been asleep for the past four years and had now awakened to realize that she had a life to live. But kissing Mark?

How foolish was that? She'd done some stupid things in her life and they all had to do with choosing the wrong men. There'd been that crazy year she'd dropped out of college and run off with the lead guitar player in a rock and roll band. Oh, how her grandfather had ranted over that one. When she'd finally grown tired of motel rooms, groupies, stoned musicians and traveling from city to city in a converted school bus, she'd gone home. Her grandfather must have wanted to shout, "I told you so" from the slate rooftop of the family mansion. Her grandmother had wept tears of relief.

Mark, her handsome private detective who in no way resembled a rock guitarist, returned to the car and tossed a package in her lap.

"There," he said, sliding behind the wheel. "It's the next best thing to art."

Diana dumped the contents of the bag into her

lap and saw three disposable cameras. "You are brilliant," she said, leaning over. Without thinking about what she was doing, she kissed him on the cheek. He turned, surprised, and her lips touched the corner of his mouth. Diana pulled away, struck again by the shock of passion that went through her. It was the same feeling as the one she'd experienced earlier, though she'd managed to disguise it by laughing at the poodle in his air-conditioned car. She'd told Mark she "liked it," when the truth was that the simple kiss almost knocked her to her knees right there in the Hungry Haven parking lot. She would have looked sillier than the poodle.

"My father was a pianist," she said, leaning back in her seat. It was an excellent way to divert herself from her reaction to the man beside her. Mark gave her an odd look and started up the car again.

"Really?"

"He used to take me with him backstage," she said, while watching an elderly couple walk carefully down the sidewalk. She wondered if they had known Warren Cooper. She wondered what they would think if she hopped out of the car and asked them. "My mother would give parties. It was very exciting, watching all those people dressed up in beautiful clothes. I would stay up late and listen to my parents sing, and then I'd curl up on a stack of fur coats and go to sleep.''

''You must have been very young.''

''I was seven when my grandparents took Sally, Richard and me to live with them. My parents died in a fire—did you know that?''

''Warren told me your grandparents raised you. I didn't know why.''

''You grew up with a mother and father, didn't you?''

''Yes. My mother died a year after my father, and that was eight years ago. I still can't get used to the idea that they're both gone.''

''I'm sorry.''

''Thanks.'' He turned left at the next street. ''We're heading toward Oak Road. You should be able to see his farmhouse soon.''

Diana was grateful for the change of subject. She shouldn't be so maudlin, not when she was about to get her first view of Twin Oaks. ''I can't wait.''

''You're in for a real surprise,'' was all Mark said, but it was enough to have Diana sitting on the edge of her seat and gazing ahead for a glimpse of a driveway lined with oak trees.

''There,'' Mark said, pulling the car over to

the edge of the road. "That's the driveway. Incredible, isn't it?"

She hadn't expected such a dramatic entrance to a farmhouse, but this wasn't just any farm. The house, oversize and well-kept, sat on a hillside overlooking the town. Farmland rolled down from each side, but the driveway was what took Diana's breath away. Enormous oak trees lined the drive, exactly the way Warren Cooper had described in his letter.

"Do you want to go up there?"

She put her hand on Mark's arm to stop him. "Wait. We should take a picture just the way it is, while the light is good."

"All right."

"I won't be long." She unbuckled her seat belt and scooted out of the car, then turned back to pick up one of the disposable cameras. She eyed the buttons and figured if she balanced the camera on her cast, she could use her left hand to operate the buttons. She refused Mark's offer of help and managed to take several shots of the oaks, promising herself she would paint them as soon as her wrist healed.

When she was back in the car, she smiled at him. "The camera was a fabulous idea."

"I have photo equipment in the trunk," he explained, "but more than once I've had to rely on disposables when I was in a bind."

"I can't imagine you ever being in any kind of trouble."

"I was when you met me," he said, his eyes dark. His eyes were his best feature, she decided. But she liked his hands, too. She remembered them sometimes, particularly at night when she thought about their brief time in the Bahamas.

"You were grieving," she said. "You had a right to be in pain."

"Everyone does, Diana. Even you."

She turned back to look at her grandfather's oak-lined driveway. "How did he do it all those years, Mark? He was devoted to the one and only woman he had loved his entire life. They had children together. And yet they lived apart for most of their lives and could never tell anyone what happened during the war."

"Your grandfather was a very principled man. And he loved your grandmother. I think it was as straightforward as that. He loved her. He would never do anything to hurt her," Mark said. "Isn't that what love's all about?"

"You make it sound so simple."

He looked as if he wanted to say something, but he turned away instead, swung the car into the driveway and followed the shaded road up the hill to the main house.

Diana readied the camera.

"MY UNCLE was a fine man," Maureen Cooper told her guests. "Everyone loved him very much."

"I really appreciate your letting us see the oak trees," Diana said, trying to sound as casual as she could. This tall chestnut-haired woman was her cousin, and had introduced herself as Warren Cooper's grand-niece. After hearing Diana's stammered explanation of visiting her grandmother's town, Maureen invited them inside the farmhouse.

"We inherited the place from Uncle Warren and, as you can see, we're remodeling. My brother and I are planning to turn Twin Oaks into a bed-and-breakfast." She smiled at Diana, who tried not to stare at the huge living room and its stone hearth. "So, your grandmother grew up with Mr. Cooper, did he?"

"Yes, so I thought I'd see the place she talked about so much. I never met Mr. Cooper, though."

"He was a wonderful man, one of my favorite relatives." She waved them over to the fireplace.

"I have his picture on the mantel, if you want to see what he looked like. Of course, he was much younger then."

Diana practically flew across the room. In a gilded frame was a kind looking man, tall and rangy like her brother. He stood next to a cow, whose halter he held in one of his large hands. "What a wonderful photo."

"I have several copies," Maureen said. "That's the picture they published in the paper with the obituary. Give me a minute and I'll get you one, if you like. I've stored important papers in the library while we're working on the house."

"I'd like that very much. Thank you."

Mark moved closer to stand beside her, then took the picture from the mantel to examine it closer. "Do you see a family resemblance?"

"I have to share this with Richard," she murmured. "He'll want to see what he'll look like when he gets older."

"You have his smile."

"Really?"

"Yeah." He cupped her chin with a gentle hand. "But not his eyes."

She thought he was going to kiss her, but Maureen's return caused him to release her.

"I have it," she called, pausing in the doorway of what Diana assumed to be the library. She waved a folded newspaper at them. "You can have this copy. It tells a little history of the town, too, and about the Coopers. That's why it's called Cooper's Corner, of course." She smiled. "You'll have to forgive my enthusiasm. I love it here."

"I can see why. It's a beautiful town," Diana said. Mark replaced the picture on the mantel.

"Well, since you've never been here before you should take your time and see everything." She gave Diana the paper.

"Thank you. I'll have to come back when you're open for business."

"Please, do that. And if you don't mind the mess, come out to the kitchen with me and I'll show you the view from the back. Uncle Warren had such a pretty place."

She led them out of the living room, through a large dining room that looked as if it hadn't been used in years, and then into a bright kitchen that looked as if the last time it had been decorated was the 1950's.

"I have ten things going on at once," Maureen continued, pointing to the opened boxes of clothing that sat along the wall by the back door. "My uncle left instructions that I was to clean out his closets and donate his clothes to the church bazaar. I've been doing my best, but there's so much to do around here.''

"I'm sure there is." She couldn't help leaning over to touch one of the worn denim work shirts that topped the pile closest to the door. Her fingers smoothed the soft cotton as if she could almost touch her grandfather.

Maureen's voice softened. "If you know anyone who could use some shirts, please help yourself. I think the church will end up cutting them up for rags."

"Well—" Mark stopped when Diana spoke up.

"Are you sure?" She lifted the shirt and saw that there were several others, folded and clean, in the box.

"Sure I'm sure." Maureen pushed open the back door. "Take a look at those hills. Ever seen a prettier place?"

"Never," Diana said, gathering three shirts and draping them over her cast. Now the three grandchildren would have something that belonged to their grandfather. She looked up and smiled at Mark. "It's hard to find shirts like these."

"We'll make a donation to the local church," he whispered.

Mark and Diana admired the view from the back of the farmhouse, but Diana was anxious to see the trees in the front. "Would you mind if we looked at the famous oak trees before we leave?"

"You go right ahead. You can go right around from the back here. Make sure you look at the markers. There's names on them, you see. Family names. My uncle was very proud of those trees."

"Yes," Diana said, remembering the words in his letter. "I heard he was."

"You take your time," Maureen said, beaming on them. "Do you have any other special places to visit before you leave town?"

"No. My grandmother's family home was torn down years ago."

"That's a shame. The older homes have so much character." She shook her head. "Well, you two enjoy yourselves. You have a lovely afternoon for taking pictures."

"Thank you for showing us around," Diana said, holding tightly to her newspaper and the shirts. "I can't believe I was able to see my— Mr. Cooper's farm."

"You're very welcome."

Mark held the back door open and Diana stepped onto the porch. He took the shirts and the newspaper from her, offering to put them in the car while she looked at the trees.

She found her mother's oak tree easily, and then the one of her twin, who died in infancy. The brass markers gave their birth dates and the dates the trees were planted.

"Diana?" Mark looked at the marker and then at her.

"I was named after my aunt. She was my mother's twin—and she died when she was six months old."

He put his arm around her shoulders. "Are you okay?"

"I think so." She sounded a little shaky, even to her own ears, so she gave him the camera. "Will you take pictures for me? I don't think I can hold the camera still."

"Your wrist is hurting?"

"A little."

He frowned, but Diana was getting accustomed to his concern. He frowned like that when he was worried about her, she realized. "This day's been long enough. We're going to call it quits after this."

"So soon? I wanted to go to the library and

see what I could find out about local history and—"

He put his index finger across her lips. "You can. We won't drive back to Hyannis today, that's all." He smoothed his hand over her jaw and tucked a strand of hair behind her ear. The intimate gesture weakened her knees as if she were an innocent schoolgirl. "I guess I'm stuck with you for another day."

"I'll buy you dinner," she said.

"All right." He looked at his watch and then down the hill, towards the roofed buildings of Cooper's Corner. "And we'll have to find a place to spend the night."

"Right," she agreed, but suddenly despite having learned so much about her new family, all Diana could think of now was hot sand, warm sheets and eighteen hours of passion.

CHAPTER SEVEN

MARK PARKED downtown and, while Diana hurried off to the library to discover more about the Cooper family, Mark went to a café called Tubbs and ordered a cup of coffee. There was a lot left to discover about Diana Webb, and he would need more than a trip to the local library to get to the heart of this woman. For a private detective, he didn't know much. He could have found out who she was, if he'd really wanted to. He'd made a couple of attempts three years ago, but he hadn't pursued the few clues he'd dug up. There was a part of him that wanted to forget the darkest time in his life—and yet he'd always wished he could find the woman who'd rescued him. He'd been close to suicide that week, not that he would ever admit that shameful secret to anyone. And then Fate had put him on a beach with a woman who somehow understood, whose kindness and understanding led to passion and something more. Something that made him believe he would survive.

Mark looked out the window of the café and watched the various people walk past. Life here looked simple, but Mark knew there were secrets in a picturesque place like Cooper's Corner just as there were in any city. The waitress refilled his coffee and he ordered a piece of lemon meringue pie to go with it. He picked up a couple of thick guides for tourists stacked by the door and thought about where to stay tonight. Diana was a five-star hotel woman, no doubt, while he preferred any motel with a clean bed, cable TV and quick access to the interstate.

But tonight he wanted someplace special. Not because he had a chance in hell of making love to Diana, but because he wanted to make her happy. He'd fallen in love with her again—if he'd ever fallen out of love with her in the first place. But Mark realized he'd never get close to this woman until he discovered what kept her living alone on an island, what made her paint tumultuous oceans and what she was so afraid of.

He'd kissed her, which had been easy. But now came the hard part: he had to get her to talk.

"YOU'RE KIDDING," Diana said, when he'd pulled into the parking area of the Red Lion Inn. Its huge front porch, with white wicker rocking chairs and hanging baskets of flowers, looked exactly like the advertisement, which was a relief to Mark, though Diana didn't seem too pleased.

"The place was an inn in 1773 and it's supposed to be the most historic bed-and-breakfast in the Berkshires." Now he sounded like a damn travel guide. Mark shut off the engine and decided he needed a stiff drink. "If you don't like it, we can get on the turnpike and find a Marriott somewhere along the way."

"Why wouldn't I like it?" She turned those green eyes on him and waited for an answer.

"Too old?"

"Of course not. It's perfect. How did you find it?"

"I'm a detective, remember? I found some tourist brochures and I have a cell phone. I've already made reservations." He relaxed and even smiled. "You don't know how smart I am."

"I'm catching on," she said. "But don't forget I'm buying dinner tonight. We have to celebrate."

He didn't let her pay for the side-by-side rooms on the second floor, though she protested so much he pretended to agree to letting her reimburse him tomorrow. At dinner they ate grilled shrimp and pasta, and shared a bottle of champagne which they drank along with their dessert of homemade biscuits piled high with fresh strawberries and whipped cream. She related the history of Cooper's Corner and Warren's ancestors, having been helped by the Cooper's Corner librarian and given access to the local history room. After the waiter brought cappuccinos laced with brandy, Mark asked her what he wanted to know.

"Tell me," he said. "Why you were on the beach that day? Why you were in the Bahamas?"

"I told you. I have terrible taste in men." Then she smiled. "Present company excluded, I think."

His eyebrows rose. "You think? You haven't figured out that I'm one of the good guys by now?"

"I'm not the best judge of character," she admitted, looking pained. "And it's embarrassing to think I, um, slept with you when I didn't even know you."

"And now that you know me?"

"I'm not that person any longer."

"Who were you then?" He watched her carefully. He would know if she wasn't telling the truth.

"A fool." She grimaced. "I fell in love with my faculty advisor when finishing my MBA. My grandfather insisted I major in business, remember? He was furious when I told him that Kyle and I were going to move in together. Grandfather raised holy hell, threatening to report him for unethical behavior, so I stopped taking my grandparents' phone calls." She took a sip of her coffee and then continued. "I was so sure of myself, so positive that Lawrence was wrong and I was right. My grand love affair lasted a year, until Kyle told me he was going back to his wife."

"Ah."

"He had a wife and a child and I never even knew he was married. I told you I was a fool."

"It happens," Mark said, wishing he could get his hands on that piece of slime for just fifteen minutes. "Guys like that are good liars. I see it all the time."

"Oh, it gets worse," she warned. "I was eight weeks pregnant when he left."

Mark didn't know if he wanted to hear the rest, but he gripped his coffee cup and waited.

"I had a miscarriage a few weeks later." Her

eyes filled with tears. "It broke my heart. I really wanted that baby, wanted to be a mother."

"So you went to Nassau."

She nodded. "I'd been living there a month, trying to get myself together, before I met you. Between losing the baby and my grandfather's insistence that he'd been right all along and when would I ever listen to reason and why had I thought living together made sense—" She shrugged. "He had a lot to say."

"Maybe he was worried about you."

"He worries about the family's reputation. Before my parents died I heard him tell my grandmother that my parents weren't taking good enough care of us and he thought he should step in and do the right thing." Diana absently rubbed her knuckles at the edge of the cast. "Can you imagine the arrogance of such a statement?"

"He sounds like a man who is used to being in charge, Diana. And he must have been concerned about his grandchildren. All grandparents would be, no matter what. *I* would."

She smiled. "You're planning on having grandchildren?"

"After my children grow up, sure."

"And when are you going to have these children?"

"Soon," Mark declared, hoping they would have green eyes and their mother's smile. "Very soon."

They fought over the dinner bill, and he let her win. But when he walked her to her bedroom door Mark didn't kiss her good-night. He was in love with her, but the next time they made love it had to mean more than a way to ease each other's pain.

IT WAS NOT EASY to take a shower and keep a cast from getting wet. She'd covered her right arm and hand with a plastic laundry bag she'd found on the closet shelf, but when she rinsed the shampoo out of her hair she had to stick her injured arm outside the shower curtain and hope for the best. Diana vowed never to climb on the roof again, even if she thought the view would be an inspiration. She had foolishly assumed replacing shingles was a simple task that could be done by almost anyone.

She toweled off, but it was awkward. Her grandfather's shirt made a perfect nightgown, the cuffs unbuttoning wide enough to allow room for the cast and, because Warren had been a tall man, the tails of the soft blue cotton covered her thighs. It smelled of fresh air, as if it had been hung outside on the clothesline for hours. She didn't think her new grandfather would mind her wearing it, especially when she planned to open the rest of his package and examine what he sent her.

Procrastination was one of her worst faults. She also felt too much, thought too much, spent too much time by herself. Tonight would be no exception, she realized, sitting cross-legged in the middle of the four-poster bed in a room that could have been decorated sometime around the American Revolution. Saying good-night to Mark at her bedroom door had been difficult. She'd wanted to lean against his wide chest and wrap her arms around his waist—well, one arm—and then haul him into her room and into her bed.

Which was exactly what she'd been trying to avoid. But did he want her? She thought he did, but she was no longer in the mood for running away with musicians, living with married men or having sex with anguished strangers she met on a beach.

Diana eyed the bulky package in her lap and managed to tear the paper enough to reveal a scrapbook. She'd thought that was what it was last night, but reading her grandfather's letter had been enough to deal with. She tore the front of the package open wider until she could remove the worn leather-covered book. Diana was engraved on the metal oval trimmed with gold-embossed flowers and when she opened the cover, she saw the first page held a picture of her mother holding her when she was an infant. The lettering under the photo was in Warren Cooper's handwriting: *Donna with Diana, my first grandchild, July, 1970.*

She was startled when she heard a knock at her door, but when she heard Mark's voice it made her smile. "Diana?"

"Come in. It's not locked," she called, and hurriedly slid underneath the bedcovers so she was covered. He stepped inside and shut the door behind him. "What do you mean, it's not locked? Anyone could walk in here and then what would you do?"

His frown made her laugh. "I'd scream, of course, since you're right next door and could run right over to rescue me." She saw that he held a small bottle and two liqueur glasses. "What do you have there?"

"Cognac." He set the glasses and the cognac on the marble-topped table by the bed. "I thought you might like a nightcap. The Inn let me borrow the glasses.'' Mark looked at her as she rearranged the bed pillows. ''I didn't think you'd be in bed this early.''

''Look.'' She scooted over so he could sit down on the edge of the mattress. ''He kept a scrapbook with my name on it.'' Diana turned another page to reveal a photo of her blowing out the candles on her first birthday.

''You were a cute kid.''

She pointed to a tall, dark-haired man to the right of the high chair. ''That's my father. And next to him, my mother.''

''Very beautiful. I see the family resemblance.''

''They were always so happy.'' She turned page after page, reliving times she remembered, surprised at events she'd forgotten. There were pictures of Christmas mornings, of learning to ride a horse, and dressed up for her very first prom. Glued into the black pages were copies of her report cards, diplomas and various awards. There was a pressed and dried rose, labeled From Donna's Funeral. ''My grandmother must have sent him all of these things.''

Mark handed her a glass of cognac. ''Here. I have a feeling you're going to get weepy.''

"Too late," she sniffed. "I feel sad and lonely and old."

"Excuse me, but you do have a man on your bed, so technically you don't have to be lonely."

"True." She took a sip of the cognac and then another. It was not easy trying to forget the last time they'd been on a bed together. At least this time they had their clothes on—or one of them did. She wore no underwear under her shirt, something she was suddenly uncomfortably aware of. "You're not exactly a social butterfly yourself," she added. "Jess told me you work too much and you haven't had a date since your dog died."

"A coincidence," he said. "I set up another office in Cambridge and—"

"There are no women in Boston? What a shame." She drained the rest of her glass and handed it to him. "It's getting very warm in here. Is the window open?"

"Just like there are no men in Nantucket," he said, He stroked her cheek with his warm fingers. "I wonder where they all went."

"Maybe they've decided to leave grouchy artists alone," she said.

His hand dropped to her shirtfront, where he

slipped the first button from its hole. "Not me. I like my women cranky and hermitlike."

"I'm kind of partial to frowny-faced detectives."

"Frowny-faced?" Another button was unfastened. "What kind of word is that for a big tough guy who brings you cognac and drives you around New England?"

"Sorry." She inhaled when his lips trailed along the side of her neck.

"We're hopeless, aren't we?"

"Completely." She lifted her mouth to his, but he surprised her with only a soft brush of his lips on his.

He undid another button. "If we make love tonight, then technically the last time wasn't a one-night stand."

"What would we call it?"

Mark chuckled. "Getting lucky?"

"That's much too crude." But she smiled and looped her arms around his neck. She did feel lucky, actually.

"An affair, then," Mark decided, releasing the last button. He slid his hand inside her shirt and cupped her breast. "We'll call it an affair, which means I spend the night and neither one of us disappears in the morning."

"You have a deal."

CHAPTER EIGHT

THE PASSION, hot and swift and strong, was the same as before, during that long night in Nassau. Diana found it difficult to breathe and yet, impossible to stop touching him. Her cast made it awkward to help Mark unbutton his shirt, but she tried until he stilled her left hand and instead carefully removed her arms from the sleeves of her denim shirt. Then he pushed her gently back against the pile of lace-covered pillows and placed her grandfather's scrapbook and torn package on the nightstand.

"I don't want to hurt you," he told her.

"I'm not worried." She watched him peel off his clothes. Mark's body was muscular, his skin paler than she remembered. His chest was covered with curling dark hair that tapered to his abdomen, all aroused male and, for tonight, all hers.

"I meant what I said." Mark switched off the light, leaving the room in semidarkness and she reached for him, curling her fingers around his shoulder and bringing him to her.

"Which was?" She was finding it hard to concentrate now that his skin was touching hers. He moved the covers back and smoothed one hand along her leg.

"You can't disappear in the morning." His fingers stopped at the juncture of her thighs. "I think you'd better promise."

She'd promise anything if he would continue to touch her, and she told him so.

"I remember the first time I touched you," he said, moving his lips across hers. His fingers urged her thighs apart, found her, claimed her. "I was shaking."

"So was I."

"And now?"

"Still shaking," she whispered, as he moved above her.

"Remind me that we have all night?"

Diana shifted her body so that he was between her legs. "I think I need—"

"Yes." He entered her, a long smooth motion of absolute perfection that halted her in midsentence. And from then on the magic continued as if it had been only days and not years since their bodies had joined. It was as if she knew what he wanted and, she realized, he knew instinctively how to move inside her, where to touch her, when to move slowly and when not to. When he slipped his hand under her buttocks, holding her tighter against him, Diana was lost. He moved deep within her, taking her closer to release with every thrust.

And long moments later, when they lay together and caught their breath, he still didn't release her. Instead he leaned on his elbows and looked down into her eyes. "I've missed you."

"Yes." She was too choked with emotion to say anything else, but Mark didn't seem to mind.

"Go to sleep," he told her. She shook her head.

"No. I don't want to waste time by sleeping," she insisted. "Last time—"

"—we made love all night," he finished for her, laughing down into her eyes. "I will if you will."

"Is that a challenge?" She touched his face, dropping her fingers to his lips. She liked his mouth, even when he frowned. *Especially* when he frowned and she knew he was simply being overprotective.

"Sweetheart," he said, moving his body within hers. "That's an absolute guarantee."

MARK WOKE AT DAWN, but he couldn't move. At first he didn't know why, until he felt a woman's body curled next to him and he remembered. Diana. Her right arm lay on his chest, the white cast holding him down. Not that he wanted to move. He'd waited years to wake up and see her sleeping next to him and he was in no hurry to end the experience. He didn't want to start the day and discover that she regretted last night. He didn't want to hear anything about mistaken judgment or even worse, like the song said, "it was just one of those things."

It wasn't. He'd been in love several times, but he had only truly loved one other woman until Diana. And he'd married her. He had no doubt he would still be married to her, would be a homicide cop and a family man, if she hadn't been killed.

Now he'd been given a second chance, with the one woman he could picture spending the rest of his life with. He doubted if Diana would think of their relationship as anything other than a convenient, passionate affair, but Mark was a patient man. He could wait a while longer for this woman to realize they were meant to be together. In fact, he decided as he closed his eyes, he could wait a while longer to get out of bed, too.

IT WAS RAINING and her roof wasn't finished. Diana tried to remember where she'd put the ladder. She thought to open her eyes and get on to the roof, but her pillows were so comfortable and she didn't want to leave the bed to go out into the rain. Not today. She began to roll over, but her cast was in the way. Her cast was always in the way, but at least her wrist had stopped aching.

But, come to think of it, other parts of her were pleasantly sore. Her eyelids flew open when she realized exactly where she was and what she had been doing for most of the night. The covers, except for the sheet over her shoulders, lay in a jumbled mess at the edge of the mattress. And it wasn't rain she heard, but the shower. And from what she heard of Mark's muffled voice, he was a better detective than a singer.

She needed coffee. She even thought she'd smelled coffee, so she sat up to see if by some bed-and-breakfast magic a pot of coffee had appeared. Sure enough, a thick yellow mug sat on the nightstand. Diana reached over for it and took a sip. It wasn't hot, but it was drinkable and she was grateful for the caffeine. She needed all the mental energy she could get, now that she'd spent the night with Mark.

Meeting him in Nassau had changed everything for her. She'd been hurt in so many ways and there on the beach stood this man who carried heartache of his own, who was intrigued by her paintings and yet asked nothing of her except what she wanted to give. She thought she was grieving too much to feel passion, but she'd been wrong. And the realization had terrified her. What kind of a woman was she that she could grieve so much and then sleep with a stranger?

In the morning, before he woke, she'd left as quickly as she could. She knew she couldn't bear to face another mistake, or face the humiliation of awkward morning-after conversation. She never gave herself a chance to find out who this special man really was.

And now she knew. But she didn't know how he would fit into her life, her careful, quiet island life. Diana thought she might be too old and set in her ways to reinvent her life to include a man, especially one who lived in such a different world.

A loud rendition of a raucous country-and-western song began, so loud that Diana hurried out of bed. She pushed the half-open bathroom door wider. "Mark, you're going to wake up everyone in the inn!"

His head appeared around the shower curtain. "You've got something against Willie Nelson?"

"'Mamas, Don't Let Your Babies Grow Up To Be Cowboys'? No," Diana said, stepping into the steamy room. "It's just the volume. And wasn't that by Johnny Cash?"

"I hate to argue with a naked woman, but it's Willie Nelson, and *you* are a vision this morning." He pushed his hair off his face and held out his hand. "Come here."

"No way," she said, knowing he'd pull her into the shower with him. "I can't get my cast wet."

"I'll hold your arm out of the water."

She approached with caution. "You will?"

"Sure. I'll even wash your hair." He gave her a wet kiss. "Among other things."

"Hmmm. Maybe this isn't such a good idea." She put her left hand in his and stepped over the edge of the tub. He supported her right arm and, keeping her backed up against him, protected her cast from the warm water cascading over his head.

"This," he said, touching his lips to her shoulder as he tucked her body against his, "is an excellent idea."

"You make love better than you sing," she

teased, as his left arm slid the washcloth over her breasts. She wasn't surprised that she wanted him again, but having a broken arm made sex in the shower unlikely.

"I can do both," he offered, slipping the washcloth lower, moving it with gentle friction between her legs. "Want to hear?"

"You shouldn't tease an injured woman," she said, as he began to sing close to her ear.

"You're right," he said, turning to shut off the water. "I think we should head for the bed."

There was no argument from Diana, but they didn't make it any farther than the fluffy blue bathroom rug.

CHAPTER NINE

"WHAT DO YOU THINK about Norman Rockwell?" Mark asked, looking up from his tourist brochure. "We could spend another night here and we could go to his art museum. It's only a few miles from Cooper's Corner."

"I love Norman Rockwell," Diana said, picking up her clothes. She folded them on the bed, next to her opened suitcase, and then retrieved her grandfather's package from the nightstand. "But I think I should go home and talk to my sister about everything's that happened. And I want to find Richard, too."

"By 'home' you mean the estate in Dover?"

"Yes." The package that held the letter and the scrapbook wasn't empty, she realized. She could feel more paper in the bottom of it, so she sat down on the edge of the bed and managed to retrieve another packet of letters. "Look at this, Mark. More letters."

"Are they Warren's?" He came closer to peer over her shoulder.

"They're addressed to him and they're from Oak Meadow—that's what we call the place in Dover. My grandmother must have—no," she said, frowning. "This isn't her handwriting. It's—"

"Whose?"

"My grandfather. Lawrence Webb, I mean. This doesn't make any sense." She looked at Mark. "Why would he write to Warren Cooper?"

"You'll have to read them and see," he said, joining her on the edge of the bed.

"Help. My hands are shaking." She handed him the pile of correspondence, and Mark took the top envelope and withdrew the letter from it. He handed it, still folded, to Diana to read. "This is very strange," she murmured, reading a description of her high school graduation.

"What does he say?"

"I don't think this had anything to do with my grandmother," she said. "And here I thought she was the one who had kept in touch with her true love. They couldn't see each other, but they could write."

"So your grandfather—your *Webb* grandfather wasn't such a bad guy after all?"

"I don't know."

"Check this out," Mark said, holding up a postcard of a tropical beach. "It's from the Bahamas and it's addressed to Warren."

"What does it say?"

I believe our sweet granddaughter's tragedy is behind her now. She met someone yesterday and flew home today with a smile on her face. From what I've been able to learn about the man, I think it's safe to say Diana learned last night that others bear pain as big as her own. Will write more about them later. L.W. Mark handed Diana the card. "I wondered why Warren Cooper hired me to deliver these packets. He could have hired anyone for an easy job like that. And he wanted them delivered personally by me, not one of my employees. He was very specific."

"Why?" She thought she knew why, but she wanted to hear Mark's take on it.

"It's simple. He wanted to bring us together again. He wanted to give us another chance."

"Warren was a very romantic man." She gathered the letters together and tucked them into the torn packet. "How did my grandfather—

Lawrence, I mean—know who you were? We didn't exchange names.''

"I imagine Lawrence Webb could have made a few phone calls,'' he said. "It wouldn't have been that difficult for a man with his connections.''

"I have to talk to him,'' Diana said, turning to look at Mark. "Will you take me?''

"Of course.''

They skipped having homemade blueberry muffins and juice on the inn's front porch, opting for the drive-up window of a coffee-and-doughnut shop instead.

Diana waited until they were heading east on the highway before she asked Mark, "Did you know about this ahead of time?''

"I had a feeling something wasn't quite right,'' he admitted. "But I wasn't positive it was really you until Nantucket, when you opened your door.'' He glanced toward her. "Why? Does it matter?''

"I don't like being spied on. And I don't like feeling manipulated,'' she said. "And Lawrence Webb is the master of that particular skill. Which is why I don't let him into my life anymore.''

"You might want to wait and hear what he

has to say before you make any judgments,'' he cautioned.

''You don't know him,'' Diana said.

''Well, from the looks of things, I don't think you do, either.''

Diana sipped her coffee and looked out the window. Lawrence Webb had a lot of explaining to do.

''HELLO, HARTFIELD,'' Diana greeted the gray-haired butler on the doorstep of Oak Meadows, the family mansion. The man's face broke into a smile. Mark kept his distance. He recognized an adversary when he saw one, and he remembered how the delivery of Sally's package had alarmed the butler. Alistair Hartfield would not be happy to see him again if he had upset a Webb.

''Diana.'' Hartfield allowed Diana to give him a hug, but he remained straight-backed and kept a careful watch on Mark during the embrace. ''It's good to see you here again. Mr. Webb will be so pleased.''

''Perhaps,'' Diana replied. ''Is he in?''

''Mr. Hartfield?'' Mark held out his hand after Diana released the butler. ''I'm Mark Solomon. I was here—''

''Yes, I remember.'' He stepped back and al-

lowed them to walk into the large foyer. "I believe Mr. Webb is in his office. I'll go—"

"Diana?" A tall, regal gentleman hurried
down the hall. "Is that you?" Mark knew he
could only be Lawrence Webb, owner of Webb
Worldwide Industries and a force to be reckoned
with. He was gray-haired and smiling, which surprised Mark. He appeared pleased to see his el-
dest granddaughter, despite their differences.

"Grandfather," Diana said, her voice cracking
with emotion. She stood as stiffly as Webb, the
two of them gazing at each other as if neither
one knew what kind of physical greeting was appropriate—or welcome.

"You're injured," the man noted, turning a
little pale. "It's not serious, I trust?"

"A simple broken wrist," Diana explained,
but Webb's attention was focused on Mark. "I'd
like you to meet my private detective, Mark Solomon. Mark, my grandfather, Lawrence Webb."

There was a brief flicker of recognition and
curiosity, but Webb masked it soon enough.
"Welcome to Oak Meadow, Mr. Solomon."

"Thank you." Mark shook his hand and was
impressed with the strength of the older man's
grip. There was an expression on his face that
said, *If you mess with my granddaughter, I'll*

make you pay, but Mark met his gaze and didn't drop eye contact until Webb turned back to Diana.

"Have you had lunch? If not, I'm sure Lucia would be more than happy to fix something for you."

"Not right now," Diana said, clutching Warren Cooper's package against her chest. "I need to talk to you."

"Ah," Webb sighed, noting the package for the first time. "Yes, I see." He turned and walked down the hall, leaving Mark and Diana to follow him. Webb led them through a large office that Mark assumed was his, then into a small room that served as library and den. The walls were dark maroon, the books on the shelves appeared ancient and the leather couch and matching chairs were a shade of brown that looked almost black.

"Sit down," the older man said, gesturing toward the sofa. He settled into a chair across from them and Diana dumped the pile of letters onto the glass-topped table that separated her from her grandfather.

"You wrote these," she said, and the man nodded.

"Yes."

"You knew who he was?"

"I did." Webb leaned forward and rubbed his trembling hands together. "I knew before the girls—your mother and your aunt—were born that they weren't mine. Oh, Helen said they were born premature, but I knew better. She told her mother she was pregnant with Warren's baby. Her parents had told me how devastated she'd been when she heard I was dead, how she'd turned to Warren for comfort and for love."

"Did you hate her for it?" Diana asked.

"Hate Helen?" He shook his head. "Of course not. I loved her dearly and I knew she loved me. And I loved those babies, too. We never had any other children, because my war injury... Well, I couldn't father a child."

"But Grandmother didn't know that?"

He took a deep breath before he continued. "No. And I never told Helen I knew about her...intimacy with Warren, because she would have been humiliated. She loved two men and I was the lucky one to have her all those years. So I kept her secret and I kept mine."

"But what about Warren Cooper?" Diana asked. "He wrote us—Richard and Sally, too— letters before he died. He sent me a scrapbook.

He knew about our lives, every detail. *You* did that?''

"I owed him that much," Webb declared. "He deserved to know that you all were well taken care of. He was a fine man. They don't come much finer than Warren Cooper, my dear. You should be proud to have him as a grandfather. Just as proud as he was of you."

Diana stood and gave Mark a shaky smile before she walked over to Lawrence Webb's chair. She leaned forward and put her left arm around his neck and her right on his shoulder. "I'm proud to have both of you as my grandfathers," she sniffed. "I'm ashamed of myself. I didn't know you two were watching over me all these years."

"I was, I concede, a bit heavy-handed at times," the old man admitted. He patted her awkwardly on her back. "You and I must start over, my dear. Life is too short and too fragile for misunderstandings."

"I do love you," Diana said, and Mark watched Lawrence Webb's eyes fill with tears. He'd bet not too many people had ever seen that particular sight before.

"And I love you, too, Diana." When she withdrew and took the handkerchief her grandfather supplied, Lawrence fixed his attention on Mark. "But you will have to excuse me for a moment, my dear. I need to have a few words with your young man."

Diana kissed her grandfather's cheek, winked at Mark and went to the door. "I'll ask Lucia to fix us a tray of sandwiches and coffee."

"Take your time," Webb replied, straightening himself in his chair. "Mr. Solomon and I need to get to know each other better."

"WELL?" Diana led Mark through the empty dining room and out French doors to a brick patio that overlooked a large, sprawling lawn and beyond, a view of the sea. They were alone, after a lunch spent reminiscing over old photographs and memories. Her grandfather had finally waved them away so he could return some business calls, but Diana suspected he needed some time alone to get his emotions under control. He missed her grandmother terribly, she realized.

"Well, what?" Mark shoved his hands in his pockets and looked out toward the distant ocean.

"What happened with my grandfather just now?" She tugged on his shirtsleeve. "And don't tell me it was only guy talk. I know him better than that."

Mark looked down at her, but she couldn't read his expression. He was frowning again.

"He wanted to know if I was going to make an honest woman out of you."

Diana's initial thought was to go find the man and tell him to mind his own business, but then again she supposed grandfathers had the right to ask questions. "And what did you say?"

Mark placed his hands on her shoulders as if he thought she was going to move away. His dark eyes were serious, his voice low. "I told him I was prepared to marry you any day, anytime, any where. But—"

"But...?" she echoed, telling herself it was foolish to be disappointed. Mark wasn't smiling.

"*But* I told him that when I asked you and where I asked you and even *how* I asked you was none of his business."

"Uh-oh." The last time she had told her grandfather something was none of his business they hadn't spoken in three years. He bent and kissed her, a long searing kiss that made her wish they were back at the inn.

"He was not amused." Mark chuckled, lifting his mouth from hers. "But he wished me luck and suggested having the wedding reception here, on the grounds of Oak Meadow, as soon as possible. Then he muttered something about wanting great-grandchildren while he was still alive to see them and poured us each a glass of fifty-year-old whiskey.''

"Male bonding,'' she murmured. "At my expense.''

"Of course. Don't you want your husband and your grandfather to get along?''

She stepped back so she could look into his eyes. "Is that a proposal?''

"Yes.''

"It wasn't a very good one,'' she teased, hoping he'd frown at her so she could tease him again.

"If you hadn't left me in Nassau, I might have asked you four years ago.'' He brought her left hand up to his lips. "You can't leave me now, not after all the trouble Warren Cooper went to getting us together again, you know.''

"That's a good point,'' she conceded, wondering how it was possible to be so filled with joy. Had Warren felt this way when his Helen came to him, needed him, loved him? He hadn't sent her away; instead he'd held her in his heart for the rest of his life.

"I'd offer to give you some time to think it

over," her detective said, "but we've already wasted too many years, don't you think?"

"Yes," Diana replied, knowing she wanted to spend the rest of her life with this special man.

"Yes?" A slow smile creased Mark's face as he stared down at her. "So I'm not going to have an affair with you after all?"

"No?"

"We'll call it a honeymoon instead," he declared, gathering her into his arms. "On any island you choose."

"No more islands," Diana whispered, leaning into his warm chest. "Unless we're together."

"That's an easy promise to keep," Mark assured her, resting his chin on the top of her head. "As long as you never run away from me again."

"I've decided to stay in one place," she agreed, realizing she was loved more than she had ever thought possible.

Her grandfathers had made sure of that.

EPILOGUE

NO ONE PAID any attention to the regal old gentleman who stood under one of Warren Cooper's famous oaks. He held a glass of expensive champagne and, with great satisfaction, surveyed the scene around him. His family—*his family*—were reunited once again.

And what a reunion it was.

Despite the short notice in change of venue, the present owners of Twin Oaks, Maureen and Clint, put together a wedding and reception for Diana and her new husband that the town of Cooper's Corner would talk about for years afterward. Lawrence had spared no expense, of course, having been deprived of giving Sally a wedding because of that Las Vegas fiasco. The orchestra had been a nice touch, he thought. And the lovely soprano from Boston's Opera Aperta certainly did justice to her two solos, one of which was from his late wife's favorite Bellini opera. Baskets of multicolored flowers hung from the huge oaks along the drive, where he had escorted Diana to her future husband.

Lawrence thought it may well have been the proudest moment of his life.

Now the various members of his family and their invited guests enjoyed a rather elegant luncheon. Of course, he noted with some amusement, Richard was too busy chasing his two little boys to sit down and eat. His great-grandsons had already changed the nature of family gatherings, and the lovely Janelle appeared to Lawrence to be a fine addition to his brood.

Yes, he thought, patting his jacket pocket where a photo of his beloved Helen lay tucked against his heart. It was good to have another "Mrs. Webb" in the family.

And then there was Sally, who at this moment, Lawrence noted, was being kissed by her husband David in the shade of a distant oak. Ah, well. They were on their honeymoon, so they could be forgiven the lapse in propriety. With any luck, there would soon be another great-grandchild on the way.

Lawrence stood in the shade and looked for Diana in the crowd of well-wishers, but saw only Mark, deep in conversation with his young nephew. He frowned, scanning the crowd for a glimpse of a dark-haired beauty in a wedding gown.

"Grandfather?"

"Ah," he said, turning to see Diana approach from behind him. "There you are, my dear. I was looking for you."

"While you were hiding here in the oaks," she said, looking happier than he'd ever thought possible. "What are you doing here by yourself?"

"Admiring my family," he said, a sudden lump in his throat. "How your grandmother would have loved this. And how I miss her."

Diana touched the pearls at her throat. "Thank you for letting me wear her necklace. It makes me feel as if she's here with us."

He nodded, too choked to speak, but Diana stood on tiptoe and kissed his cheek.

"And thank you for my wedding," she whispered, blinking back tears. She took his hand and tugged him toward the dance floor built for the reception. "Come dance with me."

"My dear, I would be honored," Lawrence managed to say. He straightened his shoulders and collected himself as he and Diana headed toward their guests.

"I think they're here with us, Grandmother

and Warren Cooper together," Diana murmured. "Don't you?"

"Yes," Lawrence heard himself agree. "Yes," he repeated with more conviction as he realized how much the thought pleased him. "I do."

Neither noticed the slight breeze that gently shook the leaves of the massive oak they'd left behind. Two oak leaves drifted down from a lower branch, mingled with rose petals and fell gently to the earth.

EMERGENCY!

The Family Doctor
by Bobby Hutchinson

The next Superromance novel in this dramatic series—set in and around St. Joseph's Hospital in Vancouver, British Colombia.

Chief of staff Antony O'Connor has family problems. His mother is furious at his father for leaving her many years ago, and now he's coming to visit—with the woman he loves. Tony's family is taking sides. Patient care advocate Kate Lewis is an expert at defusing anger, so she might be able to help him out. With this problem, at least. Sorting out her feelings for Tony— and his feelings for her—is about to get trickier!

Heartwarming stories with a sense of humor, genuine charm and emotion and lots of family!

On sale starting April 2002

Available wherever Harlequin books are sold.

HARLEQUIN®
Makes any time special ®

Visit us at www.eHarlequin.com

HSRE

Coming in April 2002
from

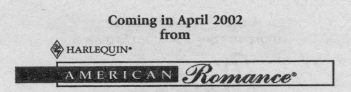

and

RANDALL RICHES
(HAR #918)

Desperate to return to his Wyoming ranch, champion bull rider Rich Randall had no choice but to accept sassy Samantha Jeffer's helping hand—with a strict "no hanky-panky" warning. But on the long road home something changed and Rich was suddenly thinking of turning in his infamous playboy status for a little band of gold.

Don't miss this heartwarming addition to the series,

Available wherever Harlequin books are sold.

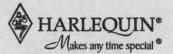

HARLEQUIN®
Temptation.

Look for bed, breakfast and more...!

COOPER'S CORNER

Some of your favorite Temptation authors are checking in early at Cooper's Corner Bed and Breakfast

In May 2002:

#877 *The Baby and the Bachelor*
Kristine Rolofson

In June 2002:

#881 *Double Exposure*
Vicki Lewis Thompson

In July 2002:

#885 *For the Love of Nick*
Jill Shalvis

In August 2002 things heat up even more at Cooper's Corner. There's a whole year of intrigue and excitement to come—twelve fabulous books bound to capture your heart and mind!

Join all your favorite Harlequin authors in Cooper's Corner!

HARLEQUIN®
Makes any time special ®